HIS
DARK
REFLECTION

MARVELLOUS MICHAEL ANSON

PRAISE FOR
MARVELLOUS MICHAEL ANSON

His Dark Reflection is laced with sharp twists and surges of emotional intensity. This is not a prognosis on the human or social condition; it's a thriller. And all lovers of such will find themselves drawn to the boldness with which Marve has crafted her first gem.

Gbenga Adesina Poet and Essayist, *Joint Winner of the 2016 Brunel International Poetry Prize*

Marve was very discursive with her words and that kept me inquisitive to know what was next. She mixes maliciousness and gentility in this poetically written blockbuster tale of conditional love.

Stephanie Chizoba Odili, *Author of 'Deafening Silence'*

Marve takes the reader through kept secrets, tragedy, and twisted relationships that question everything about what we often project as our authentic selves and who we truly are.

Tope Owolabi, Editor/Writer at *eclectictope.com*

His Dark Reflection is an example of what I call 'fine writing'. The story, the characters, the juxtaposition, and the little bits of surprise that keep you on edge after each chapter are simply exquisite.

Mercy Kwabe, Founder and Lead Coordinator, *Eccentric Reader's Club*

This is a masterpiece of fiction. Its use of time is excellent as the past, the present, and the future are intertwined. It feels too real to be a work of fiction.
Olubiyi Adeniyi Adewale, PhD Director, *Lagos Study Centre National Open University of Nigeria*

His Dark Reflection is a gripping detail of a love story with a tint of the thriller and the fabulous. It has the elements of the mysterious and the realistic. It tells a story we can relate to because it's our story told in such a mature way it blows us away.
I. O. Daniel, PhD Associate Professor of English *National Open University of Nigeria*

A compelling tale . . .
His Dark Reflection is an intriguing story, full of suspense with unexpected twists and turns. The reader is immediately drawn into a maze of fathomless emotions and keeps turning the pages in anticipation of a key to unlock the secrets.
Prof. Deji Adekunle, *Nigerian Institute of Advanced Legal Studies*

His Dark Reflection is a wheel of secrets that seems to have an unending cycle. Marve takes you on a thrilling journey of twists and turns with smooth plot manoeuvres using a terse but descriptive writing style. It's the type of literature you bring to life on the big screen.
Olayinka Yomi-Joseph, Winner of *Creetiq's Critic Challenge 2017*

Art is a rare relation between the originality of any human and the connection of their soul, and this book has a way to always use it to reach out to the reader and have them connect with the narrative of the book. Everyone seems to have a big secret hidden beneath their sleeves, and how the writer uncovered each person's secret was suspense bound.
Priscilla Philips, *Poet and Writer*

His Dark Reflection is a fictional work of intrigues and suspense, which attempts to build a complex web of malice and vengeance around simple plots; coupled with a pinch of differentials in Western and African parenting models—particularly in relation to father/daughter ideals and its concomitant often negative effects! It comes highly recommended for its frills and thrills!
Akeem Sadiq, *Writer*

His Dark Reflection is an interesting read with a riveting plot that gradually unfolds to leave the reader gasping for breath, lost in the gripping suspense that characterises the unpredictability of human emotions.
Bridget Anthonia Yakubu, *PhD Department of Languages National Open University of Nigeria*

His Dark Reflection spirals into breath-seizing thriller. Betrayal and harboured secrets between a couple, Jack and Mote, destroy their idyllic family. Marve keeps the reader invested in connecting the dots from all perspectives. It will be interesting to watch her balance and fit, the multicultural and racial characters in her imagined world.
Chikelu Chinelo, *Arts Writer, Leadership Newspaper*

HIS

THEY'LL TAKE HIS SECRETS

DARK

TO THEIR GRAVES

REFLECTION

MARVELLOUS MICHAEL ANSON

Published by Anson Press

Copyright © 2023 by Marvellous Micheal

First paperback edition February 2023

Book Editing by Emma's Edits
Book cover design by SeventhStar Art
Formatting and Interior design by Jennifer Laslie

Paperback ISBN 978-1-7392087-0-7
Hardback ISBN 978-1-7392087-1-4

Look out for more books from Anson Press at www.justmarve.org

This book is dedicated to my grandma, Mrs Omobamitale Ayodele Adewale.

FOREWARD

BY OMOBAMITALE AYODELE ADEWALE

This book borders on the reality of life. There is no one without a past or without experience of various challenges in life. No one is a saint. Most people have secrets haunting them all their lives. This book has done a good job in dwelling on the diversity of humanity and its peculiarities.

The language is very rich and deep. In this novel, there are some mysteries which the reader requires deep introspection to understand. The author uses suspense and intrigue to hold the reader captive until the end of the story.

The captivating transition from one chapter to the next and the variety of intriguing episodes make the book an interesting read worthy of intellectual exploration.

Lovers of literature and anyone who wants to sail through this life successfully should have the perseverance of Mote and the courage of Ara. I therefore recommend the book for all and sundry.

Omobamitale Ayodele Adewale

CHAPTER
1

Mote walked out to the balcony barefoot and half-dressed. The cool breeze brushed against her face, and she let out a deep breath. She stood thirty storeys above the ground, staring down at the people beneath. She had never been more afraid. Not because she feared falling, but because she was about to take the biggest leap of her life. She was about to be married.

She shifted her gaze from the ant-sized people below to the sky above her. The night had just begun to fade away. Even today, she found beauty in the first light of dawn.

She went back into the room and brought out a bedside stool, her canvas, and her bag of tube paints and brushes. She was glad she'd brought them with her; she'd hoped to find time to paint, even with all the wedding preparations. She sat on the stool, placed the canvas on her knees and let it fall back against the railings. The sun rose slowly, and when it filled up more space in the sky, she brought out her brushes and began. Nothing else would calm her at this point.

Her hands shook as she painted but she continued still, her brush stroking the canvas, carefully recreating all that she saw. Her mind would not calm. Dancing thoughts became heavy fears, crippling her so much that she had to stop. She began to lose her breath; she felt faint, and the brush in her hand fell to the ground. She dropped the canvas and closed her eyes.

There were so many reasons this could become the worst day of her life. She was sure she wanted to marry Jack. She loved him, and she had proved that to herself over and over. She had triumphed in every fight against her parents' opposition to her marriage; that in itself was enough to make her want to elope, but Jack refused. He was convinced they could get her parents on their side, win them over.

Her Nigerian roots made her marriage to a white man the

most unbearable situation. She was so stressed out; she was almost ready to give in to their endless criticism and snide comments.

It wasn't too hard to keep fighting for her life with Jack. He was such a beautiful soul. He was warm and kind and passionate about everything he did, and most importantly, she trusted him with everything. With her life, with her family—but somehow not with her darkest secrets. If she did, she wouldn't be here, staring at this half-painted canvas, hoping that her truth would not destroy the future she so desperately wanted.

She tried to rationalise the situation, what telling him would do to him. He loved her, and she knew this, not just because he had said so countless times but because he had always been with her when she needed him; he'd never given up on her. He was her anchor, constantly reminding her of who she was and what she could be, and when he promised that he was never going to leave her, she believed him. But if he knew the secrets she harboured deep in her heart, he just might change his mind. He might resent her for keeping them, and even more for lying to him.

This ache in her chest was sure to be permanent if he left her because she'd been careless, because of a mistake she didn't have the courage to undo. Sometimes she wondered if marrying him was the worst kind of betrayal to the love he had shown her through the months he had been with her, but leaving him at the altar, she imagined, would be much worse.

He'd come into her life just when she'd needed someone to share her burdens. She'd felt an encumbrance of responsibility that she just could not bear alone.

She had lost everything, and the thought of starting over was terrifying. She'd left Nigeria, never to return. Not because she wanted to but because she no longer had a home there; her father had made it so. She was scared then just as she was now: walking into unknown territory, hoping to find a path that led to a happy ending.

Fear. She knew it way too well. It made her hands shake and her voice tremble every time she bid her parents goodbye from her grandmother's stairs. She'd felt it whenever the matron turned off the lights, and she'd sobbed into her tear-filled pillow and allowed the stories of the lady in red that lurked in the halls to scare her to sleep. Secondary school had been a rather difficult time for her; try as she might, she just couldn't fit into the boarding system. The time she'd spent in Isokun Grammar School, Oyo, was the most trying time in her life. Thinking back, the corner of her lips lifted when she remembered the girls who'd made schooling there bearable enough to graduate.

At the time when she was leaving Nigeria, she was pretty much on house arrest. Her father forbade her from seeing anyone. 'They are all the reason you have gotten yourself into this mess,' he would shout every time she asked to leave the house. She didn't even get the chance to warn Komi that she would be moving to the United States or why. She couldn't bring herself to talk about it then, now, or ever. Her father had been unbearable; he'd gone on and on and just wouldn't let her hear her own thoughts. She had tried to stay, but his demand for her to leave their home, to leave the country, was absolute. She remembered her mother's stern advice, she remembered the pleading tone of every harsh word that rang in her ears. *Don't bring any more shame to our family. Keep your head down, make no friends, focus on your books and nothing else. Nothing else matters.* She had heard all those words before—that was why they had sent her to her grandmother, wasn't it? To be well trained and disciplined and the perfect daughter they still didn't want?

Many months later, the memories of the life she'd left behind still haunted her.

She hadn't done much in the months leading up to when she'd met Jack. Actually, she'd done nothing but draw and paint whenever she managed to drag herself out of bed.

Komi was the most understanding housemate she could have hoped for. She didn't ask questions she knew had no answers, and she didn't impose too much on her. She was always too busy, juggling nursing school and night performances at the bar, to give Mote anything other than what she wanted: space.

Komi was different from most girls she knew, which was why they'd remained friends even when Komi had left Nigeria a few years earlier to pursue her career in nursing.

Komi was a beauty, with long legs and dark skin. Her long, thick, curly hair framed her face, falling perfectly beneath her shoulders, and her small waist gave her an hourglass shape. That wasn't what made her different, though. None of that was rare when walking the streets of Oyo. The girls there were beautiful— the dark, the brown, and the light-skinned all wore their skin perfectly—but most of them had their eyes set on an early home, a picture-perfect family. They wanted the whole package in order: secondary school, husband, children, and that was it. Some went as far as a degree but few went further, especially after getting married and becoming occupied with the husband and kids.

Komi was different; she wanted more and so did Mote. They had very different dreams, but dreams all the same. This was what had kept them together all these years.

Komi had managed to convince Mote to put her paintings on display in a new gallery her friend had just opened. She didn't give Mote much room to decline the offer—she had already spoken to the owner, whom she had met on one of the nights she performed at the bar. It wasn't a surprise to Mote that Komi had met such a wealthy man there; most nights she came home with tales of different men who had offered her more than was safe to accept.

She was beautiful, and they felt the need to remind her of it every night.

Mote had given in to Komi's tireless requests. She'd felt like she needed a push. All her pieces were dark and dreary, and she seemed stuck in that pattern. Perhaps if she saw her work in a new environment, she'd be inspired.

Whenever she saw a piece of art, she was always consumed by its beauty. She could stare at a piece for over half an hour, just trying to understand the artist and their mind. She had been to a few exhibitions since she returned from Nigeria. She'd found that serenity lurked between the walls where art hung, but hadn't displayed any of her pieces.

She'd been lost in thought, staring at her work hanging on the white wall of the gallery. It was such a contrast; the canvas was filled with an array of dark colours. The gallery wasn't noisy, but she could still hear a lot of chatter. Komi wasn't too far away; Mote could hear her giggle and flirt with the owner of the gallery. Mote knew she would try to convince him to keep her art on the walls for a couple more days. Komi didn't know the first thing about art, but it didn't hurt that she knew when to laugh and when to stroke his arm, and with that short blue dress she wore, Mote was sure she had his attention for the night.

Mote suddenly felt naked. It told too much of what her heart wished to keep secret. She wanted to take it down, but the room was already crowded. She felt exposed, like everyone who looked at the painting could see right into her soul.

Mote had blocked out everything and everyone else in the room. She stood alone in the white space and all that was left was this painting on this wall. She hadn't seen Jack come up to her, so she was a bit startled when he spoke.

'You've been standing here for a long time.' He held out a glass of champagne to her.

She looked at it as though she wasn't supposed to touch it, but she would. She took the glass from his hand. 'You've been watching me for a long time.'

He smiled at her. Komi always told her that she looked unapproachable and stern, so she cracked a faint smile. It had been especially hard to smile those days, so she turned back to the painting on the wall.

'This painting looks sad. Whoever did this must have been in a dark place.' He paused, stealing a glance at her. 'What do you think?'

'It is sad, and I was hurting.' She placed her empty glass in his hand and walked away from him, towards the next painting on the wall.

He followed her still. 'My name is Jack, and I am an ar—'

'Artist?' she said, cutting him off. 'Very nice, I am an artist, you are an artist, let's elope to Paris and get married.'

He chuckled. 'Oh, that's a bit cliché, and I'm an architect. But we could get married, if that's what you want. Although, why Paris? Is that where eloping artists get married?' He smiled. 'You wouldn't speak to me, but you'd marry me? You're an interesting lady.'

She giggled. 'I'm Mote.'

They'd spent the rest of the evening together. She'd tried not to be interested in what he talked about, and he'd tried to break through to her. She'd found herself saying more than she had thought she would. The whole time with him, the thoughts that had clouded her mind the past months seemed to fade away. Every word drove those thoughts further out. She continued to speak until the gallery closed for the night.

He'd offered to walk her home, and she had briefly considered it, but as they'd stepped onto the sidewalk, the cold breeze blew stronger and she started shivering. She did not know where the breeze was coming from or where it was going, but it had done something to her. It came with all that haunted her and left without it. She quickly left him standing on the streets, running in the opposite direction to get a cab home. She could feel him looking at her as she entered the taxi but did not look back. He'd made her happy that night, and she did not deserve to be happy.

The next time she'd seen him was at the opening of a museum he had designed. Since the night she'd met him at the gallery, she'd been going out more, sometimes with Komi and other times alone. This was one of those times.

He had seen her a few minutes before she saw him, so he approached her. She'd tried to take off before he could, but he'd reached out to her, held her hand, and pulled her closer. 'You don't have to run, not from me.'

She remembered how shocked she'd been at his move, how she'd listened to all he had to say that day and every day after that until this moment. She wasn't quite sure why she'd stayed, why she'd looked him up, or why she'd agreed to have dinner and then breakfast, but she was happy she had. It had been ten months since then, and here she was in Paris on the morning of their wedding, trying to keep those haunting thoughts away, and once again, the cold morning breeze blew across her face, causing her to shiver.

There was a knock on the door; she was sure it was her mother. She tossed the painting on her bed before walking towards the door.

You'd think it was her mother's wedding. After months of back and forth, Mote liked to believe her mother was genuinely happy. Her mother had often given her not-so-subtle hints that she expected a husband and grandchildren.

She imagined her mother had already been saying similar things to her sister, Tolu. Although Tolu was much younger and

7

wouldn't be thinking of marriage for another five years, Mote knew that after she had left home, all the pressure would be on Tolu to be better than her older sister. She tried not to imagine what life was like for Tolu back at home, and she always managed to convince herself that it really couldn't be that bad; at least Tolu didn't have to live with their grandmother.

She knew how angry her father was with all that happened and how strict he would have been with Tolu. Frankly, she was a little surprised he'd actually come for the wedding; she was sure her mum must have persuaded him to—after all, he had only two daughters. That didn't stop him from complaining that Mote couldn't even find a Nigerian man to marry because she had ruined her reputation back at home.

Her mother didn't seem to care so much, and Mote adored her for that. She just wanted her daughter to be happy, and all Mote wanted was to be happy, so they had been on good terms for most of the planning period.

'Coming!' she called. She opened the door and found her mother smiling with outstretched arms.

'Ẹ káàárọ̀ mà,' Mote said, kneeling halfway to the ground.

'Káàárọ ọmọ-ọ̀ mi, Aṣakẹ,' her mother replied and, from the hallway, called out to the dress-up crew to hasten them. 'Ó yá, ẹ ṣe kíá o, ẹ yá'ra - ẹyá'ra - ẹ tètè ẹ jọ̀ ọ́.'

The room filled up quickly with makeup artists, hairstylists, videographers, and the bridesmaids: Tolu, Anna, and Komi. It was a bit of a cluster, each person trying to squeeze themselves into their clothes and have their faces done, and of course, she needed to be ready as well. Mote stood in the middle of the room, watching everyone hurry as quietly as they could. She suddenly felt woozy and light-headed, and before she could call out to her mother, she hit the floor.

As she came around, she found her mother staring at her with teary eyes. She tried to sit up, but her mother wouldn't let her. She could hear distant voices, the room filled with panic; she tried to keep her eyes open, but she was weak. Soon, it was quiet. Her mum cleared out the room and called for her father.

He walked into the room, scared, but that quickly changed to anger when he saw Mote's eyes open and her attempt at getting off the floor.

'Temi, leave her be,' he said. 'Let her get up and fall again! I don't know why she is acting like a child, fainting like she has no stamina. Everyone is here for her. She can't even respect them. Maybe she is pregnant!'

'*Ah-aaah*! Baba Tolu? Don't say that. Why must you always say things like this?' her mum replied. '*Ìwà líle rẹ náà ló sún ọmọ déipò yí. Má pa ọmọ-ọ̀ mi fún mi!*'

He shrugged and headed for the door. '*Ẹ da omi s'ójú ẹ̀!*' He slammed the door behind him with a loud bang. A couple of the men with the photographers came in after he'd left and carried Mote to the bed.

About half an hour later, she had regained some of her strength, so she tried to sit up again, holding her head with her hands. '*Maami*, call the girls. We must not be late for the service.'

'Wait.' Her mother whispered although there was no one else in the room. 'You woke up earlier before your father came in, and before you passed out again, you said you wanted to tell Jack about what happened. You should have told him the minute he asked to marry you, Mote, but you cannot tell him anymore. What if he doesn't want to marry you anymore? What if he leaves you? What will your father say?' She paused and frowned. 'No, my daughter, you cannot tell him. You will marry this man today and hope to God that he never finds out. Otherwise, it will be your undoing.'

Her mum got off the bed and called everyone back into the

room, giving her no chance to respond. They moved Mote to the chair, fixing her hair and make-up, fitting her dress and shoes. They were nothing but blurred images to her. As the empty eyes in Mote's reflection stared back at her, she knew that the more this secret ate at her, the less of herself she would recognise.

CHAPTER
2

J ack had been up for a while before he rolled out of bed. The sun was yet to rise, and the moon had stayed up late, shining through his window onto his bed. When he finally got up, he walked out to the balcony, barefoot, wearing the T-shirt and shorts from the night before. The cool breeze brushed his face, and he keenly felt the thirty storeys between him and the ground.

He was about to be married. This was the singular thought that had kept him awake all through the night.

As he watched the moon slowly disappear and the sun take its place, he realised that this was the dawn of a new chapter in his life, and although he was determined to make sure nothing ruined it, he could not ignore the fact that it might already be on the fast track to its end.

He wondered if she too was awake at this time, if she watched the sunrise as he did, and if she had the same thoughts that he did. He knew she was a couple of rooms down the hall, and for a brief moment, he wished he could go to her and tell her all that had kept him awake and afraid. He had a secret; he had an untamed monster lurking in the corners of his life, threatening to destroy all he had built and hoped to build. He wanted to tell her everything, but he was afraid. He could not live without her, he didn't want to, and he was going to do everything in his power to keep her, to love her, and to protect her.

He loved her; he truly did. He had never felt this way about anyone else, or even known he could. He had tried and failed many times before, but with her, everything came so easily. Everything seemed to fall right into place. She made loving her so easy that he couldn't imagine a world where she wasn't all that she was to him. He loved her smile, her eyes; she was the most beautiful woman he had ever met. She was kind, generous, and compassionate, and although she couldn't always see herself that way, he was determined to always remind her. The past months had been challenging for them, but he'd known from the moment he'd watched her run away from him on the night they first met that he never wanted to lose her.

His smile soon faded. He couldn't think of her without being reminded of someone else. Someone he'd rather forget.

About a week ago, just before they left for Paris, he'd had the most unexpected guest. He had just returned from Ethan's new house. Ethan was his best friend since college; they'd shared the apartment until a few months ago, when Ethan had got engaged to his pregnant girlfriend, Anna. Jack had spent a couple of weeks helping him move out so Mote could move in with him.

He remembered the fear that had gripped his heart and stopped him motionless as he opened the door and saw the man waiting on the other side. Before he could gather his thoughts and find the words to speak, the man had smiled.

'Hello, brother,' he said and walked past him into the apartment.

The stranger walked around, scanning the room and making small side comments. 'Nice tux, royal blue—did she choose that?'

He made his way to the windows and peered out, then checked behind the doors as though to make sure they were alone. Then, he finally sat at the kitchen counter.

Jack was scared; he only hoped it wasn't obvious. He regretted opening the door wide enough for the man to walk through, but it was too late for regrets now. He just wanted to know what was going on.

'Who are you?' he asked with a shaky voice as he closed the door, leaving it ajar in case he needed to run for his life.

This man looked exactly like him; it felt like he was watching his reflection walk around his apartment. He didn't even know what to ask other than 'Who are you?' What else could he ask? What else could he say to the mysterious doppelgänger?

The man ignored him. He picked up a photo from a table not too far from the kitchen counter.

'She's beautiful,' he said.

'What is going on? Who are you?'

'I'm your brother, if that wasn't already evident,' the man said plainly.

'I don't have a brother.'

'Well, I knew our mother lied to the world about me, but I thought she would have told you at some point.' He sighed. 'That's interesting. However, I'm sure you see the resemblance. You can run a test if you want. It won't change who I am.'

'I don't want a test. I want you to leave. I don't know what this is. I ... I don't have a brother.' His voice began to shake again; he was pacing and almost lost his ground. Then he stopped. 'You need to leave.'

'I met her a few days ago—beautiful woman.' He turned his attention back to the photo of Mote he'd picked up, and smirked. 'She was pleasant. I can see why you chose her.' He paused. 'Although it might be a problem if she doesn't know the difference between her husband and his long-lost brother.'

'Leave, now!' Jack said more firmly, holding the door open.

The man stretched out his hand. 'Don't you have any more questions? Where I have been all these years? Don't you even care to know what I want?'

'I don't care about anything you want. I don't want to know anything about you either. I just want you to get out of my house.'

The man smiled. 'Our mother named me James, but you can call me Jay,' he said.

'I don't care. Get out!' Jack shouted.

'I know you don't. Not now anyway, but you will. I am here to take the life that should have been mine, and I *will* take it, and I'd love to see you try and stop me.'

Jay said nothing more and dropped the picture in Jack's hand before walking through the door. 'I'll be back, brother, and all this will be mine.'

As he watched Jay walk out, Jack felt like a part of him left the room with him. He shut the door and leant back against it. He slowly fell to the ground, his fingers shaking. Suddenly, he sprang up and rushed towards his mobile phone and had begun to call the police, when he stopped and thought. He was scared, but not scared enough to break up his family. His mother had just battled with her health and barely won, and he didn't know how true anything this man had said was, but he didn't want her to be in any trouble or cause her to relapse.

He knew his mother and he could not believe that she would ever do such a thing as abandon her child. But even if she had, he couldn't mention it to her; he couldn't live with himself if he did anything that caused her to be ill again.

He was still staring at his phone, deep in thought, when he heard someone at the door, trying to open it with a key.

He didn't want to be caught off guard this time, and although he couldn't protect himself emotionally from whatever this man would throw at him, he didn't want to feel helpless again. So he put down the phone and picked up a golf club from the corner of the room and headed towards the door. He took in a deep breath as he opened the door. When he realised it was Ethan, he let out a deep sigh.

He unbolted the door and stepped back, throwing the golf club on the couch.

'Jack? How did you get back here?' Ethan said, looking confused.

'I left your house a while ago. I walked home.'

'Yeah, I know that, but I just saw you at the reception, told you I was coming to get a couple of things before I go back home. So how are you here and changed so quickly?'

'Oh, that wasn't me.' Jack felt light-headed and off balance, took a few steps back and forth. Ethan's voice seemed further away with every word he spoke. Jack couldn't hear him, but he could only imagine all the questions, the confusion he must be feeling.

He would rather have Ethan doubt himself than find out the truth about Jay. He wasn't ready to deal with that reality just yet.

'Jack, that looked a lot like you, and I spoke to you—'

'It wasn't me, Ethan. I've been here for over an hour, leave it be,' he said sternly. 'Lock up when you leave,' he muttered before he slammed the door of his room behind him.

Now, on the morning of his wedding, Jack walked back into his room. The balcony had become too chilly for him. Remembering all of this upset him. He couldn't tell Mote; he knew it was a lot to take in, and he couldn't risk losing her if she freaked out or got scared. He barely understood what had happened himself; most days he just convinced himself that he had been exhausted that night and imagined it all, but that thought didn't hold for long. He knew what had happened was real, and he remembered every moment. More importantly, he remembered the fear that had crippled him as he'd watched a man with his exact image walk about his apartment and threaten his life.

Mote deserved more than all of this. He kept saying it over and over again until he was as convinced as he could ever be. He would not tell her, and hopefully, that man would never show his face again.

He figured he should tell Ethan, though. He didn't want to be the only one with this secret, and if anyone could understand the bizarreness of the situation, it would be him.

He tried to call Ethan's room, but Ethan didn't pick up. Jack sighed and sat on his bed. He had shut Ethan out since that night; he'd felt he needed to keep this to himself. He'd even tried to look up this man who claimed to be his brother, but he couldn't find a single document or record that he was born a twin. He'd hired a private investigator, but all his efforts ended up empty. After everything, the man he had met was a ghost—perhaps really a figment of his imagination.

He hoped Ethan wasn't passed out somewhere; he always burnt himself out when he had something to do, especially if it was important to him. He'd somehow managed to go the extra mile at his own wedding. Jack remembered the day Ethan had got married to Anna: Ethan had worked so much, he'd been the last person to clear out after the rehearsal dinner and the first to help set up the next day, even though he was the groom. Jack laughed to himself. Ultimately, Ethan had worked so much during the days before that he'd barely been awake at the ceremony. Although it had been a small wedding with only a few witnesses, it was beautiful.

Jack was still on his bed when Ethan used his spare card and walked right into the room. 'Hey, man, why are you still on the bed? Mote is almost ready.'

Jack smiled 'cause he'd been pretty sure that was what Ethan was going to say. 'Yeah, I know, I know. I need to tell you something, Ethan. Please sit down,' he said, patting the bed. 'This is important.'

'OK, now you have my attention. What's wrong? You don't have cold feet, do you?' Ethan said with a smirk.

'You might need to sit down,' Jack said, and waited for him to do so. 'Remember the night of the party a few weeks ago?'

'Yeah, the night you threw me out of your house—I remember,' Ethan said with a bit of a frown. He was obviously still upset about it—and fairly so—but he hadn't brought it up since that night.

'So, this is what happened ...' Jack began.

As he narrated the events of that night, recalling every moment of fear and anger and recounting every word spoken, he watched Ethan's face go from straight-out confusion to worry and then anger. His reactions were everything Jack had expected them to be, except what he said next.

'You have to tell Mote. If this man means what he says, whatever he does will affect her too.'

Jack was surprised, not because Ethan was wrong but because he knew Ethan usually saw omission of truth as being protective of the other person and not as a lie. Many times before, Ethan had laughed at him because he felt Jack shared too much of his life with Mote, and now here he was telling him to do exactly that.

Ethan continued, 'I know this is unlike me, but this is different. There are things you keep to yourself—like the strippers at the party or anything like that. Not this. There is someone out there claiming to be your brother who, by the way, looks exactly like you and is threatening to hurt your family. She becomes your family today, Jack. You have to tell her.'

'I can't,' Jack replied in a low voice. 'I can't ruin what we have on the speculation that this man isn't lying. We don't even know if he could cause any real damage. If he shows up again, I'll tell her, but for now, I just want to get married and live happily with my wife.'

He went quiet. He knew he couldn't keep this a secret for much longer, but he hoped, he truly hoped, that he would never see Jay again.

His fear kept him silent, and he was even more convinced to not tell Mote, because if she was even half as scared as he was, she would leave. He just couldn't live without her.

19

CHAPTER

3

Seventeen years later

Ara had been standing in front of her mirror for about ten minutes, fixing every stray edge and putting on the finishing touches. This included the biggest decision of her night: Ruby Woo or Snob. It wasn't just about picking the right lipstick; it was about looking perfect for her senior prom, for him.

A few months ago, she'd had tougher questions to answer, like where to study for her first degree. It had been a bumpy ride, choosing to go away from home, convincing her father that an acting career was good enough to keep her off the streets. Although he was an architect, he wasn't as in love with the arts as her mum, whose paintings were the most breathtaking images ever, and she wasn't the only one who thought so, which was how the AM Gallery had been born.

Ara was to start her freshman year at UCLA in the fall, and he was already a student there. She tried to convince herself that she wasn't choosing this college because of him, but she knew better.

A couple of days ago, after the movies, they'd walked for a while, talking and laughing and having a beautiful time together. She remembered how blown away she'd been when he stopped and kissed her.

'I love you,' he'd whispered.

She'd held her breath and stared at him; she was shocked that he did, but happy. But she couldn't find the words to tell him this. She'd panicked and left him on the corner of the street near her house. She knew she should have stayed; she'd wanted to. She could not explain even to herself why she'd run away from him, but she had.

She was both overjoyed and terrified, but tonight she was going to tell him. She couldn't wait to see him and run into his arms. He was her best friend, and she wouldn't want anyone else; she wanted him.

She smiled at her reflection in the mirror. 'I love you.' She paused and smiled even wider. 'I love you too, Andrew.'

She giggled to herself and continued practising how she would say those words back to him.

She strapped on her heels and got her purse, checking for all the necessities: lipstick, powder, a small mirror, phone, pocketknife, and pepper spray. She wouldn't need the knife or spray, but since the three weeks of compulsory self-defence classes her dad had made the whole family take, it had become a habit. She couldn't blame him for his paranoia; he was shaken up by the burglars that broke into their house about a month ago. Although they hadn't taken anything, and the cops said they weren't likely to return, he was still so scared he'd requested a police detail for as long as they were willing to indulge him.

Today, though, there was no hint of worry on his face. 'You look beautiful,' Jack said as he watched his daughter walk down the stairs.

Still holding the camera, he called out to Mote and Tale. 'Guys, come on. She's ready.'

After taking lots of pictures and the seemingly endless hugs and kisses and congratulations, Ara finally got them to let her leave the house. It was bad enough that her father was driving her to her senior prom; she hoped that no one would see her get dropped off. She wasn't the most popular kid in school, but she wasn't going to let go of what little reputation she had.

Before she left, Mote gave her a beautiful silver necklace that had a sapphire pendant. She put it around her daughter's neck.

'If you lose it, don't come home.' She laughed.

Everyone laughed a little, but Ara knew better than to think her mother was joking. She knew how important that necklace was to her mum. She remembered very clearly when her grandfather had given it to Mote a few years ago. They weren't always on the best of terms, and this was very obvious to everyone, so it had been a really big deal when he visited with Grandma. They hadn't come back since.

Somehow her little brother, Tale, managed to convince her father to take him with them. Ara sighed with frustration as she remembered the conversation she'd had with Andrew the night before, when he told her that he couldn't pick her up for the prom and would have to meet up with her when she got there. April, his sister, who'd been her backup, got a date, and so when Ara's father volunteered and insisted on taking her, she couldn't say no. So, a family trip to the prom it was. She rolled her eyes as her mum laughed at how this would make for a funny story someday.

As soon as she got in the car, she got to thinking about Andrew again. She could slip him a note and have him read it when he got home, or she could just whisper it to him—oh, she couldn't, her nerves would get the best of her.

She played out different scenarios about how the night would end. Either she would get together with her best friend and first love, or lose him because of what had happened the other night. She was so nervous her hands began to sweat.

She had tuned out her dad's voice, and her brother's. She was facing the window, and with each house they passed by, she could feel herself slipping further away from their voices.

The last thing she'd heard was Tale going on about the girl next door; they had a rather complicated relationship for seven-year-olds. They were always in each other's way, shouting all the time, yet refusing to spend time apart. Chinwe was just a couple of months younger than he was. She had fair skin and dark, thick, curly hair. Her parents were both Nigerian and had moved to the United States years before she was born. They'd recently moved to

Bowie. Her father owned and managed a string of African restaurants in the city, so he was out of town more often than not, and her mother was an active participant in many of the town associations. Therefore, Chinwe spent most of her days with Tale. The family all loved her very much, but whenever she came around to play with Tale, there was always a chorus of shouts and screams from every corner of the house. They always played too hard or quarrelled, but they always ended the day as friends again.

Their friendship seemed much easier than her friendship with Andrew, Ara thought. Falling in love with him had made everything so complicated.

She could still hear Tale talking from the back seat; he was strapped in but his voice still filled the car. However, it was easy to space out because she had heard the story he was telling at least ten times today. He and Chinwe had been making sketches for the 'remodelling' of their treehouse, but she wouldn't let him choose the colour of the inside walls, and when he got mad, she ripped up the sketches and ran home. He had been upset all day about it. He had said a mean word, he explained to Jack, but she was mean too, so he didn't want to apologise—she'd caused it.

Her dad reached out and held Ara's hand. 'Are you OK, honey?' he said, one hand still on the wheel as he glanced at her.

'I'm OK, Dad,' she replied, smiling, hoping to convince herself as well.

'I said, what do you think, Ara?'

'What do I think about what?'

'You're being absent-minded again. I've told you to be more present, Ara, you can't keep spacing out.'

She could already feel herself blanking out again. However, to reassure him, she squeezed his hand a little tighter. 'Dad, I'm here, what is it?'

'I'm going out of town tomorrow,' he said, taking his hand out of hers and placing it back on the steering wheel.

'Well, that doesn't sound like a question, Dad,' she scoffed. 'You aren't asking my opinion, you're telling me.'

'I am going to see Grandma.'

'Is she OK?' she asked, sitting up and facing him.

'Can I come with you, Dad?' Tale asked from the back seat, leaning forward.

'No,' Jack replied firmly.

Tale sat back down and whispered, 'May I come, please? I want to see Grandma.'

Jack, realising he had raised his voice and frightened him, stretched his hand to the back and rubbed Tale's knee. 'We'll all visit Grandma for Christmas; this is a quick trip. I'll be back at the end of the week.'

'OK, Dad. Tell her I love her,' Tale said softly as he leaned into the door.

He was soon distracted by something outside the car. Ara couldn't be sure what had caught his attention this time; he was easily taken away by the weirdest things. One day he'd made everyone stop talking so he could hear the birds singing. 'Because they sing beautifully,' he had said.

'What's so urgent that you can't wait for Christmas, Dad?' Ara asked. 'Don't you have that big presentation next week?'

'I'll be back in a couple of days. Just take care of your mum and your brother for me, and whatever happens ...' He paused. 'Know that I love you, both of you. Everything I do is for you, to protect you,' he said, smiling back at Tale.

'Dad, what's this about? What's going to happen?'

'I just need to ask Grandma a couple of questions. Seems there's a lot we need to talk about.'

For a while, then, he was silent.

She didn't know what to say or if she already said something wrong, but she stayed quiet. She figured she'd let him sort through all that was on his mind, then they could talk more.

There was one question on her mind, though. 'Will she remember? She barely recognised us last time, Dad,' Ara said softly.

'Oh yes, she will,' he said. 'She must.'

He was silent after that, hands tight on the steering wheel. Ara didn't ask any more questions; she turned to the window and stared out at the lights.

They were out of town when she saw the man standing in the middle of the road. She could never forget his face. He was dark-skinned and had a scar underneath his eye, and he wore black clothes and had dreads packed in a messy bun. As they approached him, she thought he might be homeless or maybe he just needed a ride. She could never have guessed what happened next.

Jack slowed the car in an attempt to swerve around the man and continue on their journey. He didn't see the piece of metal the man had in his hand, skilfully hidden behind his back. The man slammed the rod into the window on Ara's side. Glass shattered, Ara screamed, and Jack lost control, coming to a stop by the side of the road a few feet from where the man stood.

It all happened so fast. Words Ara would say over and over again in the next few days.

The man ran over, and before Ara knew what was happening, he'd heaved her out and thrown her to the ground. She could hear Tale screaming out for his dad; she was so scared and dumbfounded. Jack tried to fight the man off, but the man knocked him to the ground with the rod. Jack groaned in pain, holding his side, and lay on the ground, folding his knees to his stomach. The man struck him again, and he fell unconscious.

Ara crawled towards Tale and held him tightly, whispering to him, 'It's going to be OK.'

She didn't believe a word of it, but she hoped with all her heart that he was comforted by the lies she fed him. He was still sobbing heavily; he shrieked every time the man shouted at him to stop crying.

A few minutes later, a black van pulled over nearby. The dreadlocked man had them on the side of the car that faced the woods, making sure they didn't see anyone in the van. He covered their heads with black bags and bound their hands behind their backs and led them into the van.

It was quiet in the van. All Ara could hear was Tale's whimpering and her dad's faint groans.

They had been moving for about half an hour; she imagined they weren't going towards the city, and this scared her even more because they could be driving further away from her home. She leaned on Tale every other moment just to make sure he was still by her side. It wasn't like he could leave, but she was so afraid, anything could have made sense, and everything made no sense at all.

She gently felt for her dad. She couldn't find him, but she knew he was there; she could hear him breathing, or at least she hoped it was him she heard. She couldn't tell if they were alone.

The van finally came to a stop, and the door swung open. She couldn't see what was going on, but she heard Tale shout and struggle to get free from whoever was dragging him out of the van.

'Leave my son alone!' her father shouted over and over. 'He's just a boy.'

She choked on her tears, and shouting seemed impossibly hard.

She was next. She didn't struggle at all; she let the man drag her and lift her and drop her on the floor by her brother. He led them into the woods and made them sit on the ground, then took the bags off their heads and headed back towards the van, leaving them there.

It was the same man who had stopped their car. As soon as he was far enough away, Ara began to struggle to get free; she cursed out loud when she realised her knife was still in the car.

Then she saw the figure coming towards them from the same direction the dreadlocked man had gone. She gasped, surprised to see her father, but happy to see him unharmed.

He stopped in front of them.

'Dad, help take these off!' Ara cried out loud, but he didn't respond to her.

She called out to him a few more times but stopped when she realised he wasn't approaching them anymore. Tale didn't stop calling for him. She was just about to get up and shout even louder when he brought out a gun from underneath his shirt and shot Tale in the head.

She froze and fell to the ground. Blood rushed to her head, her vision blurred. The world seemed to stop, frozen in that moment. She did not notice when her father walked behind her and cut her free. Her eyes were fixed on the trail of blood that flowed out of her brother's head. She realised she had been holding her breath, and she inhaled deeply.

The cry that came out of her when she exhaled was like that of a dying animal. She pulled Tale's body closer to her chest. She screamed at his limp body in her arms, begging him to open his eyes, to hear her voice, to wake up.

Her father tossed the pocketknife to her and turned back the same way he had come. He left without saying a word.

Tale was no longer shouting for his dad; he wasn't crying or whimpering. He was just quiet. Ara didn't stop calling his name, trying to stop the blood with her hands.

In the distance, she heard them drive away. She cut Tale's ropes as well and carried him towards the road; blood had covered his face and soaked into his shirt and her gown. She began to walk down the road, but soon her arms were aching from carrying him and she sat at the side of the road, holding him in her arms, sobbing. He couldn't be dead. This thing she was holding ... it couldn't be her brother. At that moment, she could barely think at all. She remembered every time she had shouted at him to be quiet or keep still. Right now, she would give her life to hear him speak again.

Her father had shot him. He had killed him. How could he? What kind of father killed his child? Why did he kill his son—and why did he let her live? How would she tell her Mum? These were only a few of the questions Ara asked herself as she sat by the side of the road, covered in Tale's blood, washing his face with her tears.

She got off the ground and began walking again. She didn't know where she was or where she was headed, but she had to leave. She took off her heels and carried Tale in her arms, and taking one step after another, she kept walking.

That was all she remembered from that night.

CHAPTER

4

J ack sat still by Ara's bedside as he watched Mote pace the room back and forth, sobbing and ranting. She hailed curses on everyone and anyone who'd had anything to do with her son's death.

'Why would anyone want to hurt my family?' she questioned herself, sometimes murmuring the words out loud.

Sometimes, she sat by Ara on the other side from Jack; she'd hold her still hands and stare at the bruises on her wrists, crying softly. Other times, she'd raise her voice, trying to wake Ara up, but all she did was alert the nurses, who requested she leave the room and insisted that she take some mood stabilisers to calm her nerves.

Jack managed to convince them that he would make sure she didn't cause any more of a scene, but that just made her furious. She directed her anger at him.

'You let them kill my son.' Walking back into the room, she slumped on the couch. 'You should have stopped them, Jack. They killed my son, our son, and you just let them.'

'I didn't let them, Mote. He was my son, and I would never let anyone hurt him.'

'But you did, didn't you? You let them, and now Tale's dead and Ara is lying on this bed, hurt.'

'I know you are hurting, Mote, but do you believe I would want any of this? I tried to fight them off, but I couldn't. I tried,' he said as tears rolled down his face.

She was quiet now. She hated that she'd hurt him even more with her accusations, but she was mourning her son. She closed her eyes and curled up on the chair, calm now she had taken some of the pills they'd given her.

A few moments later, Ethan and Anna rushed into the room, waking her up. She began to cry again when Andrew walked in after them. He looked like he had been crying too. She hugged him. The hug was longer than usual; she convinced herself he needed it more than she did. He apologised for not picking Ara up himself. Mote didn't care; it seemed unimportant now. He must have known he couldn't have done more to protect them than their father would have.

A couple of officers came into the room to speak with them. Jack intercepted them, and Mote could hear him telling them to speak only to him, and not without his lawyer and friend, Ethan. She moved her gaze back to her daughter, and the tears that had dried up just a moment before came back, pouring down her face. She was in no mood to speak to anyone.

Just when it seemed like the officers would start speaking to her, Jack came to her. 'Go home, Mote. Come back later, let me take care of this.'

She could hardly see his face properly from behind her tears. She heard his words and understood his meaning, but everything felt strange and hollow. Nothing else mattered. Nothing was more important than her daughter lying unconscious in that bed. But after a few minutes of his pleading, she took one look at the officers and walked out of the room. Anna followed close behind her.

Andrew remained with Ara. He stood over her with tear-filled eyes, and he kissed her forehead and stroked her hair. He felt the bruises on her hands and closed his eyes; he prayed that she would wake up.

Just before he dropped her hand, she opened her eyes. Slowly, she turned her head towards him. He wiped his face and sprang up, forgetting that he was still holding her hand.

'I'm so sorry,' he said, kneeling beside her, patting her arm. 'I am sorry for everything, for not picking you up, for not being there for you. Your dad is here, I'll get him.' He dropped her hand on the bed and headed for the door.

'Andrew, no.'

She was weak, so she couldn't raise her voice, but it was loud enough for him to hear her.

'He's outside. He's been waiting for you to wake up.'

'My dad.' She paused, looking frantically to the door and back to Andrew. 'He killed Tale.'

She closed her eyes and was quiet after that; she fell back to sleep. He remained on his knees, staring at her, whispering her name so she could wake up and explain what she just said. Perhaps she had been hallucinating or dreaming or suffering from post-traumatic stress; the doctor assigned to her had briefed them on what she had gone through and her expected recovery. She had lost some blood from the cuts around her wrists, so she wasn't expected to be lucid when she woke up. He'd also mentioned that she might be paranoid or have panic attacks; they'd had to sedate her the last time she woke up. Before Andrew had got to the hospital, she had woken up a couple of times, but she'd only mumbled words they couldn't understand or screamed and tried to break from the tubes connected to her. Although he hadn't been here during any of her episodes, he insisted to himself that she hadn't lost her mind.

He was still lost in thought when he heard Jack's voice.

'You love her, don't you?' he asked, standing by the door, looking at him intensely, awaiting a response.

Andrew didn't answer immediately. He looked at Jack and then back at Ara.

'I love her,' he whispered, as though he was speaking to her.

He had never said it out loud to anyone but her before. He had told her he loved her, and at this moment, he wished he hadn't let her get away from him that night. He hadn't expected her to run from him, and it had startled him. He'd begun to doubt himself—maybe he read it wrong, maybe all she wanted was to be his friend, and maybe he'd just ruined that.

He hoped he hadn't ruined their friendship. She was perfect, and she was his best friend. He considered himself the luckiest person in the world, and even if she didn't love him the way he did her, he was still so happy to be in her life. Even with all of her flaws, she was the only one he wanted to be with. He wanted to be the one who made her smile, who laughed at her weird jokes and just listened to her talk about how passionate she was about being an actress.

She had so many ideas; most of them were just bits and pieces of an actual plan, but she always seemed like she had everything figured out even when she didn't. He was different from her in this way—well, in many ways, but this was most important. She spoke of how she wanted to travel the world and be adventurous, see things, meet people, experience as much as she could, and he just wanted to finish college and get a good job. He was much less adventurous and had a more stable, laid-out plan, so very unlike her big dreams that seemed to be based on whatever she felt like at that moment. It had caused more arguments than he'd like, but through it all, he'd loved her. He loved her spontaneity and hoped he would always continue to fit into her world.

As he knelt by her side, he held her hand firmly, as though he was keeping her from slipping through and falling out of this world—his world. *He killed Tale*' replayed in his head over and over again, and when Jack touched his shoulder, he shook in fear.

'You are exhausted, you should go home,' Jack said, taking a couple of steps back.

'No. I won't leave her,' Andrew replied firmly.

Jack pulled him up by the arm. 'I insist. I want to spend some time with my daughter—alone.'

Andrew was quiet. He slowly let go of her hand, took his bag, and left the room. He wasn't going to leave her alone with her father, so he went to look for Aunt Komi. She was a nurse in this hospital, and he was sure she had heard about the incident. He found her a couple of floors down, attending to a patient. He pulled her out of the room and whispered, 'Please stay with Ara. I have to go home now.'

'Is she alone, Andrew?' she replied, slightly confused.

'No, she is with Jack, but I don't trust him. Don't you think it's weird that he wasn't hurt in all of this? What if he had something to do with this?'

'Andrew, stop it.' She raised her voice. 'Jack has been through a lot. He doesn't need us doubting him. I know you are angry and probably scared, but don't say things you know nothing about.'

'Please, Aunt Komi, stay awhile with her. I'll be back soon.'

'OK, Andrew,' she sighed, knowing he would continue to ask. 'I'll stay with her till her mum gets here. Promise me you won't speak of this crazy story you've got to anyone, especially not Ara.'

He nodded, but his mind was still heavy with doubts as he left the hospital.

Back in the room, Ara opened her eyes slowly. She groaned in pain as she tried to speak. Jack was sitting by her side now, holding her hand, slowly awakening her to consciousness.

'Dad,' she whispered. 'You killed him.' She paused, trying to hold back the tears in her eyes as she recalled the events that led to her brother's death. 'You killed Tale.'

He looked at her sternly and gripped her shoulder. He leaned towards her and said, 'The police will ask you about everything that happened. You will tell them that you do not remember anything. Do you understand me?'

She could no longer hold the tears back. She took short, fast breaths, and her voice was shaky. 'Dad, I remember everything, you followed us out to the woods, and you shot him. You shot him, Dad. He was my brother, and he was your son. What about Mum? How could you do that to her? To us?'

'You don't know what you saw!' he shouted, his grip tightening. 'You should think of your mother before you say anything to anyone. Think of what it will do to her if she loses a child to death and another to mental disorder.'

Ara groaned as he let go of her arm and stood up from the bed.

'If you say this ridiculous thing to anyone, they will have you checked into a mental institution. The doctors already say that you might suffer from post-traumatic stress. Don't give them a reason to put you away.'

'Dad, what is going on?'

Ignoring her, he continued, 'Don't cause your mother any more grief. Promise me you won't say anything.'

She was still weak and was fading back out of consciousness. Her voice could barely carry her words. 'Dad, I'm scared.'

'Don't worry, baby; I will be here when you wake up. I won't let anyone hurt you.'

———

Komi came into Ara's room to check up on her as she had promised Andrew, and found Jack sat by her bedside.

'Jack, she's going to be OK.' She placed her hands on his

shoulders and rubbed them. She kissed his cheeks. 'She's a strong girl, she'll be just fine.'

He stood up from the bed and kissed her. She pulled back from him. 'Not here, Jack, Mote could be back at any time.'

'She's gone home. She won't be back for a while,' he said as he walked towards the door. He shut it and returned to her.

He kissed her again before she asked, 'What happened tonight, Jack? You can talk to me,' she said, leaning in to kiss him again.

This time, he pulled back, moving her out of the way, and walked towards the window. 'It all happened very fast. I don't remember much of what happened.'

'Oh, you have to remember something, anything. People will wonder why you were not hurt and your kids were attacked. Your son is dead.'

'That's your problem, Mote! You always care what people think.' He stopped when he noticed the look on her face. Her eyes began to tear up.

'You called me Mote,' she said with a shaky voice.

She turned and headed for the door. He stepped in front of her, obstructing her path. 'I'm sorry, Komi, it has been a long day, and my head is all over the place. It's like you said: I lost my son today, I'm not thinking right.'

He hugged her, and reluctantly she let him hold her for as long as he wanted. Tears rolled down her face still. She was in love with him, and she didn't want him to leave her. She had this gut feeling that he wasn't being truthful about what he'd seen that night, but she was going to leave it be. He had protected her once before; she owed it to him to be by his side now.

'I need you, Komi. I know it's going to be difficult but I can't do this alone.' He held her even closer.

She could feel his breath on her neck; she tried to be with him here in this moment but she couldn't. So many thoughts raced through her mind. Her heart beat faster, and her knees felt weak. She tried to remind herself that there was nothing to be scared of; this was the man she was in love with and he would never hurt her.

She remembered the first time they were together. They had met at the airport, both waiting for delayed flights, and one thing led to another, and now here she was in the arms of her best friend's husband in his sick daughter's room, hoping that the next knock on the door wasn't her—Mote.

The first few months had been difficult for her. She'd only been with him about once a month, when he would tell his family he was leaving town for a job or some other excuse. She'd missed him and longed for the moment when she could have him in her arms, but she was patient and she was apparently a very good liar. This was shocking to her because Mote had always joked that she could never keep a secret. It had been true until now, when she kept the biggest secret of all.

She would completely ignore him when she hung out with the family. She was the perfect Aunt Komi, Ara's godmother, and she truly loved Ara and Tale as though they were her children. Even more, she loved their father as though he was her husband.

He was back to staring out the window when she curled up in the chair next to him. She cried a little more when she remembered Tale and the image of his body lying in the morgue. She had flashes of the moment when they had brought him in with Ara, how she'd thought she could help save him.

She cried at the thought of Mote, what she must be going through. She wanted to be there for her best friend; Mote needed her. But how could she leave the man she loved when he had begged for her to stay and be with him?

She was still curled up on the chair, her eyes closed, when someone barged into the room.

'Boss, we have to go now!'

She jumped off the chair in a panic.

Jack stood in front of her. 'What's going on?' he said, slightly agitated, hurriedly picking up his jacket and closing the blinds.

'He got away, sir, your brother—he's gone,' replied the dreadlocked guy who'd stormed into the room.

'How could you let this happen, Stig?' He took a few steps closer to the man. The man retreated, shuffling back. 'Boss, Victoria let him go. She's with him—'

In a rage, Jack knocked over the tray of cups that were on the table by his side. Komi screamed in fright. She could not recognise him; she just stared in panic. She stepped back from him, towards the bed.

'Dad, what are you doing? Let's go,' said a girl who came running into the room. She paused when she saw Komi; she looked at her and then back at Jack. 'Dad, we have to go now. He could come here any minute.'

'What about her?' Stig said, checking down the hallway.

Jack turned to Komi. 'Come with me.'

'Jack, who are these people? Why is she calling you dad? What's going on?' She withdrew from him.

He held her wrist firmly. 'We have to go, Komi, and I don't have time to explain.'

'If you won't tell me what's going on, I am not coming with you. Who will stay with Ara? You can't just leave.'

'Boss, we have to go!' Stig insisted.

Jack pulled her closer, holding her firmly. She began to struggle and raised her voice. 'Let me go!'

Stig walked back into the room and pulled out a gun from beneath his jacket. He pointed it at her, and she froze. She looked at him in fear and confusion; she had tears in her eyes now. She could feel her heart racing, her hands trembling. She stared at the gun as she moved closer to Jack. Although she'd tried to get away from him earlier, he was still the only one in the room she trusted.

'Komi, don't fight,' he said as he kissed her. 'Just come with us, I will explain everything later. I love you, I won't hurt you.'

The girl scoffed. 'Dad, leave her.'

'Put that away, Stig,' Jack said, waving the man down. 'She understands that we have to go. Don't you, baby?'

She nodded slowly. Her hand still locked in his, they walked quickly, and she didn't understand what was going on. It all seemed surreal, as she walked down the hallway and out the doors with this man who was now an absolute stranger to her.

She took short, fast breaths, which got louder as they approached the exit. He squeezed her hand tighter any time it seemed fear was getting the best of her, either to threaten her or to comfort her, she wasn't sure, but she went quiet. She hoped that someone would see her, see through Stig's shirt to the gun he kept underneath, see through her eyes to the fear that crippled her and sealed her tongue. But no one spared their group a second glance.

As they got out into the night's cool breeze, there was a car waiting for them. The driver called out to them. He looked about the same age as the girl, the one who called Jack 'Dad'. That was the most disturbing thing that had happened—he'd let this girl call him Father. Who was she?

Perhaps Komi wasn't the only one he was sleeping with. At this point, that would not surprise her. The thought hurt her, but it was easier to think about than the fact that he might kill her tonight, just as he had murdered his son.

CHAPTER
5

J ack sat quietly beside the woman, holding her hand and staring out the window. She was his wife; they had come out to the woods to take time off and be together, but she'd had an accident and bruised her arm. They'd got lost and tried to follow the trail that led to the highway. They'd been sitting on the side of the road because she was too tired to keep walking when Greg found them.

The story she told was surprisingly believable; he couldn't have come up with such a lie as quickly as she had. Thankfully, Greg had completely believed her and offered to give them a ride into the city. She'd insisted they go to the city. He didn't understand much of what was going on, but she'd helped him escape. She'd saved his life and he didn't know why, but until he had more information, he decided to follow her lead.

At intervals, she would squeeze his hand tighter. Sometimes, she'd stare at him, assuring him that it was going to be OK. She made small talk with Greg. They talked about a variety of things, from his little girl Ruth and her new science project that had him looking for a particular kind of tree, to his wife who loved the loud city life too much to leave with him and their daughter when they'd moved to a quieter part of town.

He was uninterested in this man's life. He stared out the window, allowing himself to be distracted by anything and everything. His own life was hanging in the balance, the fate of his family in the hands of a madman, and he was forced to trust this woman he did not know but found himself stuck with. She played the part of his wife all too well; it scared him. She'd created this faux connection with him that almost made him comfortable with her, but sometimes when he looked at her, he saw something in her eyes that made him uneasy; he couldn't quite figure it out. At that moment, though, she didn't seem threatening.

She was beautiful. Her red hair was tied up in a bun that was now loose, scattered strands falling to her face. She wore pale jeans and a grey top, which was hidden beneath a long blue sweater. One of the bullets had grazed the side of her arm, cutting through the sweater and leaving a rather large wound, which she had bound with a ripped piece of her top.

She didn't need him at all, or so it seemed; it annoyed him that he relied on her for everything. Since they had escaped from the cabin, she hadn't said a word to him. He'd had to follow her lead. She knew the way around, and most importantly, she knew how not to get caught. He'd asked a few questions while they'd waited by the roadside to find a ride, but she'd ignored him, concentrating on stopping the bleeding from her arm.

She somehow managed to be both distant and intimate with him at the same time. When she told Greg about the life she wanted him to believe they had, she spoke with a tender tone that seemed genuine. Jack listened carefully and pictured everything she said. In his mind, her very words formed a reality he knew was untrue but was pleasant enough to let linger. She spoke of the child they were expecting and how this trip was to be their last getaway with just the two of them because of their busy schedules. She even had an explanation for her bleeding arm: apparently, she was a strong-willed klutz. She'd insisted on pitching the tent herself; she slipped and fell, and on her way down to the bottom of the shallow ditch, a branch protruding from the tree by the tent cut deep into her arm.

'You should have seen me fall,' she said, smiling. 'I felt so silly. Now I know I should have just let my amazing husband fix up the tent. Paul has always been good with his hands.' She said all this with her hands locked in his, and at this point, she looked up at him and kissed him. 'He saved me, just as he's done a thousand times before.'

He stared into her eyes as she tossed her gaze between him and

Greg, who watched them through his rearview mirror. Her blue eyes told a story he could not understand. Her hands felt warm and tender, but her words provoked him. She was an amazing liar; every word felt right and true. He couldn't blame Greg for believing every word of it and even sympathising with her. All that she said made for a much better story than the truth, which would have had them explaining how he'd been kidnapped and chased down by men with guns while she helped him escape, and most importantly, how a bullet had grazed her arm.

He let her do all the talking. He was already disoriented; he could not fight her on this or try to explain to this man that he was a victim and needed saving. So he let her call him whatever she wanted; he assumed the role of Paul, the expectant father. He said very little and nodded when appropriate. Whenever he wasn't playing his part in her unending tale of their perfect life, he stared out the window, lost in thought. In his world, in his true reality, he knew his family was waiting for him.

After driving for what seemed like forever, although it was only about an hour or so, he was glad to get out of the car. He waited for Greg to drive off and then he turned and ran away from the motel where Greg had dropped them.

She ran after him as fast as she could, shouting, 'Stop, wait! Stop!'

He just kept running.

'He is going to kill them all!' she yelled, panting.

That made him stop. She slowed down as she got closer to him.

'Who are you? What do you want from me?' he shouted in frustration. 'What is going on?'

'Just listen,' she said. 'Let's go inside and I will explain it all to you.'

'I am not going anywhere with you! You're one of them!'

49

'I saved you!'

'I don't owe you anything, woman.'

'You need to come with me. You can't be on the streets; they are looking for you, for us, and I will not go back there. Think about your family.'

'I *am* thinking about my family!' His eyes let go of the tears they harboured as he paced around her. Sympathy flashed in her eyes, but she kept her mouth in a hard line as she held his face, cleaned his tears, and hugged him. He sighed, giving in, as she held him in her arms. Her right hand rubbed his neck, convincing him that staying with her was the only option he had at surviving the demons that haunted him. She smelt like sweat and blood.

She pulled away, rubbing her arm. 'We have to go inside now. I am going to need you to trust me.' She let down her hair and fixed up his shirt. 'You are Paul Whitman, and I am your wife Sarah. We are expecting a child. We got lost in the woods after a minor accident—'

'Yeah, I know, I heard your story. Very convincing,' he said with a snort.

'It will be if you play your part,' she said sternly.

He followed her into the motel. They got a room and settled in fast. She went out to get dinner and a few changes of clothes while he remained in the room. She got back in about an hour later. He was on the bed, watching the TV. He was so engulfed in the news, he didn't even hear her come in. She walked towards him and stood in front of the TV set, obstructing his view before turning it off.

'Don't torture yourself—it's not the cops looking for you,' she said as she put her shopping bag down on the bed. She took out a small towel she had bought and headed for the bathroom.

He heard the shower running, and he quickly began searching the bag, rather noisily, hoping she had got a phone. He found a burner at the bottom of the bag. He fixed up the battery and made a call.

'Please pick up ...' he whispered, but before they could answer, her wet hands grabbed the phone from his ear and smashed it against the wall.

'What is wrong with you?' she shouted. 'Are you trying to get us killed? Are you trying to get me killed?'

'I need to reach out to my family; I need to know they're safe,' he said as he stood up and turned to face her. 'I need...'

He paused; she was naked and wet. Her red hair was dark and long and fell midway down her back. She wore a necklace that had a small locket that fell in her cleavage. Her eyes seemed brighter under the pale yellow light, and her skin was fair and bare, with droplets of water running down. He tried not to look anywhere other than her face; he focused on the frown that caused her eyebrows to fold up together, the hint of pink on her cheeks, the strands of hair glued to her forehead. Most importantly, in all of this, he looked at her.

She took a couple of steps towards him. 'What do you want?'

'I—I want my family,' he stuttered.

'Then let me help you. Just trust me.'

'How can I trust you? I don't know you. I don't know anything about you. I don't know your name.'

She looked him in the eye. 'I just saved your life, and risked my life in more ways than you could ever understand. So trust me or don't, but listen to me, otherwise you will not survive this. I can promise you that!'

He didn't know what to say, and as the silence stretched between them, her frown slowly faded.

She walked toward him, closing the gap between them, so close that the water on her body seeped into his clothes. Her voice was softer, the anger seemed to have burnt out. 'I want to help you, and I will if you can just stop getting in the way.' She held his face in her palm, and looked at him pleadingly. 'Let me help you,' she whispered.

He was conscious now that her body was pressed into his, and her voice was softer than he'd ever heard it. He could hear the desperate plea in her voice and was weary, but he could not deny that she had all the answers he needed. So he slowly nodded, and she smiled, mirroring his nod.

She walked back into the bathroom and stayed there another fifteen minutes. The shower was off for about five minutes before she finally came out. As she unlocked the door, he stood and faced the wall; he had laid out her clothes on the bed. She laughed a little as she put them on.

'All done,' she said as she sat on the bed and leaned against the headrest. 'What do you want to know?'

'What is your name?' he asked.

'Victoria. Victoria Sherman.'

'What were you doing in that cabin in the woods? Why were you there?'

'I have lived there for about thirteen months.'

'Are you his prisoner too?'

'Not in the conventional way, or in the way you were. I'm his wife.'

He sprang up from the bed. He picked up a plastic fork and pointed it at her as a weapon.

She got off the bed.

'That won't do you any good,' she scoffed. 'I am not trying to hurt you; I saved you from him.'

'Why?' he shouted. 'Why did you help me, why are you doing all of this?'

'I needed to get away from him. He is a dangerous man. It

wasn't until he came after you that I realised I couldn't stay with him anymore.'

'How could you marry a man like that? How ...' He paused. 'I don't even want to know anymore. I don't care. I will not stay here with you.'

He grabbed the keys and headed for the door.

'If you leave, you'll never know what he wants from you. Without me, you will never have answers to the questions that have been whirling in your head since the minute he took you. He is always going to be two steps ahead of you—let me help you catch up.'

He stopped.

She sighed, relieved, and took a couple of steps closer to him. 'If you stay, I'll tell you everything you want to know. Who he is, how he found you, what he wants, and most importantly, how to stop him from destroying you.'

He stood at the door for a while. He let his head rest against it, his hand still on the knob as he contemplated his next move.

She waited patiently.

Without turning away from the door, he said under his breath, 'Tell me everything.'

She nodded in approval.

CHAPTER

6

'My father was a mercenary,' Victoria began. 'He would do just about anything for the right price. Many years ago, he was sent to kill a man and his family.

'The man, a wealthy politician, had a price on his head, and my father, without reluctance, took up the job. My father did the job, just as expected; he shot the man and burnt the house to the ground, with the man's family inside. Before he left the burning building, he heard a little boy, just a few days old, crying in one of the rooms, and got him out. I cannot say what made him do that in the moment, but he did. He would later hear on the news that the wife and their only child had escaped from the house before it burnt down.

'She completely denied the existence of their second child and had his birth certificate and every proof of his birth erased from the system. My father brought him home, and that was the beginning of the life of the man you now know as Jay.

'I didn't know Jay until he was about seven years old. I grew fond of him and soon he was my best friend. He spent hours studying everything about how my father ran his empire. Soon, he was the perfect puppet to do my father's bidding.

'He trained him to fight, to steal, to lie. He wasn't just a good assassin; he was an excellent conman. He was the heir my father always wanted. I wasn't ever good enough to take over his empire.

'Jay never knew about you or your mother, because Father never told him. He loved my father so much, he would do anything for him.' She sighed. 'He loved me too. Until he found out the truth. Until I told him the truth.

'I wanted to get out. My father's life was toxic and dangerous, and I wanted to start a new life alone with Jay, with the love of my life, but he wouldn't listen. He was devoted to my father and he was held down by his blinding principles. I hoped that the truth would cause him to leave, but I was wrong. I turned him into the monster that haunts you today.

'I told him my father murdered his father—your father—and my father had only kept him alive for the money he would get by replacing you and accessing the wealth your father left to his children, which was now all yours. I assured him that my father would kill him as soon as he delivered what he was supposed to and was no longer relevant. I told him that your mother abandoned him and lied to the world that he never even existed, to save herself from the shame of leaving her child behind in a burning house. I hoped to convince him that this life he'd been trained to live wasn't his and he could truly be himself with me, far away from all of this.

'I regretted telling him as soon as the words came out of my mouth, because I saw the hatred grow in his eyes, and there was nothing I could do to save him from this path of revenge I had put him on.

'My father soon realised that he may have trained Jay too well, because as the time got closer for him to replace you, Jay wanted more than to just take your money. He wanted your life, your family, he wanted all of it. There was nothing stopping him. Nothing except my father.

'I loved Jay and he loved me, but the day he killed my father and took his place in his empire, turning his men to do his bidding, was the day I lost the man I loved.

'He's been watching you closely for years. He knows things about you only you could know. He doesn't just look like you, he is your exact replica. He likes golf, just like you do. He was born left-handed, but he writes with his right hand now just because you do. When he takes over your life just as he has spent years planning to, no one will ever know that he isn't you. This is the moment he has been waiting for.

'Jay will stop at nothing to take what he wants. He blames you for the life he has lived. Father loved him, but he did not shield him from the horrors of his world as he did for me when we were kids. He took him to make deals and close contracts. He witnessed so many murders and has killed his fair share of people. He is not afraid to kill or to die. He wants revenge for being left behind, and he will get it.

'Over the years, he has made contact with every member of your family: your wife, your daughter, your son, and even your best friend. That was a test run, and if none of them noticed that he wasn't you then, they won't notice it now.'

Jack was on the floor of the motel room now, his head leaning on the door and his eyes closed. Tears rolled down his face. He was so confused. His mother had never told him about a brother. He'd known his father was murdered, although he didn't know much else about him. His mother didn't talk much about the past; she said it did nothing but hold you back from what the future held. Perhaps this was the past she was running from, the one where she had abandoned her child. How could she have done that? Why wouldn't Jay be furious and out for blood? He might be the one with the gun, but she had condemned his family to the wrath of a madman.

Even in all this, he couldn't get Mote out of his head. Now he was lying on one side of the bed with the sheets covering his head. He brought his knees up to his chest. He had failed his family. The thought slipped into his mind and held tight.

His thoughts drove him into despair. As he lay on that bed in a motel room with a woman he barely knew, his family's lives flashed before his eyes. He remembered the day Ara was born. The joy in his heart had been so overwhelming he could not hold back his tears when he heard his little girl cry for the first time. She was so beautiful. He'd looked at her, and in that moment, he realised that he was the most afraid he'd ever been. He knew nothing about being a father, but he would do his best to be perfect for her. He had always been proud of her; she was smart, beautiful, and incredibly strong. Every moment with his little girl was imprinted on his mind, from the first time she said *daddy* to when she'd emerged at the top of the stairs in her prom dress; he loved his daughter more than he ever thought was possible.

Tale's story was a bit different. There had been some complications during the delivery. Mote had almost lost her life; her parents even suggested she go back home to Nigeria so they could take better care of her during her recovery, but she wouldn't agree to that. She'd had a falling-out with her father shortly before Jack met her, and although she didn't talk much about it, he knew that she had never completely got over whatever took her away from home.

Tale grew very fast and healthy, to their surprise. Mote loved him so much, and he was her precious little gift. He had just turned seven a few weeks ago, and he was very excited about his new age. 'All the cool kids are seven already,' he'd say in a whiny little voice in the weeks before his birthday.

He'd found a friend in Chinwe, their neighbour's daughter, whose parents were seldom around. Jack had built them a treehouse in the yard last summer, and that was their haven. They hardly ever left it. Although they fought more than half the time, they were very protective of each other, and Jack believed they would have it no other way.

Bits and pieces of their lives played in his mind, from vacations together to family dinners, to right before they'd left the house that evening. He wished more than anything that he hadn't let Tale come with him to drop off Ara. He wished Andrew had come to get her as he had earlier planned, and for a minute, he hated him, but he was his best friend's son, and it was irrational even in this moment to blame him for any of this.

The ache in his chest grew with every breath he took, and he just could not understand one thing: why his mother had abandoned her child.

'Why did she leave him? Why did she not go back for him? How could she go on knowing her child might have survived and never bothered to look for him?'

'I don't know, Jack. She could have tried—I don't know, but she will have to answer that herself,' Victoria responded softly.

'She's his mother! How could she not save her child?' He shook his head. 'Jay never bothered to find out? He could have just asked her! All these years, I'm sure he had the chance to.'

She sighed. 'There are truths that bring more pain that lies. I don't think he has ever had the courage to ask why. The chance that she really didn't want him or simply abandoned him terrifies him. I think it haunts him more than anything else.'

He kept his eyes closed to keep the tears from falling. He heard, almost as clearly as he did the first time, the loud bang that had echoed in his ear when he was in the van. He sprang up in a panic, and he asked the one question he knew could break him.

'Did he hurt them?'

'What?'

'Did he kill my children?' he shouted, staring at her. Tears rolled down his face.

'I don't ... I ...'

'Tell me!'

She looked away, but he wasn't going to let her get out of this. He would be silent until he got his answer, or he would leave.

'I don't know, Jack,' she said in a clear, low voice.

He was outraged. 'If you won't tell me the truth, then you have nothing to offer me.'

He began to look for his shoes; he found them underneath the bed and reached out to get them. One was a little further back than the other, so he had to go under. On coming out, he hit his head on the bedframe. He let out a loud cry; he shouted and cursed. He remained on his knees and buried his face in the pillow.

He didn't care if knowing the truth would hurt—it couldn't hurt as much as not knowing. Victoria's lips twisted as she watched him. She crawled over to his side of the bed and knelt beside him.

'Yes,' she said.

'What?' He raised his head.

'He killed your son, Jack.'

Jack closed his eyes for a moment as her words replayed in his head. *He killed your son. He killed your son.* He clenched his jaw, forcing his anger to stay pressed down until he was ready to release it. When he opened his eyes, she was still there. The bearer of his worst nightmare, the wife of his enemy.

He thought he glimpsed tears in her eyes—but that couldn't be. She didn't have that in her. He walked to the bathroom and shut the door. He climbed into the bathtub and sobbed quietly until his head throbbed in pain. It was in that moment, in the dark of night, lying in a bathtub in the middle of nowhere, that he knew his life would never be the same again. It was there he knew he would have to become his brother.

The first light had just begun to shine through the cracks in the blinds when he opened the door. She was still sleeping, curled up near the headrest. She looked calm and peaceful, nothing like someone who had grown up with assassins, although he had no idea how he felt she *should* look.

'Victoria,' he said, standing above her, his shadow cast over her face.

She didn't answer, so he leaned in closer and tapped her. She woke up frightened. She screamed and kicked him away, fighting and scurrying away from him.

He shouted at first—her foot had hit his mouth—but he stopped when he saw the look on her face. She no longer looked peaceful or even fierce, as she had the day before. This was a new look, one he'd never thought he would see her wear. She was scared.

She took in a deep breath and got off the bed, frowning. 'Don't ever do that again,' she said, then headed to the bathroom without looking at him even once.

He did not understand why she was afraid. He had barely touched her, but she'd screamed as though he was attacking her, as though he wanted to hurt her. Then it came to him: she'd probably thought he was going to.

He waited for her to come out of the bathroom. This time, she was only partly dressed.

'Are you scared of me?' he asked, taking a few steps away from her.

She looked over at him and turned away. 'No, I'm not.'

'Then why did you scream? I wouldn't hurt you.'

'I know that.' She paused. 'It's just ... you have his face. And you may not hurt me, but he would.'

He felt pity for her.

She put her clothes on quickly and began to pick up their trash and clean up the room.

'We can't leave anything behind,' she said without looking back at him.

He could see that he had caused her great pain. He didn't know much about her life; she'd conveniently left out information about herself when she'd told him about her father and Jay. He wanted to comfort her, but it was probably best to not touch her again. He was still angry, furious, but he directed everything he felt at his brother, not at her.

He wanted to help. If for nothing else, he needed her to trust him. Like she'd said, he couldn't get out of this without her. She was his entire arsenal. Just as Jay knew everything about him, she knew everything about Jay; he hoped she would be enough.

He let her pack up without interrupting her. When she was done, he asked, 'You told me he loved you. Why would he hurt you?'

'Jay no longer has room in his heart for love. He is consumed with a burning desire for vengeance.' She sighed. 'He did once, but I took that from him when I told him about you and your parents, and he never lets me forget it. I took his life from him.'

'When did you tell him?'

'About a year before he first met you. After studying you for months, he decided to finally meet with you, face to face. So I followed him to your apartment that night.'

'You were there? Why didn't you come back to warn me? You could have told me then. My son is dead! I could have protected him.'

'There was nothing you could have done for him!' she shouted. 'Would you have believed me? Also, that was many years ago. I thought I could change him back to the man I fell in love with.'

The entire situation provoked him. Every time she said something about Jay, he was filled with rage all over again. He found it very difficult to not hate her, to not hurt her the way she'd hurt him with her words. She had also caused him pain; willingly or not, she was part of this elaborate plan to destroy his family, and he hated her for it. She might have been a victim once, but she'd stayed with Jay all those years. He had been married for sixteen years, and for those sixteen years, she'd chosen to stay with a psychopathic murderer.

'We have to go. We can't stay here any longer,' she said, holding the door open.

'Where will we go? How will we stop Jay? Where is he now?' The questions went on and on.

'We will start with his daughter,' she said as she walked out the door.

CHAPTER
7

M ote was awake all through the night. At first, she tried everything to take her mind off all that had happened, but she later gave in to the grief, and it consumed her. Everything she saw was a reminder of her children, the one she had lost and the one she hoped would wake up. She stared at the pictures on the wall; she stared into the eyes of her kids, and her heart sank. She sank into her bed, hoping to drown herself in her tears, but soon even the tears dried up. She was tired and exhausted; she just lay there, waiting to wake up from this nightmare she had stumbled into.

She jumped when she heard a knock on the door. She wasn't sure who she was expecting to see, but she was slightly disappointed. It was just Anna. Anna had been one of her closest friends since she met her years ago when Ethan introduced her as his girlfriend. She had always been an amazing friend; she was also Tale's godmother and was pretty much family already. Mote knew that this broke Anna's heart just as it did hers, but she could give her no comfort. In this moment, her heart knew no peace, so she had nothing to offer. She just lay there on her bed and stared at the ceiling.

Anna let herself in. She placed a cup of tea by the bedside, climbed on to the bed, and just lay there with her, holding her hand and letting her cry whenever she needed to. Although it was a summer night, the breeze from the cracked-open windows was cold and filled the room very quickly.

Anna stood up to close the windows and the blinds when she saw the police car stationed outside the house. She recognised one of the officers from the hospital; they must have followed them home.

She climbed back into the bed. She had no words to comfort Mote, although she usually did. In this moment, all she could do was hold her hand and cry with her. As a therapist, she was used to telling her clients the best ways to deal with grief, that they'd ultimately feel comfort if they allowed themselves to grieve, but in this moment, all of that seemed like lies. She'd tried everything her books recommended, but it didn't help much.

A few hours ago, she had been standing in a well-lit, cold room in the hospital, holding Ethan's hand and crying into his shoulder as the medical examiner drew back the cloth and revealed Tale's body. She'd thought she just might pass out; the chemicals they used to mask the smell of death did nothing but nauseate her. She reached out and felt his cold hands, and for a minute, she had hoped he would squeeze her hands in return. She closed her eyes, and shook when she felt hands cover hers. She took in a deep breath, but they weren't Tale's.

She watched as the blue gloves took her hand out of Tale's and covered him up. The man's voice was calm and weary. She knew he tried to be sympathetic, but his words bounced right off her skin. This was his job; he probably had the same conversation with a dozen people before noon every day.

She knew she had no basis for the rage she suddenly felt towards him, but his supposed words of comfort hurt her. She shoved a tray of bean-shaped bowls to the floor and screamed at the top of her voice, falling to her knees beside the table where Tale's body lay. Ethan quickly held her in his arms and led her out of the room.

She wondered how he found the strength to even console her. He had lost his parents in a car crash when he was really young. He'd been stuck in the car with them for hours before he was rescued. He was terribly affected by the entire incident; for years, he relived images from that night, which caused panic attacks. His boss had ordered him to have therapy sessions after he'd had a panic attack in court, which was triggered by a car accident case he was working on.

She remembered the first time he'd come into her office; the cold attitude and distant voice had been enough to make her want to move him on to another doctor. However, before the end of their first session, he showed something. As he talked about the case he was working on and the events that had led to his episode in the courtroom, she'd noticed the compassion he had for his client, and although he was very angry, she'd been determined to help him heal and grow.

This night, he'd proved that he really had overcome his fear of death and all the anger that came with it. He held her in his arms for as long as she wanted; he let her cry and comforted her. It didn't make it hurt less that her godson was lying dead on that table, but she found comfort in his calmness.

It was almost morning when Mote got off the bed. Anna was asleep, having rolled over and nestled beneath the headboard. Mote drank the tea Anna had placed on the side table. It was horrible; the cold sweetness had an awful aftertaste and made her want to puke. She had taken tea cold before, but this just tasted like gall. She knew it probably wasn't that bad really, but everything was awful.

She looked out the window and noticed the police car stationed in front of their house. The men inside were sleeping with the window wound up.

She took the cup of tea and quietly went downstairs. She tried to avoid looking at the walls where the pictures were hung; she just headed straight to the kitchen cabinets. She placed the cup on the centre table and climbed one of the side tables to reach a top shelf. She sighed, relieved to have found what she was looking for.

The bottle.

She'd quit drinking shortly before she got married. She had wanted a fresh start then. No baggage, no addictions, just a perfect wife to her husband and mother to her children. Ironically, she'd had her first drink shortly after the birth of her first child.

It had been a very long time since she'd felt herself on the brink of depression, as she felt now. Jack had never seen her like this; she never wanted him to see her like this. As she sat down on one of the high stools and poured some of the whisky into the cold tea, she let out another deep sigh.

She was back here, the place she'd promised to never return to. She was back to being engulfed by the false reality where she would find solitude at the bottom of the bottle, drinking through its contents, hoping every burn would bring healing.

She held the cup up to her nose and breathed it in. The smell of the whisky was so familiar even though she hadn't had a sip in over a decade. She'd quit because of her children, and now she had nothing keeping her from indulging.

She thought about Jack again. He knew she'd struggled with alcoholism at the time when they met, and he was proud of her for quitting. She closed her eyes, and she could hear his voice telling her of the strength she had, but in this moment, here and now, she knew she had no strength left. She was weak and frail and once again troubled, and the scent of the whisky called out to her, waking a lust in her she'd thought she had put away.

She was there another five minutes, staring blankly at the curtain above the sink as it swayed in the wind, up and down. It knew no rest as long as the window remained open. She felt like that piece of cloth, slave to life's troubled breeze.

'What are you doing, Mote?' Anna asked, walking into the kitchen.

Startled, Mote dropped the cup, spilling some of the tea and knocking over the bottle. It crashed to the floor.

She got off the stool and looked at Anna. 'I was just thinking. It's nothing.'

'Are you drinking again?'

'Again?' She frowned. 'Ethan told you.'

'He is my husband, Mote. Yes, he told me.'

'Well, my life's not your business, is it?' Mote shouted and stormed out of the kitchen. Before she could reach the stairs, there was a knock on the door.

She sighed and reluctantly headed to the door. She knew Anna only meant to help, but she was angry and she couldn't control her rage; she was angry at everyone and everything. She felt her blood boil. She was mainly embarrassed; she wanted so much to be calm and reasonable, but she couldn't pull herself together, and if the bottle would help calm her nerves, then so be it.

She stood at the door and let out a deep breath before she opened it. Standing there was one of the officers stationed outside the house.

'We heard a loud noise and some shouting. Is everything OK, ma'am?' he asked in a concerned tone. He was tall and well built, standing at ease with one hand on his hip near his gun and the other on the door, as though he wanted to push it open and come in.

'Everything's fine, just a broken bottle,' she replied as she took a step back, allowing him to come in and look inside the house.

He took a quick look around and then headed back out.

He turned back at the porch. 'We'll be right outside if you need us.'

'Thank you, officer,' she said, and she closed the door behind him.

When she turned around, Anna was already out of the kitchen, standing by the foot of the staircase.

'I'm sorry,' she said softly, folding her arms again. 'I didn't mean to upset you. I care about you, Mote, and I know this is a tough time, but you need to be strong, for your husband, for Ara.'

Mote pulled out a chair from the dining table set. She sat down and placed her face in her palms, crying and sobbing. 'I have lost all my children, all three of them.'

'Oh, don't say that, Mote, Tale may be gone but Ara will be fine. The doctors said she'll recover soon.' Anna paused, clearly thrown by *three* children, but she didn't question it.

She tried to lead her back upstairs to the bedroom, but Mote insisted on staying in the parlour. She curled up on one side of the long sofa, raised her knees to her chin, and buried her face in them. Anna sat on the other end. The room was filled with silence, interrupted by Mote's occasional sobs.

'Would you like another cup of tea?' Anna asked.

Mote nodded slowly. Anna got up and went into the kitchen. Mote didn't really want the tea, but she wanted to be alone. She realised she had said *three* children; she was grateful to Anna for not asking more about it.

The truth was she did have a third child, and she had lost that child too. Lara was just a baby when Mote gave her up all those years ago. She remembered it like it was yesterday.

She was in love, but even more, she was young and careless. At least those were her mother's words when Mote had knelt before her and told her she was pregnant. There was a lot of crying and shouting from both sides. However, her mother's words could not have been worse than her father's. He was mad with rage; he'd instructed her to get rid of the child or be disowned. She was humiliated, engulfed in shame.

Lanre Olayinka, often called Yinka, was the father of her child. He lived with his single father, a few compounds away from their house in Oyo, and was training to take over his father's mechanic workshop. Mote couldn't even tell him she was pregnant; her father forbade her from telling anyone.

'You have disgraced this family!' he would shout at the top of his voice.

He was still active in the army, then, and he ruled his household just as he did his men at the barracks. His voice was so loud when he shouted; it echoed and bounced off the walls. She would never forget the ringing in her ear from the slap he threw across her face when she dared to say she was with child.

'For that mechanic's child? The one who has no future? You want to marry that poor boy?' he asked in rage.

She decided to leave Nigeria before she began to show, and her father was more than pleased to see her go, taking the shame she had conceived with her. He'd been sure to let her know. From the day she'd told him, she was never allowed to leave the house. She would write letters to Yinka and get them to him through Tolu, her younger sister. Tolu passed by his father's workshop every day on her way to school, so every morning, Mote would wrap up her letter and sneak it into Tolu's school bag and wait eagerly for dusk when she got to read her lover's soothing words. In her letters, she wrote of her undying love for him. Without giving much reason, she attributed her house arrest to her father's overprotection and paranoia with regards to her outings as a result of the tension building in the eastern parts of the country.

'He fears war, most importantly its aftermath,' she wrote, hoping Yinka would understand and not ask of her more than she was willing to share, and he did. At least she hoped he did, as he did not ask any more questions about it. He seemed to care only about her well-being.

A few weeks later, she left for America to live with her Aunt Ayo until the baby was born. She had begged and cried for her father to not kill the child, but he still would not let her keep it. She remembered his loud voice echoing through the phone when she called him the night before her delivery.

'You must not come home with that child. Just leave it there and come back,' he said before he cut off the call.

Aunt Ayo helped her give her child up for a closed adoption about two months after she delivered. She had no ties to her daughter's new family, and they had no idea who she was, either.

'It's better this way.' She remembered the words Aunt Ayo had said to comfort her the night her child was taken from her. 'You can go home now. Your father will take you back. It will all be like nothing ever happened.'

She'd been miles away from home, and her heart hurt every day. She grew weary from missing Yinka. For the first few months after she left, she wrote letters to him but never got a response, so she eventually stopped writing. Their love had become one across the oceans, and just like her mother often reminded her, such long-distance relationships seldom worked out. She decided to stay in America. She had grown to despise her father for what he made her do. She was never going to return to his house.

She met Jack months later. She smiled as she remembered their life together, how much her love for him helped her heal.

She was still lying down on the sofa, tracing imaginary lines with her finger across the floor, when Anna came back with the cup of tea. She looked like she had been crying again. Mote got off the chair and put the tea on the table. She hugged her, and they both cried again.

'It's been a long night, let's get some sleep. It's going to be OK,' Anna said as she let go of her and led her up the stairs.

Mote didn't know whether or not it would be OK. All she knew was what the pastor always said to comfort them in difficult times: 'This too shall pass.'

CHAPTER

8

K omi was still held up in the back seat of the car, between Jack and the girl. Well, not Jack—Jay, she had heard one of them call him. He looked just like him, smelt like him. How could he not be Jack? Or was he just pretending not to be? It was all so confusing. Who was this girl, and why did she call him Dad? So many questions twirled around in her mind, and she found no answers.

She sat quietly, trying not to say anything that might put pressure on his trigger finger. She could feel the gun pressed into her side, not as firmly as in the hospital but enough to let her know all she was allowed to do was breathe. She was in love with him, and she hoped he loved her just as much. So none of this could be happening, could it? It wasn't real; there must be some misunderstanding. She told herself that until she believed it. It seemed the only way she could stay calm. She reached out her hand and placed it over his, squeezing it lightly.

He turned and looked at her. 'I don't have to hurt you, so don't make me.'

His words sent chills down her spine, and she choked on her tears. She was scared that if he saw her crying, it might give him another reason to lash out at her.

His voice was calm as always but had a cold tone to it. When she looked into his eyes, she no longer saw the man who kissed her, who surprised her with late-night visits, the man who had promised to love her; she could not recognise this man. He looked just like Jack, but she was starting to realise she had either gotten mixed up in something horrible or fallen in love with a stranger.

Mote. Had her best friend also been in love with a stranger all these years? It broke her heart to wonder which truth might hurt Mote more: the fact that her husband had betrayed her love or that her best friend had betrayed her trust.

About half an hour into the drive, Jack put a black bag over her head. The journey continued for what seemed like forever, but eventually they arrived at a cabin somewhere in the woods. She tried to look through the tiny holes in the bag, but all she could see was darkness. Jack led her into the house while the driver and Stig, the dreadlocked guy, stayed outside.

'Follow their tracks, find them!' Jack shouted to someone, squeezing her arm even tighter and leading her up the stairs into the cabin. She could tell the stairs were old from the creaking noise and the soft wood that felt like it might give way if she stomped hard enough.

He put her on the couch near the fireplace and bound her hands together. He took the bag off her head and leaned into her ear. 'Be quiet.'

He walked through into the other room, and the girl followed him. Her name was El; she seemed to have a bond with him that none of the others shared. He didn't bark orders at her as he did to the rest of them—until now. Komi could hear bits of their conversation. Someone had got away from the cabin, and he wanted to know how she'd let it happen. She tried to explain, but he shouted and threw a tantrum, knocking things over.

'The entire plan will fail if we don't find him!' he said finally, in a lower voice.

'Don't worry, Dad, we will find him. You will get your revenge. He will pay for everything. Victoria couldn't have gone too far,' she said, trying to calm him down.

Komi had heard the name Victoria before. Whoever she was, she must have escaped with whoever they were looking for. She was just another mystery in all the events that had happened that day.

The cabin had a unique smell; the whole thing was made out of wood. It looked like it had just recently been furnished and decorated. A dim bulb hung from the ceiling in the middle of the room and a standing lamp was just a few feet away from her. The sofa she was sitting on was backed up against the only window on her side of the room. Opposite her was a small wooden table separating her from a rocking chair, with a few knitted blankets on it. It looked like someone had been working on them quite recently.

The room on the other side of the cabin was quite similar. The same yellow light hung from the ceiling, over the middle of the dining table, which had four chairs, one of which Jack had shoved to the ground in the middle of his tantrum. He also knocked over the flower vase on the table. The flowers were fresh; they must have been picked recently. In the corner of the room was an old TV set placed on top of a wooden cabinet with glass doors. Inside the cabinet was some china and a few glasses and bottles of alcohol.

El took out a glass and poured out two fingers of Scotch. She placed it in Jack's hands. 'Get some rest, Dad. I'll let you know when the boys get back.' She kissed his cheek and led him up the stairs.

He paused at the foot of the stairs and looked at Komi. 'Don't lose her too,' he told El.

She nodded slowly and gave Komi a stare that made her almost as scared of her as she was of him. El walked into the room where Komi was; she picked up the blankets from the rocking chair and threw them into the dusty, coal-filled fireplace. Komi wasn't sure what to say, whether to beg for her to release her while her father was upstairs or if she should just try to escape. El was just a girl, and apparently, she wouldn't be the first prisoner to escape that night.

Komi tried to figure her out from where she sat. El couldn't care less that Komi was staring at her. She picked up the pack of cigarettes that lay beside the ashtray on the small wooden table, took out a lighter from her back pocket, and lit up. She took in a long drag and let out a sigh, letting all the smoke she'd inhaled come out of her nostrils and mouth, directing it right at Komi.

Komi tried to keep her face away from the smoke. Who was this girl? Why did she call Jack Dad? She let herself get distracted with different guesses. Why she was so comfortable surrounded by men with guns, kidnapping, and probably murder? She couldn't be more than twenty. Her dark makeup made her look a bit older, but her voice gave her away. Although she had such a stern look all the time, her voice was as soft as the summer breeze. She was a few inches shorter than Komi; her eyes were dark and her skin even darker. She was beautiful, her face well defined. She pursed her lips.

'It's getting cold. May I close the window?' Komi asked.

El ignored her request and kept staring at the smoke that came from her mouth as she shot it towards the ceiling.

'Please,' Komi asked again, a bit agitated.

'Do it yourself.'

Komi stretched out her hands to show she was bound. El reluctantly got off the chair, pulled out her pocket knife, and unbound her.

Komi watched her as she returned to her seat. 'You trust me not to run?' she said, rubbing the marks on her wrists.

El scoffed. 'If you try to run, the men outside will empty their bullets into you.' She paused. 'Take a blanket from there.' She pointed at the dusty fireplace where she had thrown them earlier.

Komi did as she was asked. She quietly got up and picked out the topmost blanket and dusted it off. She returned to the sofa and wrapped herself in it. She pulled her knees up to her chest and buried her face in the blanket. She could not cry; she was terrified. Every minute she remained in this cabin, she lost hope of ever leaving this place alive.

If Jack could kill his own son, how much more easily could he kill her? She had no evidence that he had killed Tale, but with recent events, it was the only thing that made sense. Andrew had warned her of his fears that there might be more to Jack's story about the incident than he was letting on, but until Ara woke up, no one could really know what happened that night.

Jack was either a liar or a murderer. She hoped so much that it would be the former, but she also knew better than to blindly hope for the best in this man she no longer knew.

The edge of the blanket had a name embroidered on it: *Tori*. She feared to speak, but she did anyway.

'Who is Tori?' she asked, turning the inscription towards El.

'Victoria—it was hers. She spent hours knitting those damn things in the middle of summer. She obviously was losing it.'

'Who was she?' Komi asked. 'Was she your mother?'

'God no! She was his wife. If you ask me, it's good riddance. I never trusted her. She was weak, and she was going to get us killed.'

'Get who killed? Jack?' Komi asked. She had put her feet on the ground to sit upright, wrapping the blanket around herself.

El looked at her with a smirk. 'It must haunt you to not know who he is. I can just imagine the thoughts you have taunted yourself with. "Does he love me? Does he love her? Is he the man I thought he was?"'

She laughed to herself, watching as Komi's heart sank.

'You were sleeping with your best friend's husband. That's a new kind of low.'

Tears rolled down Komi's face. She could not find the words she needed to deny this claim or convince this girl otherwise, or even convince herself that she didn't deserve all of this. *This is just karma,* she thought to herself.

For a long time, she'd been consumed with guilt every time she saw Mote, but her love for Jack was overwhelming. She comforted herself in his arms, and with every kiss, her fears faded away. She was reassured by his words, and she allowed herself to be free of any lingering guilt, but that was then. All that was when he'd looked at her as though he could not have enough of her, not like he did earlier, when she'd looked into his eyes and feared that he might rip out her heart right where she sat. She was terrified, but in all of this, Komi cried even more because, stranger or not, she was in love with the man El called Father.

Komi tried to change the subject. She wanted to seem stronger than she really was. She wanted to seem fearless; she wanted to hide every bit of fear or regret for as long as she could.

'Did he kill Tale?' she asked.

El looked at her. 'You don't deserve to know the truth.'

She said the words so plainly. Komi could hardly believe that such a young girl could be so cold and unfeeling.

'Yes I do! You have kidnapped me, and I—'

'There's no need to shout. Why don't you ask what you really want to know?' she said with a giggle.

She got off the chair and walked into the other room, pouring herself a drink before returning. She must have known what that question would do to Komi. As much as she tried to hide her fear, Komi began to sweat. She longed to hear what El had to say, hoping falsely that she would find peace in her answers.

'Who is he?' Komi finally asked after a long pause.

'He is my father,' El responded.

'I heard you call him Dad, but how is he your father? How is he married to this other woman, Victoria?'

El returned to her seat. She sat upright and began to speak, slowly, so every word sank right into Komi's heart.

'You have been sleeping with someone's husband—he's just not your best friend's.'

'I don't understand. What does that mean?' Komi asked. Her trembling hands could barely keep hold of the blanket. She stared at El as though she could change the words she'd spoken.

'I've said too much already.' El got up and headed towards the stairs. 'Make yourself comfortable,' she added.

'Wait! You can't just leave. I don't understand. Why would you even tell me all of these things?'

'Well ... who are you going to tell? He'll keep you here for as long as he thinks you are important to the plan. Good thing is, you get to decide how long you remain relevant for, but one way or another, you won't leave here alive.'

She walked up the stairs without looking back at Komi.

Komi's heart dropped with every step El took farther away from her. She looked around the dark room where she was held prisoner. She had fallen in love with a friend turned stranger turned monster, and it was starting to look like she would pay for that mistake with her life.

CHAPTER

9

W hen Ara finally woke up, Mote was asleep on the chair next to her bed, and the TV set was on with the volume turned all the way down. The room was cold and the smell of the drugs nauseated her. She tried to sit up, and the noise woke Mote up.

Mote moved closer to her. She hugged her and kissed her cheeks and hugged her again before finally letting go.

'I'm OK, Mum,' Ara said in a soft, calm voice.

'I know, baby, just lie down for a bit.'

'No, Mum, I want to sit up.' She pushed herself up.

'OK, that's all right. I'll get the doctor.' Mote hurried out of the room and came back moments later with a doctor.

His name was Edward Arig, and he was pretty dressed up for a doctor on duty. Beneath his loose white coat was a black suit, and beneath that was a white shirt with a blue tie.

'How do you feel today, Ara?' he asked, wearing a wide smile that completely exposed the gap in the middle of his upper teeth.

'Uh ... My head hurts and I feel tired.' She paused. 'I guess all that's from carrying my dead brother in my arms for over an hour.'

The room fell silent. He did not know how to respond, and Mote was even more surprised.

Ara saw her mother's glassy eyes and wished she hadn't said that. She didn't want to be the one to remind her mother that her child was dead. She lowered her gaze, wishing she could take back the words.

The doctor continued to ask a series of questions and perform some tests. He avoided asking about the specifics of last night; instead, he tried to cheer her up a bit. He took off his coat and walked to the end of the bed and turned around slowly.

'Do you want to know why I'm all dressed up?'

Ara did not respond to his question. He didn't mind. He went on to answer as though he'd intended it to be rhetorical.

'I'm taking my wife out to lunch,' he said. 'It's a surprise,' he added.

Ara was still not interested in his conversation, but she indulged him with a nod and a forced smile, hoping it would make him leave sooner rather than later.

'My wife—it's her birthday today. You know, it's been years since she celebrated her birthday last.' He paused. 'It's been my fault really—I've been busy. But, you see, today I have planned a day she will not forget.' His smile was even bigger than the last.

He walked around the bed again, turned around slowly. Mote smiled as she watched him. He didn't seem to care if his gestures made him look funny; he kept turning.

'How do I look?' he asked.

Ara smiled. The cloud of grief that weighed on her heart wasn't lifted, but she appreciated his effort. 'I'm sure she'd love it, Dr Edward.'

'Oh no, Ara—my friends call me Eddy. I'd hope we could be friends,' he said, stretching out his hand to shake hers. 'Or would you rather I called you Ara … mide?' he added when she didn't take his hand.

She let out a chuckle now. He had pronounced her name all wrong as he read it from her chart, but she still smiled. He wasn't giving up.

'No, Ara is just fine, Eddy.' She stretched out her hand to his. 'Have fun at lunch,' she added.

She watched the doctor leave the room with her mother and she knew they would be talking about her. So she switched off the TV and listened keenly for the voices from behind the door.

She leaned closer to the door, tempted to leave her bed, but too weak to stand. Faintly, she could hear the doctor's deep voice below the hum of hospital chatter.

'Her vitals are fine. She'll need to rest up for a couple more days, but physically, she's good.'

'But what?' Mote asked. She could tell her mother was agitated by the rise in her pitch. The doctor was in for it, Ara thought.

There was silence for a while and she thought they had moved further away or stopped talking but then she heard the doctor say, 'But I think she'll need to see someone.'

'Like another doctor? You said she's fine.'

Again, the silence, then again, he spoke. 'Yes, she is fine. Her body is fine. But I'm afraid she needs more help than I could give her here. She went through a great ordeal, and she might need someone to help her sort through all that she's feeling right now. I would recommend she sees a therapist.'

She heard her mother exclaim in Yoruba, and though the doctor would not know what she was saying, Ara knew exactly what those words meant.

The doctor clearly did not know the weight her words carried, because he continued in the same tone as before. 'I have a few recommendations for you. You could check them out when you are ready.'

Ara imagined her mother shaking her head vigorously like she often did. The silence came again, and she did not hear anything until her mother came into the room, a tight smile on her face. Mote sat back next to Ara, who was now pretending to be eating.

She stroked her Ara's face with her palms and smiled even wider. 'You're going to be OK.'

'That's not what he said, is it?' Ara asked sharply.

'Oh, my baby,' Mote said, moving closer to Ara. 'You'll need to rest up here for a couple of days, but you are fine.'

'You think I'm losing my mind.'

'Oh, Ara, why would you say that?'

'I didn't. You did. He may not understand Yoruba, but I do. I heard you from the hallway,' Ara said as tears filled her eyes.

Mote hugged her. 'No, I'm sorry. You are not losing your mind. He suggested seeing a therapist, to help you, but you don't have to go if you don't want to.'

Ara didn't hold back the tears anymore. 'I don't know what I want, Mum. Everything just hurts.'

Mote held her even tighter.

'It was horrible, Mum. They attacked us and took us in a van. It was very dark, and we didn't know where they were taking us to.' She began to sob so much her words were barely audible. 'Dad was there, he ...'

She paused. She remembered what he'd said to her earlier.

She couldn't believe that her father could be so wicked, so evil, he would kill his own son and threaten her. More than anything, she wanted to tell her mum everything, but she couldn't. She couldn't tell Mote that her husband was a murderer, or he would hurt them, just as he had promised.

She remembered the words he told her to say when anyone asked for details about that night, and she repeated them to her mother as she removed her arms from around her, resting back into the pillow. 'It all happened so fast.'

'Your dad is fine, Ara, you don't need to worry about him. He also managed to get away from the people that took you. He stayed here with you all through the night. He must be with Ethan now. Everything is going to be OK, Ara. We will get through this. Lie down now,' Mote said softly as she helped Ara find her way back under the covers. 'I'll go find out what's taking Anna so long.' She kissed her forehead and went to leave.

'I want to see him,' Ara said.

'He'll be here soon, baby.'

'Not Dad—Tale.'

Mote paused at the door. She didn't look back at Ara, but she nodded gently and walked out.

Ara turned on her side towards the window and wept.

She remembered every minute of it. From the first moment when the van overtook them, she remembered how afraid she was and confused Tale was. Her dad had done many things that night: he'd fought the dreadlocked guy and lost, begged and been knocked out, and stood over them and pulled the trigger. Whatever was happening, he was at the centre of it all. He had to be. All that begging and pretending to care about them must have been a ruse.

Thinking about how her father had pulled this off made her head hurt. How had he known that Andrew would cancel on her? Was that why he'd agreed to having Tale come along with them? If Tale hadn't been there, would he have killed her? If he hadn't driven her that evening, would he have done this in their home? Was Tale always his target, or did he just pick at random? The questions went on and on.

The questions that sent shivers down her spine finally came in last. Would he kill them too? Was her mother safe with the man she called husband?

Ara stopped crying. She was not going to protect him. She was not going to save him from his doomed fate. He was a murderer, and he deserved to die for what he had done. She hated him. The thought of him being anywhere near her or her mother made her skin crawl. She would tell the truth. She would tell anyone and everyone the truth about everything that happened that summer night, and he would not get away with this evil he had done.

She sat up again, staring at the door, waiting for whoever would come in so she could tell her story, tell the truth. She wouldn't hide behind the cowardly words her father had threatened her to say. She would be brave; she would be strong, for him, for her brother.

'For Tale,' she whispered gently.

A few minutes later, a young woman walked into her room. She introduced herself with her badge; she was a detective from the police department.

'Hi, Ara. Do you mind if I ask you a couple of questions?' she said as she walked closer to Ara's bed.

'Yes, please. Oh, no, I mean no, I don't mind. I'll tell you everything.'

The woman looked at her strangely, thrown by her eagerness. But still, she got out her notebook.

Ara began slowly, giving every detail from the minute she walked down the stairs. She told the woman about her brother, how amazing and high-spirited he was, and how he insisted on coming along with them to drop her off. She explained why her father had to drop her off and why Andrew cancelled last minute. She told her about the conversation they had in the car that led up to the attack.

It was the first time she'd told anyone what happened that night, and as she spoke, she sieved through her memories, hoping to see any signs her father had shown that would hint at what he'd been about to do. As she got further in the story, she began to cry again.

The detective handed her the box of tissues from the side table. 'I know this must be difficult to talk about.' She paused. 'Did you see anyone?'

'Yes, I did,' Ara replied. 'There was a man, the one who took us out of our car and put us in a van. He was tall and dark-skinned and had long dreadlocks. He had a full beard and a scar on his face. He spoke with a funny accent, like he wasn't from around here.'

Ara noticed the woman was no longer writing in a notepad. Instead, she was staring at her.

'Are you sure about this, Ara?' she asked with doubt in her eyes.

Ara wasn't sure why she wouldn't believe her.

'Why would I lie about that?' she said, frowning. Her eyebrows closed up together, and her lips were pursed.

'I am not saying that you are lying. It's just that I spoke to your father earlier, and he said the man that attacked you was wearing a mask. You could not have this description of him if he wore a mask—that's what has me confused.'

Ara sprang up. 'He is a liar. You must not believe whatever he tells you.'

The detective paused, then started the questions from a different perspective. 'That looks expensive,' she said, pointing at the necklace Mote had given Ara before she left the house.

Ara looked down at it and wrapped her hand around it. 'My mum gave it to me,' she said passionately.

'Well, that makes it less likely to be a robbery. If they didn't take that, they probably weren't after money. What do you think they were after?'

'What's going on here?' Jack shouted as he walked into the room in a hurry. 'I already told you all that happened that night. What else do you want?' he asked, looking at the detective.

'I need a statement from everyone who was at the incident,' she responded firmly.

'No, what you need to do is find the people that killed my son,' he barked at her.

Ara scoffed.

They both looked at her. His eyes burned holes in hers, and she looked down, avoiding his gaze.

'You cannot question her,' he told the detective. 'Not until she gets better.'

'That's OK. I'll come back another time. Get well, Ara,' she said, handing her a card. 'Call me if you remember anything.'

Before she left the room, she turned towards Jack. 'I was going through my notes again. Seems I don't have the description of the man that attacked you.'

'He was wearing a mask, I couldn't see his face,' he responded irritably. 'If you can't remember simple information, how will you ever find these people?'

'People?' she asked. 'You don't think he was alone?'

'I don't know. Like I said, it—'

'It all happened so fast.' She completed his words. 'Got it.' She took a sharp glance back at Ara before she left the room.

'What was that about?' Jack asked Ara, lowering himself to her side. He held her arm tightly against the bed and began to squeeze it.

'Nothing,' she whimpered. 'She came in asking questions, and I told her what you asked me to say. Dad, please stop—you're hurting me.'

He released her arm. 'You need to be very careful, Ara. Say the wrong thing, and the wrong person will get hurt. It's just you and your mother left. You must think about her next time you feel like saying anything to anyone.'

Mote walked in. 'Jack, there you are. I've been looking for you. Ethan said you left him last night. Where were you?'

Still leaning over Ara, he kissed her forehead and turned towards Mote. 'I just needed some time alone, and I know you did too—that's why I didn't come home. I'm sorry.' He hugged her. 'Where is Ethan now?'

'He took Anna home.'

'She was up for a while. We both were.' She began to sob. 'I couldn't sleep, Jack. I couldn't do anything but cry. I feel so lost, I don't know what to do. How could this happen to us?'

He rubbed his hand over her back and led her to the chair beside the bed. He knelt beside her, holding both her hand and Ara's, squeezing Ara's a bit more.

'We will get through this together, as a family, I promise.' He smiled at Ara.

She closed her eyes so she didn't have to see his face. His smile stirred up anger inside of her, and she could not hold back her tears.

She held her eyes shut and said a prayer under her breath. 'Please God, don't let him kill us.'

CHAPTER
10

A few days had passed, and Mote didn't feel any better than the night she picked up the phone and the voice on the other end asked her to come over to the hospital to identify her child.

Tale looked just as peaceful as he had that night. His eyes closed, dressed up in his favourite tux with a SpongeBob necktie. He'd loved that tie; she had got it for him a few months ago, and he'd worn it almost every Sunday to church ever since.

She smiled as tears rolled down her cheeks. She shivered; the cold in the room had got into her bones.

Her husband led her out of the room. 'You don't have to do this. Go home. I'll take care of this.'

'They're going to put my baby in the ground.' She sobbed and held on to him tightly. She didn't let go for a while. She could hardly breathe, and she felt the walls closing in on her.

She knew she could not bear to watch the service, so she asked him to drop her off at home while he went with Ara to the funeral.

Ara had tried her best to avoid her father these past few days. He hadn't allowed her to have any visitors, claiming she needed to rest, so she hadn't spoken to Andrew either. She was stuck in her house with a murderer, and she did not know what to do or who to tell. He had taken the detective's card away from her; he had completely disconnected her from the internet, and her mother had let him. She'd let him do all of these things, thinking he was protecting Ara when he was just protecting himself.

How long did he really think he could get away with all of this? Someone would find out, someone would ask the right questions, and one day she would be bold enough to tell the truth.

However, today wasn't any of those days. Today, she sat in the passenger seat and felt his sharp eyes on her. She clutched the door and held on tight like she was ready to jump out once it stopped. She tried to distract herself from the fact that he was right beside her, probably thinking up new ways to keep her quiet.

She let her thoughts roam until they settled on Chinwe. Chinwe had come over to the house the night before, as she had done every night since Tale died, but last night she went home crying, her face revealing every hurt her heart felt as Mote knelt beside her and told her that her best friend was gone.

'When will he come back?' she'd asked innocently.

Tears had filled Mote's eyes. 'He isn't coming back. I'm sorry.'

Mote watched her and waited for her response. She was ready for anything Chinwe would do next: throw a tantrum or scream and cry. She was ready to comfort her.

But what Chinwe said next shocked her. 'He has to come back. I promise I won't fight anymore. He can even choose the colour of the walls and even give it a new name; I know he'll want to do that. He can do whatever he wants. I promise.'

She choked on the next few words and sobbed loudly as she went on talking. 'I can't go on the bus alone. I can't climb up to the treehouse alone. I can't do my homework alone.'

Mote hugged her tightly, holding on for a long moment that seemed like it would never end. Then, finally, she let out a deep sigh and released her. Her eyes were red with tears, but she managed a smile for the little girl. She wiped the tears from her eyes and walked Chinwe back to her home.

Ara had watched from the top of the stairs for a while before her father sent her back into her room. She frowned as she remembered his words in the hospital again. He was her warden and he had turned her home into her prison. She was consumed with fear for her mother's life. Every night, she watched Mote go into the same room as this man, this dreadful man, and there was nothing she could do about it.

As she continued to think of a way out of this dreadful limbo he had her stuck in, she had an idea. She would cooperate with him. She would be the daughter he remembered, the one he promised he loved, the one he took everywhere with him, the one he swore to protect. Maybe if she reminded him of the family he was destroying, he would reconsider. Maybe she could reach out to him through all of this and find the man she had once called Father.

He felt like a lost cause. She'd watched him closely over the past few days and it was as though nothing had changed. He was the same amazing husband he'd always been to her mother, but he simply wasn't the father she remembered.

She forced herself to stop thinking about him. Today was the first time she would see Andrew since the night he came to the hospital. She couldn't remember much of that night; most of her memories revolved around her father's face and threatening words. These past few days, she'd wished for nothing more than to see Andrew and talk to him about everything. He was the only one she could trust right now, and so the one her father was most determined to keep her away from. He knew how she felt about Andrew; they had spoken about it so many times. He knew that he was her best friend and she loved him. So she wasn't surprised when he made up some excuse every time she asked to see him.

She had only been able to communicate with Andrew through his sister April, who had come with her mother a couple of times to see Mote. Anna was one of Mote's best friends, and since Aunt Komi had been too busy in the hospital to come over, she had come over every day since the incident.

Andrew hadn't always been close to April. Sometime last year, she'd got on his motorbike, though she did not know how to ride.

She drove it into a tree and broke her arm. He'd been tasked with nursing her back to health, taking her for her doctor's appointments, helping her out when she needed a hand. Soon it wasn't as much a burden as it had started out as. He grew fond of her, and the next few months together made their bond grow stronger. They were nearly inseparable now, and Ara was grateful for this because now more than ever, she needed April to be her middleman.

Ara resorted to writing letters because her father had convinced her mother that access to the internet and social media would cause more harm than good while she was grieving. He took her phone and her computer.

'The kids nowadays could be so insensitive,' he'd said, with faux concern for her mental health. She could see right through his pretence and lies.

Behind his back, she found a pen and paper and wrote:

> Andrew,
>
> I know you have tried to see me but my father won't allow you. I need you to keep trying. I need to see you. I have so many things to tell you. I don't know if I can do this alone. I don't know what to do, I'm scared.
>
> Please come to the funeral, he won't be able to keep you from coming.
>
> I miss you. It
> ~~My father may not~~
> Ara.

She had stopped the letter abruptly; she wasn't sure what she could write in it about her father. If he ever got hold of that piece of paper, he might choke her to death one night, right where she lay.

She'd folded it up and stuffed it into April's hands.

'Please make sure it gets to him,' she whispered as she led her out of the room.

Her first letter to him had only been brief. She had no idea what to say; she'd never written a letter to him before. However, his response was a full three pages. He asked questions that she could not dare give answers to, but even in all his anxiety, his words calmed her.

She wanted more than words on paper. She wanted to see him and hold him in her arms. She wanted to hear his voice and his soothing, calming words. She wanted him.

Her father terrified her. His face was what she saw when she closed her eyes to sleep, and the nightmares lingered. She woke up to that same face every morning. She knew it was all a ruse for Mote, and she hated that she let him deceive her mother, but she was terrified at the thought that any plans she had to stop him would fail and her mother would pay the price, just as he had promised.

She sprang upright where she sat in the car when he touched her arm.

'We are here,' he said with a smile. 'It will all be over soon. It'll be just about an hour. If you want to leave before it's over, just tell me—I'll take you back home.'

She nodded slowly.

They got out of the car and she walked slowly behind him, taking every step carefully so she didn't fall. She felt weak and tired; she hadn't slept through the night since the incident, and her insomnia grew with every passing night.

Why did he pretend to care about her? Nobody else was here; there was no one in the car, no one to lie to. She knew the truth.

She had seen him pull the trigger; she saw the blank look on his face when he did. She saw it all.

Why, then, would he do all of this? Why was he here? He could just leave if he didn't want them anymore. He didn't have to stay and threaten her; he didn't have to pretend to love them, pretend like nothing had happened and force her to wake each day to the face of the man who murdered her brother. Or did he?

Was someone making him do this? That actually would make sense. He could have been compelled to do these things, to hurt his family, to kill them. Someone out there could have him on a leash just as he had her.

Maybe he was also a victim. As soon as the thought crossed her mind, she frowned with disgust. How could he be a victim? If anything, he was a coward. If he truly was someone else's puppet, then he was a shameless coward. If he'd allow someone to use him to cause such harm to his family, he deserved to die just as much as whoever was behind all this. They all should be the ones lowered into the ground this afternoon. Not her brother, not Tale.

Tears filled her eyes again. Rage spread through her as they approached the gathering and she watched him hug friends and family that had got there before them. He went up to the minister and embraced him. She saw him shed a few tears as the pastor whispered quiet words to him. What was he crying about? He was the reason for the entire gathering. He had done this. He had put this boy in this coffin. She wanted to shout at the top of her voice; she wanted everyone to know the psychopath he truly was. She wanted him buried six feet under, just as her brother would be.

She was startled by the hand she felt on her shoulder but sighed, relieved, when she saw who it was.

Andrew opened his arms and let her sink into his chest. She hugged him tightly and stayed in his arms for as long as he let her. A few moments later, he pulled her back and looked into her eyes.

'I'm sorry. I'm sorry about everything.' Tears rolled down his face.

She lunged back into his arms. 'It's OK, Andrew. There's nothing you could have done.'

'I should have come for you. I should have been there.'

'Then you would be dead. You have nothing to be sorry about. I'm just so happy that you are here.'

'I'm sorry I was away. Your father said you couldn't have any guests.'

'I know. He cut me off from everything. He—'

'Let us begin,' the pastor said from where he stood with her father by his side.

He opened the Bible in his hands and read out a few scriptures. Despite her anger, those words settled around her like an embrace, and she sighed, wiping away tears.

'We find solace in knowing that we will meet again. Let us not grieve like those who have no hope, for since we believe that Jesus died and rose again, so, through Jesus, God will bring with him those who have fallen asleep. We have peace because we know our brother, son, and friend is with the Lord.'

Everyone chorused the hymn he started, and they lowered the casket into the ground.

Cries and sobs got louder as they began to pour the sand back into the grave. Each lump of sand made a loud thud when it hit the wooden casket, and Ara shook a little every time she heard it. She was still standing with Andrew; she folded herself into his arms and let herself cry out all she could.

The pastor said a few more words and sang a couple more songs, and soon the service was over. Ara stood as close to Andrew as she could as she greeted all those who came to pay their condolences. She forced a smile every time she said thank you.

Everyone dispersed, although most of them would go back to the house to see Mote.

'I don't want to go back with him,' Ara said to Andrew, looking at her father as he thanked the people that had come for the service.

'You don't have to. You can come with us—we're going to your place. April is still with your mum.'

'Would you tell him?' she asked.

'Yes, but what's going on? Is this because of what you told me in the hospital?'

She looked confused. 'What did I tell you?'

He leaned into her ear and whispered, 'That he killed Tale.'

'Oh goodness.' She moved away from him. 'I said that?'

'Yes, you did. I figured it was the trauma talking, but you look scared of him.'

'Don't say another word,' she said as she noticed Jack coming towards them.

'Are you ready to leave?' he asked politely.

'I will go home with Andrew and his parents,' she said hurriedly as she left both of them standing there.

Andrew hurried after her and led her towards the car.

Jay watched them walk away and drive off. He waved at Ethan, who was driving the car, and then turned towards his. He picked up the phone and dialled a number.

'El, get her ready. I'm coming to get her now.'

CHAPTER

11

J ack was growing more impatient with every passing minute. It seemed as though Victoria had no solid plan; she was just trying out different leads, hoping one would turn out well. He had followed her everywhere the past couple of days, and he was tired of hiding, of doing nothing. Everyone she had met was either too scared of her husband to tell her anything or tried to kidnap her again and claim the bounty he had put on her head.

She had returned last night with even more bruises than she'd had when they escaped from the cabin. Something twisted in him to see her this way, and he hurried through the door. He wasn't sure why he worried about her so much. She always insisted on going into the meetings alone, but he was usually right outside. This time, she hadn't even taken him along. She'd brought this on herself, he thought, as he cleaned off the blood dripping from her arm with a damp towel.

'Hold it firmly for a few minutes,' he said as he got up and walked away.

'Thank you,' she replied calmly.

'This isn't working,' he murmured under his breath.

'What?'

'Your plan,' he said louder. 'This plan. Whatever it is that you are doing. It's not working.' He slumped onto the bed. 'You are going to get yourself killed. Without you, I have no chance of winning this. You are my only way out; you can't keep being careless.'

She took a glance at him and looked back at her wound, wincing at the pain. He wanted to do more to help, but what could he do?

She was right: he needed her. He was blind and lost in this new reality without her, but he still could not decide how much he wanted to or could trust this woman.

She got onto the bed, spacing herself from him. She played

with her fingers, opening and closing her mouth before finally saying in a single breath, 'We have to go back to the cabin.'

At first he looked up at her, and then back at the ceiling, ignoring her.

She said it again, this time more insistently.

He took the lamp beside his bed and threw it against the wall. 'What is wrong with you?' He raised his voice in anger. 'Do you have no good ideas? My family is out there with this man—this man that you brought into our lives—and all you want is to go back to where we were shot at?'

She flinched when he shouted, but she came back even harder. 'Stop it! You need to calm down. You'll get us caught if you go about shouting like this,' she said, looking out the window, checking if the loud thud made by the lamp had attracted anyone.

He put on his shoes and headed for the door. He thought she would physically stop him as she had before, but she didn't.

'You can't keep threatening to leave every time it gets difficult, Jack.'

He opened the door and stepped out.

'Jack, there's evidence against him back at the cabin. Actual evidence you can use to get him away from your family forever,' she continued. 'What's your plan? Still the same one, where you go to your wife and you confuse her and tell her that you've been lying to her all these years?'

'I never lied to her,' he said under his breath.

'No, but you didn't tell her the whole truth either.'

'What is your truth? Why are you here? Did you just bring me here to get more information out of me then take me back to your husband?'

She frowned. 'I cannot leave him. He will always find me. If I help you stop him, we will both be rid of him,' she said plainly.

Jack walked back into the room. 'So you are using me.'

'I am helping you. You have no idea what you are up against. Your first reaction to everything is a head-on attack. You need me just as much as I need you,' she said. 'I won't go any further with you until you assure me you're in this till the end. We'll both get what we want and go our separate ways. I can't spend every moment thinking you will quit and hang me out to dry. Jack, are you in or out?'

'What evidence is in the cabin?'

She walked up to him, so close she could feel his breath on her face. 'Are you in or out?'

He stared into her eyes. 'I'm in.' His gaze lingered for a moment, then he returned to the bed and asked her again what was in the cabin.

She explained to him that Jay's ultimate plan was to ruin Jack's family and leave; that was why he hadn't killed him. He planned to return Jack to his broken family, where everyone would think he'd killed his son. He wanted to drop him back in the midst of chaos and watch from a front-row seat as his life fell apart.

'Even if you go back now, no one will believe you. What proof do you have that you aren't crazy? Nobody even knows you have a brother.'

'My family will believe me. My wife will know I'm telling the truth.'

'The way she knows you're not the one sharing a bed with her?'

Her words kept him quiet.

'Someone else knows,' he said.

'Who knows?'

'Ethan, my best friend. I told him what Jay said when he came to my room that night. Ethan had seen him leaving the hotel.'

'Ethan—he's a lawyer, isn't he?'

'Yes,' he said reluctantly. He hadn't got used to the fact that there was so much about his life she already knew.

'Well, he can't help you without evidence. All you have is what you told him years ago, and he probably didn't believe you then. Anyone could be convinced that he is lying on your behalf. You need proof, Jack.'

She told him more about how Jay had been watching him and practising to be him for almost two decades.

'He made tapes of himself when he was in character and watched them over and over again so he could perfect his act,' she said.

She claimed to know where those tapes were hidden in the cabin. 'Those tapes will show him practising to be you. That's the first step to getting him out of your house. I know it's not a smoking gun, but it's a start—a good start.'

He was finally convinced to go back to the cabin. They waited till the sun was going down before they cleared out the room and left the motel.

Victoria stole a car from the motel car park. She forced the door open with a long piece of metal and hot-wired the car. He stood by the passenger's side, watching to see if they attracted any attention. As soon as the car started, he got in and they went off.

The sun had set by the time they got to the cabin. They parked somewhere along the road and went to the cabin on foot. He walked quietly behind her; he hadn't said anything the whole ride and he wasn't going to now. Although he realised he needed this evidence she claimed to have, he hated this plan. She was putting his life in danger; she was putting her life in danger, for him. He oddly felt protective of her.

He might have spent almost a week with her in the same room, in the same bed, but she was still as much a stranger as she was the first time he met her. Every word she said that made him feel like he was getting closer to understanding her seemed to just reveal another layer with countless more underneath. Still he found himself caring for her, wanting her to be safe. Trusting her. This scared him. At any time, he knew, she could turn him in and spin the story in her favour. He had watched her lie her way out of so many situations in the past few days; he knew it was something she was more than capable of doing. Yet, he trusted her.

They finally got up to the cabin after a long walk. She signalled to him to be quiet, which he felt was unnecessary; he wasn't going to make any noise while quite literally entering the enemy camp. He saw the van parked in front of the cabin—the van that had stopped him and his children on the road earlier that week. He rushed towards it and tried to open the door.

Victoria ran after him and pulled him out of sight. Behind the cabin, she shoved him against the wall.

'What are you doing?' she whispered in an angry tone.

'I ... I ...'

'What is it?'

'He put us in that van. That's where I last saw my children.' The fear from the night rushed back through him, and his heart jumped.

'There's nobody there.'

'I heard a voice,' he insisted.

'I shouldn't have brought you here,' Victoria muttered, looking around frantically.

Even in the shadows, Jack could see the pity in her eyes, and it made him feel weak and small. Somehow reminding him that he'd fallen short when his family needed him, like they needed him now.

Victoria placed her hand on his. 'Will you go back to the car? It's OK if you can't do this.'

He shook his head. 'I'm fine. I'll keep it together.' He let out a deep breath.

She nodded and led him through the back door, through the kitchen, and soon they were standing in the middle of the dining room. They quietly went up the stairs and she pulled him into Jay's room. As soon as she closed the door, they heard the door to the next room open. They stood still as footsteps approached the door, and stopped.

The footsteps began to walk in the opposite direction and down the stairs. They heard a girl's voice, and Victoria tensed up beside him. As soon as the voice had faded into the distance, Victoria began searching the room, frantically pacing from one end to the other.

'I thought you knew where they were,' Jack said. 'We don't have time for this.'

'He's smart—he won't leave them where I can find them easily. Just give me a minute,' she said with her hand held to her head.

She went towards the desk at the other end of the room and searched the drawers again. This time, she found a false bottom with some files beneath it. She skimmed through the documents and replaced them with random documents she found on the table.

When they were sure no one was outside, they quietly left the room and went down the stairs. She hoped they would be out of the house before anyone saw them, but as soon as they turned into the kitchen, they saw a girl waiting for them.

She must have heard them coming down the stairs.

The girl pointed the gun in her hand at Victoria. 'Drop the bag.' Her voice was low, almost a growl.

She moved her aim to Jack, and a deep frown settled on her

face. She seemed to not be able to decide who was the better target as she waved the gun back and forth.

She finally settled on Victoria. 'What are you doing here? I truly didn't think you'd be foolish enough to leave, but apparently you have a death wish, coming back here.'

Victoria stared down the girl. 'Get out of my face, El.'

El pushed the gun closer to Victoria's head and Jack flinched. 'Just drop it,' he whispered to Victoria, who did not take her eyes off the girl.

'She won't shoot her own mother.'

'You're not my mother, Victoria!' El shouted. 'You never were, and you never will be!'

Jack stepped forward and tried to intervene—she was getting agitated. She pointed the gun at his face, and he flinched and stepped back.

'You are the coward he said you are,' she scoffed. 'You chose this brother?' she said, looking at Victoria. 'You always did make bad decisions. Why should this be any different?'

She turned back to Jack. 'She's using you. Whatever she tells you is a lie. She's his wife. You think he could have pulled this off without her?'

Jack slowly turned and looked at Victoria. She ignored him and kept her gaze on El.

'While you stand here being her pawn, your son is buried today. I doubt she told you that. I'm sure she's convinced you that going back home would be the wrong choice.' She paused and looked at Victoria. 'She is very convincing, but I'm sure you figured that out on your own. She must have told you the tale of her "unhappy marriage",' she said, using air quotes. 'She is not your friend or ally, she is using you, and surely even you must see that.'

Victoria reached for Jack's hand, trying to pull him closer to her and away from El, but he jerked his hand out of hers.

She let out an angry sigh. 'Let us go!'

'You still think you can order me around?' the girl said, irritated. 'Wherever you go, he will find you.'

'El!' Victoria shouted. 'Get out of the way. You cannot kill me, even if you had it in you, which you don't. Your father will never forgive you.'

'You think he would forgive me for losing you twice in one week?'

'He never has to know.'

'That's what you do best, isn't it? Keep secrets?' El lowered the gun.

'I'm not the one keeping secrets from you. He is.' Victoria paused. 'He still hasn't told you who she is, has he?'

El shook her head slowly and moved in closer to her. 'Why won't you tell me who she is? I deserve to know.'

'It's not my place to tell you.'

'Please,' she begged.

In that moment, Jack realised that although El put up a tough front, she was still ultimately a child. Victoria saw the look on her face and took advantage of this glimpse of weakness she had shown.

'Let us go and I will tell you who she is.'

'Don't lie to me,' El said, frowning.

'Not any more than he has been lying to you.'

'He won't lie to me! He's my father!' she howled back at her. She raised the gun back at Victoria's face.

'Maybe, but we both know he will never tell you the truth about your birth mother. I'm your only hope at the truth. Let us go, El.'

'If I let you go, you'll never come back.'

'It's like you said: wherever I go, he will find me.' Victoria smiled and, with Jack right behind her, slowly walked past El.

As soon as they left the cabin, they began to run back towards their car.

Jack heard the door of the van swing open, and he stopped. Victoria tried to pull him along, but stood still until he was able to catch a glimpse of the person in the back of the van.

He watched as El pulled out a female figure from the back of the van, and before the girl put a black bag over her head and sent her back into the van, he saw her face.

It was Komi.

He tried to break free of Victoria again and head towards the van, but she managed to shove him to the ground. He regained his footing quickly.

'That's Komi, she's my friend. She's Mote's best friend.'

'This is not the time to play hero, Jack. There's a bigger picture. We may have been able to talk El out of calling her father on us, but I won't risk a second chance for a woman like Komi.'

'What do you mean "a woman like Komi"? You know her?'

'All too well. She's my husband's mistress,' she said, leaving Jack to follow her trail.

CHAPTER

12

Andrew and his family were the last to leave Ara's house the evening of the burial. Anna helped Mote to tidy the house afterwards; she insisted that she needed the distraction. Ethan talked with Jack on the front porch. Ara buried herself in a couch with her head on Andrew's lap, completely ignoring the muted images on the television screen.

All round, very few words were spoken, and when it was time for him to leave, Ara could barely let go of Andrew. He led her upstairs to her bedroom, and she closed the door behind them.

'Don't leave me here with him, Andrew, please,' she begged. She sat beside him on the bed. 'He killed Tale,' she said frantically.

'Shhh, don't say that, Ara.'

'Why? I thought you believed me?' she asked, confused.

'Ara, are you sure? Do you know what this means, saying that your father killed your brother? He could go to jail. It would destroy your family. Aunt Komi said we shouldn't make such accusations.'

'Aunt Komi?' Realising her voice was getting loud, she paused. 'I saw him, Andrew—he pointed the gun at me and then at Tale, and he shot him, point blank. Just shot him. I'm not imagining this, I know what I saw. Even more, he threatened me.'

'What do you mean, he threatened you?' Andrew asked, leaning in closer to her.

She knew she could trust Andrew; she never doubted him. However, she could not deny that she was afraid for him. She began to sob, and he hugged her.

'I know this must be difficult for you. Take your mind off it. Just be there for your mum, and mourn your brother. I'm sure everything will be OK.'

'But it won't be. For as long as he lives here with us, it's not OK.'

Tears had filled her eyes, and he pulled her in for a hug. He held on to her for a long moment and she sobbed into his arms.

'I don't understand what's going on, but I won't let anything happen to you. I promise,' he said quietly over her head.

She nodded slowly.

'Come with us, stay a few days, clear your head. You could stay with April.'

She shook her head. 'I can't leave my mother with him. I know you don't understand now, but I cannot trust that man. None of us can.'

He let out a deep breath, and pondered. 'Would you want me to stay here for a couple of days?' he asked.

She cracked a smile and nodded. She hugged him. 'Yes. Please stay.'

When she finally let go of him, he held her face and looked at her. 'Ara, you need to tell me everything that happened that night.'

She sighed deeply. 'He mustn't know that I told you. You cannot tell anyone, not even your dad.'

She knew he was close with his dad. Just like with April, their relationship had grown over the years, and he told his dad everything. This was something she admired about him, but not today, not with this. Their dads were best friends, and there was no way his dad wouldn't say something about it if he heard.

She knew how ridiculous it sounded to accuse her dad of murdering his son, but this wasn't something she'd imagined. She saw him pull the trigger.

Many times, she had played back that night in her head. Was there any way it hadn't been him standing over them with a gun in their faces? Was he brainwashed? Was he threatened to do it? Whatever questions she had were answered with the loud bang that killed her brother and left him lying lifeless in her arms. She heard that bang over and over again; she feared she might lose her mind.

He snapped her back to reality by shaking her. 'Ara, talk to me. I wouldn't tell anyone. I only spoke to Aunt Komi because your dad was acting weird and didn't want me to stay with you in the hospital room.'

'Weird how?' she asked.

'He insisted on being alone with you. I figured he was still scared about losing you too.'

She frowned. 'You shouldn't have left me alone with him.'

'I didn't know what to do—that's why I went to Aunt Komi,' he said, holding her hand in his.

'Aunt Komi—where is she? I haven't seen her since we left the hospital. I think I saw her talking with my dad in the hospital room but I'm not sure. I don't remember.'

'I don't know where she is. Neither does my mum. I heard her trying to call her earlier today when she didn't come to the house, but her line was disconnected.'

Had Komi seen something in the hospital? Did she know something? Ara didn't want to think about what might have happened to her if she did. 'I hope she's OK. I hope he hasn't hurt her.'

'Why would he hurt her?' Andrew asked. 'She's a friend. She's your mum's best friend.'

'You think he cares about any of that?' she scoffed. 'If he could kill his own son, how much more easily could he kill a friend? He —' She stopped when the door was flung open in a rush.

'It's time to go, Andrew,' Jack said plainly.

He wasn't frowning or smiling.

He scared her. How long had he been standing outside her door? How much had he heard and what was he going to do next?

He completely ignored her stare and continued to speak to

Andrew. 'Your parents are ready to leave, and you should go with them.'

'I'd like to stay the night here, if you don't mind,' Andrew replied.

'I do mind,' Jack said more sternly. 'You should go.'

Andrew looked at Ara and back at him. Just as he was about to talk again, Jack said, 'Now!'

Andrew jerked up and walked towards the door. He looked back at Ara.

'It's OK, Andrew. I'm fine,' she said, looking down at her feet, trying to avoid her father's stare.

Andrew walked out first and Jack followed, closing the door behind him.

From inside her room, Ara could hear the voices on the landing. Anna had walked to the top of the stairs. 'Is everything OK?' she asked. 'We heard shouting.'

Jack spoke first, before Andrew could say anything. 'Everything is fine.'

Ara frowned at how easy it was for him to lie. When had he become this person, and how had she missed all the signs until it was too late?

She heard Anna say, 'I'd like to see Ara before I go.'

Then she heard footsteps and imagined her father blocking the woman's way. 'She needs some rest,' he said. 'Maybe some other time.'

Anna didn't argue. It was very much like her to accept anything said in a strong enough tone.

Then Andrew said, 'Let's go home, Mum.'

And then she heard footsteps going down, and then nothing.

Did her father intend to shut her off from everyone? From her friends, from Andrew? She grew angry and paced back and forth in her room. She watched them drive away from the window of her room, and tears blurred her vision.

She watched as her father held her mum, waving at the car. She hugged him and cried in his arms before they finally went into the house. It bothered Ara deeply that her mother took comfort in the man who was no longer her husband but a murderer. She was lost in thought when she heard footsteps coming towards her room.

She rushed to her bed and hid beneath the covers and pretended to be asleep. The door opened gently and stayed open for a while. She heard her mum whisper something to her father, and Ara wanted to run into her arms, but she did not want to see him again. So she stayed still on the bed until she heard the door close behind them, and she cried herself to sleep.

A few hours later, she woke up to the feel of cold fingers holding her arm. She opened her eyes slowly but jerked up when she saw his face.

'Dad?' she asked, wiping the sleep from her eyes.

He smiled at her and gently tucked her hair beneath her ear, then his fingers tightened around her head. She let out a small cry and shoved his hand away.

'What do you want?' she asked coldly.

'That's no way to speak to your father, Ara.'

'You are not my father, not anymore. You lost that when you killed my brother!' she shouted, tears in her eyes.

He placed his hand over her mouth and leaned towards her. 'You're right. I'm not your father, so you have no idea what I am capable of. Don't test me.'

She peeled off his hand. 'You can't scare me, Dad. I am not afraid of you.'

He ignored her. He got up from the bed and went to look out the window. He got a call on his phone and picked it up. For the first few seconds, he didn't say anything; he just listened. Ara tried to listen in, but she couldn't hear anything.

'Wait there, I'm coming to you,' he said to the person on the phone.

He started to walk out of the room and stopped. He turned back to her. 'I won't warn you again, Ara.'

'I have done nothing wrong,' she said with fear in her voice.

'Except talking to Andrew. I wonder what you told him that made him want to stay here with you.'

'Nothing. He just cares, that's all. He's my best friend.'

'Well, let's hope his feelings for you don't get him in trouble. Goodnight, Ara.'

'Where are you going?' she asked quietly.

He ignored her question. 'You seem to no longer care about your mother,' he said. 'Perhaps you don't think she has lost enough, or maybe it's you who needs to lose something as well.'

'Why are you doing this? Why won't you just leave? You don't have to stay with us, you can go.'

'I am not going anywhere!' he shouted.

She recoiled back against the headboard, frightened. 'You truly aren't my father.'

'You will not say anything to anyone, or I will make sure you never leave this room again,' he said.

Before he left, he asked her what she was supposed to say when anyone asked about the night of the attack.

'It all happened so fast,' she replied in sobs, barely audible.

He asked again, angrier. She cleared her throat and repeated the words.

'Get some rest,' he said. 'It's a long day tomorrow.' He smiled and shut the door.

She peeked out the window and watched him walk out of the

house. She tried to see where he was going, but he was soon out of sight.

—————

Jay met El where she'd parked the van, about fifteen minutes away from the house. She was standing outside, waiting for him.

'Why are you here?' he snapped.

'You called hours ago saying that you would come to get her, and you never did—and your phone was disconnected.'

'So you brought her here?' he said, irritated.

'I can take her back.'

'There's no point. Take her to her apartment and wait for my call. Make sure she doesn't speak to anyone.'

He saw the look of disappointment in her face.

'I know you want to help, but this was the wrong call. Follow my lead, and you will learn all you need to.' He kissed her forehead and hugged her.

'I can't wait for this to be over,' she said.

He released her. 'I have been waiting for this moment my entire life. This is what we have trained for—we will see it through.'

'I know, Father, I know. I'm sorry.'

'Wait for my call,' he said plainly and turned his back.

'How's it going in there?' she asked, just loud enough for him to hear.

'Everything is going according to plan.' He paused. 'The girl, Ara—she knows I'm not her father, or she will soon enough.'

'How did that happen?' El asked, agitated.

'I told her.'

'What do you mean you told her? Weren't you supposed to kill her? She could ruin everything.'

'Don't worry, child, the plan remains unchanged. There are many ways to keep her quiet. She won't be a problem—she's just a girl.'

'Why didn't you kill her? You must have known this would happen.'

'I have it all under control. I have her under control.'

'I hope you're right.' She sighed. 'So what's next?'

'You just take care of this, and I'll fill you in. You may just yet have a part to play in all of this.'

'Why don't you trust me? I could help you. I can do more than just babysitting.'

'You're not very good at that either, now, are you?'

She was going to defend herself, but then stopped. Victoria was right; he didn't trust her, which was why he still wouldn't tell her about her birth mother. Maybe he feared she might leave him. However, it didn't matter; she was done talking to him tonight. She got into the driver's side of the van and turned on the engine.

He followed her and stood outside her door. 'Take care of this and I'll tell you more tomorrow.' He smiled.

She glanced at him and looked away almost immediately. She nodded slightly and drove off, leaving him standing on the side of the street. He turned around and headed back to the house.

She knew this was important to him. She knew the hatred he harboured for his brother, how he felt cheated even from his birth, and she could not help but feel the jealousy that brewed inside her. She wanted to be more involved; she wanted him to fully trust her, as he had done many times before. Why was this different?

The question that tugged at her the most was what fuelled her anger even more. Why had he spared Ara? Why was he willing to risk the entire mission by letting her live?

El was, more than ever, determined to find the answers to the questions that roamed her mind, with or without his help.

CHAPTER

13

The next morning, Ara woke up very early. She stayed in her bed, crying and sobbing then falling asleep and waking up to the same nightmare she had dreamt about and starting all over again.

She opened her eyes and sat up slowly when the door to her room clicked open. She braced herself, fingers tightening in the sheets, but it was just her mum. She ran into her arms and hugged her tightly.

Mote hugged her back. She had been distant the past few days. She stayed hidden in her room most of the time, and she barely said anything or ate even. Ara knew her mother was trying to be there for her. Mote had been distant since she returned from the hospital, and had recoiled into a shell of herself. Now, she was reaching out.

'Your father made breakfast. Come downstairs,' she said.

Ara removed her arms from around her and returned to her bed. 'I'm not hungry,' she said plainly.

'Ara, why not? What is going on with you? Your father says you've barely spoken to him this week. I know this is difficult.' Mote sat on the bed beside her. 'This is difficult for all of us. A horrible thing happened and it hurts, but we need to be there for each other. We need to be a family again.'

'We can never be a family again,' Ara said in a low voice.

'Don't say that, Ara. This too shall pass. It will never be OK that we lost Tale, but it will get easier. You have to be willing to work through it, with me, with us.' Mote hugged her again. 'I am here for you. We both are.'

Ara wanted nothing more than to tell her mother everything. That the man downstairs was a monster, not a father or husband. A murderer. She wanted to tell everyone; she hated that she had to keep his horrible, dark secret for him, with him. She felt as responsible for Tale's death as he was.

Jay heard Mote and Ara coming down the stairs and smiled. Good thing Mote had convinced Ara, otherwise he'd been ready to pull her out of that room and throw her down the stairs if he had to. She was just so annoying.

He'd hoped that in the time they'd spent in the room together they hadn't been talking about what happened with Tale. He knew that Mote would not have brought it up. She was too fragile, and when he'd offered to talk about it—to prove he had nothing to hide—she could barely keep from sobbing the whole time he spoke and finally asked him to stop. She had insisted that she did not want to hear about how her son was gunned down by a madman.

It was Ara he could not trust. He hoped he had scared her enough to keep silent, but he saw the fire in her eyes every time he looked at her and knew she was on the edge of doing something stupid. He had to be ready for it—whatever it was.

Jay had finished setting the table by the time they reached the dining room. He was determined to be the best husband Mote could ever hope for. Most importantly, to be better than the one she'd had before him. From the moment he'd met her all those years ago before their wedding, he knew that one day she would be his. Every moment of planning had led to this. Here and now, where Mote was his wife, and he had the family that was rightfully his. He was going to make everything right; he was determined to make her love him even more with each passing day.

Mote smiled as she walked towards him and planted a kiss on his lips. He closed his eyes and smiled, allowing the feeling to linger on his lips, and he let out a satisfied smile. She was his. He pulled out a chair for her and motioned for Ara to sit opposite her mother.

He made some small talk, but only Mote replied to him. Ara was either absent-minded or completely ignoring him.

He studied them very closely, every moment, every gesture, every word. He hadn't met Ara until the night of the attack, and he hadn't seen Mote since the night he had spent with her during her honeymoon. He smiled to himself as he remembered that night. It was truly one of his finest moments.

He hadn't been sure he wouldn't get caught. It was the first time he had inserted himself into his brother's life, and he was nervous.

He remembered how his hands trembled the first time she touched him, the first time she kissed him. The look in her eyes, the look of a woman who was absolutely smitten and in love, was the same look she had on her face right now, seated at this table. She wasn't as full of energy as she had been that night, but she had the same look. He could never forget it. The only other person who'd ever looked at him this way was Victoria, but that had been a long time ago, before she betrayed him. He felt a frown form across his face.

'Jack. Jack?' He heard Mote's soft voice call out to him. 'Are you OK?'

He nodded and smiled and continued eating his food.

'I was just telling Ara, perhaps it would be good to leave the house today,' Mote said. 'Maybe we could go shopping, finally start getting ready for college.'

'It's still a couple of months away, Mum,' Ara said, still keeping her gaze away from him.

'I know, baby, but it would be nice to leave the house, wouldn't it?' Mote tried to convince her.

'I think Ara is right—you shouldn't leave the house just yet,' Jay said. 'It may not be safe yet.'

'We can't stay here forever,' Mote said, raising her voice.

'That's exactly what he wants,' Ara said, with her head down towards her plate.

'Ara!' Mote called out to her.

Jay ignored her comment. 'Not forever, just for a few more days. We should all be together.'

Mote was staring at him again. This time, she was signalling that he should speak to Ara. He didn't want to. The girl was becoming a bother, and quite frankly, he was starting to regret not killing her with her brother. He knew why he hadn't, but now it didn't seem to matter. She could jeopardise his plan. Nobody's life was worth failing this mission.

He turned towards her, placed his palm over hers and squeezed lightly. 'I just want you to be safe, darling. I want to keep you and your mother safe,' he said, staring into her eyes, allowing her to read the words he could not say.

She looked blankly at him, as though it all meant nothing to her, the words he spoke and the ones he didn't. It was clear that she did not care about him, and that was fine, as long as she knew the risks. He glanced at Mote and back to Ara, and instantly he had her back where he wanted her. The fear that crept into her eyes let him know she knew exactly whose life was on the line.

Ara removed her palm from his and continued to eat. She barely took two more bites before she dragged her chair back and took her plates to the kitchen.

She was about to go up the stairs when she turned and asked, 'Where is Aunt Komi?'

He paused. There was no way she could know about Komi, or was there? Why else would she look at him when she asked? She couldn't know anything for sure, but even the slightest suspicions could alert Mote.

'What?' he asked after swallowing the food in his mouth.

'She hasn't come around—that's unlike her. She should have

been here. Do you think she's OK, Mum?' Ara turned her focus to Mote.

'I don't know, Ara. I've tried calling her several times, and her phone is disconnected. At first I thought she was busy at the hospital, but still, she should have called,' Mote replied. 'I should go check her at her apartment.'

'No! I will go,' Jay said quickly. Both Ara and Mote looked at him curiously.

He knew as soon as he said the words that he had been too eager and too loud. But he was determined to keep them in the house. He needed to control the situation, and it was starting to get loose at the seams.

'I'm sure she's fine, and wouldn't want you both worrying about her and wearing yourselves out,' he added calmly.

Ara glanced at him as though she knew there was more to his volunteering than he was letting on. She continued up the stairs without looking back and went into her room.

He watched her go while Mote cleared out the table, and all he knew was he had to put Komi back in play. He quickly got up from the table and took the rest of the plates to Mote in the kitchen.

'I told Ethan I'll meet up with him this morning in the city, and I'll stop by Komi's on my way there. I'll call you when I get there.' He kissed her and walked out.

She went after him before he got to the front door.

'Jack.' She went in close to him and held his face. She hugged him. 'Please come back,' she whispered.

He slowly pulled her away so he could see her face. He stroked her cheek with his fingers and kissed her forehead. 'I'm not going anywhere. Don't be scared, I'm here to stay, forever and always.'

'Forever and always,' she replied. She leaned in and kissed him deeply.

He let out a deep sigh once he was on the other side of the door.

She was something, Mote. She always reminded him of the life he could have had if his mother hadn't abandoned him in a burning house. If she had chosen him instead of his brother, maybe he just might live in a house like this, have a family like this, a wife like Mote.

He loved Victoria, he truly did, but she was a reminder of the life he'd lived, the life he hated, the life her father taught him. She would always be her father's daughter. Mote was so different from her. The fire that burned in her eyes wasn't scorching like Victoria's; she had an innocence to her that he found refreshing.

Almost two decades after marrying his brother, she had the same look in her eyes as she'd had on their honeymoon. He had watched them all these years, but they hadn't been in the same room since that night. Now that it all was real, he wondered if he could have a fresh start with her. If his brother wasn't there to interfere and Victoria wasn't roaming the earth with her fury, maybe he could.

He was startled out of his thoughts by the loud honking that came from the car behind him at the traffic lights. He was just few blocks from Komi's place.

He couldn't seem to get Mote out of his mind. The past week he had been with her, he'd had to be the husband she thought he was, but he liked playing the part. She was easy to please. He'd already known his brother so well that being him wasn't ever going to be a problem, but he'd thought it'd be a chore being a husband to her. However, he'd found himself easing into his role rather seamlessly.

She was beautiful, almost more so than she'd been that night he spent with her all those years ago. He had gone to her with a mission, and although he'd accomplished all he had planned and more, she had planted a seed in his heart that he hadn't realised was there until he was back in her life, now as her husband again, as her lover, as her friend. He was there for her in every way she needed, and when she leant into him on the bed and whispered in his ear, he gave in to her demands, although he knew she only wanted a distraction from the grief that flooded her mind.

His first evening with her was burned into his memory. It had been just a few days after her wedding. Jack had left her alone for the evening; he'd gone in search of *him*, the brother he had just met. That week, he was obsessed with finding him, which played out nicely for Jay because he spent time with Mote. Although he spent just a few hours with her, every word she said, every secret she spilled, every tear she cried was precious. She finally told her husband all the secrets that ate at her, the secrets she had always kept from him. He watched as she cried, and the relief filled her face as she heard him say it was OK.

He listened to every word she said very carefully, every deep-rooted secret she had held until her honeymoon. Given it was a few days after her wedding, he was happy she waited till this moment to spill her guts.

He owed her for that night. Without her, he might not have had all he needed to make this plan work.

He'd had to act surprised and upset about what she told him, but he was far from upset. However, he'd convinced her that he forgave her and was willing to move on with the rest of their lives as though she had never mentioned it, as long as she never spoke of it again.

She'd been thrilled and grateful, and she'd showed it to him in every way she knew how. He'd let her. That was the first time the reality of the life he could have had was literally in front of him, lying in his arms underneath the sheets.

He knocked on the door, and El let him into Komi's apartment.

He smiled when he saw her. She was the only family he needed. She had been with him since he adopted her as a baby. He'd given her as much training as she needed to survive in his world. He'd taught her to fight, to defend herself, to be strong. She loved him and protected him, even from himself.

She'd always doubted Victoria's loyalty; perhaps if he had listened to her, his brother would still be in his custody.

El bumped into him and hugged him. 'Dad, I was worried about you.'

He smiled and kissed her forehead. 'Where is she?' he said, walking into the sitting room.

He called out to her. 'Komi, come out here.'

CHAPTER

14

Komi walked out of the room, her hair wet and dripping down her back. She had on a white robe that stopped right before her knees. She folded her arms across her stomach and walked in slowly, scanning the room. She first noticed Stig, who was in her kitchen, trying and apparently failing to make something to eat. The smell of burnt food filled the room; however, his clear incompetence in the kitchen didn't distract her for long. She quickly moved past him to El, who paid her no attention; she simply stared at Jay, who was standing behind her.

Komi had been quiet the entire time; she hadn't said a word to any of them, not even El. Since El had brought her from the cabin in the back of a van, she'd realised there was near nothing she could say to change any of their minds. She was tired of begging; she was now more frustrated than frightened.

Jay moved out from behind El and walked towards Komi. For every step he took, she took one backwards. However, he took large steps, so he caught up with her and soon he had her in his arms. She wriggled out of his grip and retied the loosened ends of her robe.

He smirked, and she hissed. He probably thought she had nothing to hide from him, but it was all she could do to not rip his eyes out and wipe that silly grin from his face.

She could not recognise the man she had spent the past six months with. He looked at her as she stared sternly back at him, proving to herself that she was not afraid. She was.

His gaze lingered on her and slid down past her face to the rest of her body. She shifted uncomfortably, warily conscious of the way the water droplets soaked the top half of her robe, and how her folded arms made her look fuller. His eyes roamed even lower.

'What a beautiful distraction you were,' he said with a sly smile.

Then he moved in closer to her again and gripped her arm and pulled her back into the room, shutting the door behind them.

Komi peeled his hand off her arm and hurried to the corner of the room. She thought he would come after her, but he didn't. He began to talk about the things he wanted her to say when she saw Mote.

He was insane, she thought. He did the most unexpected things; he said the most unusual things. And when she'd thought she could bring him back to the man he once was, she failed, and that hurt her even more than the indifference she saw in his eyes. She knew now that he'd truly never cared for her.

She tried interrupting him, but he wouldn't budge.

'I'll drop you off at the house. Mote is worried about you,' he continued without paying attention to her words. 'When you get there, apologise for not being with her, for missing the funeral. Make sure you say whatever you can to make her believe you. Whatever you do, she must not suspect that anything is wrong. Ara will also have a lot of questions—she was asking about you this morning. She may not be so easily convinced.' He turned to her. 'Be sure to remember that your life depends on how well you do. So do whatever you must, just get it done.'

She looked at him with tears in her eyes and a pained frown. 'I will not do any of this!' she shouted. 'I will not lie to her!' She threw an empty box in his face. 'She is my best friend, and you are a monster!'

'I may be a monster, but I am also the father of the child in your womb,' he said as he slowly approached her.

She gasped in surprise. 'How did you know?'

'Your self-righteous act isn't fooling anyone, Komi, least of all me. You are carrying your best friend's husband's child, but you cannot lie to her, even to save your life? Don't be a fool, Komi— she won't hate you any more than you already deserve.'

'How can you say these things? How can you do this?' She was weeping at this point. 'I thought you loved me. You said you loved me. How can you hurt me, hurt our child?'

Before he could respond, there was a loud knock on the door. 'Dad! We have a lead on where Victoria might be. We have to go.'

'I'll be right outside,' he shouted through the door.

He turned back to Komi. She didn't let him get a word out; she moved closer to him and said calmly, 'Is she your child? El. She calls you Dad.'

He stared at her without saying a word.

She continued, 'Have you always cheated on Mote? Do you even love or care about anything or anyone?'

She felt the hate grow inside her. She had never hated anyone as much as she did in that moment. The feeling overcame the fear that had lingered in her heart since she was taken. Now she wanted answers. She deserved to know the truth, even if he could lie to Mote. She was done being foolish. It was time to act.

'Yes, she is my daughter. I met her mother, Victoria, many years ago.' He paused. 'Also, to answer your question, I did care about you, but I have to take care of my family now. Mote needs me.' He rested a gentle palm on her cheek.

She shoved it off. 'Don't lie to me. She told me Victoria was not her mother.'

'El spoke to you about her mother?'

'How is that relevant? Why are you lying to me?'

'She *is* my daughter!' He clenched his fists. 'She doesn't get along with Victoria. Whatever she told you, she said out of anger. I cannot deny that I have a weakness for women with dark skin and beautiful curly hair.' He smiled at her.

She tucked her hair behind her ear and turned her back to him.

'How can this be?' she asked. 'How can you live so many lives?

How can you be the loving husband and father to Mote, Ara, and Tale, and be with me all these past months and still have a secret daughter and baby mama somewhere else in the world?' She paused. 'You are not the man I fell in love with. I don't know what's going on, but you are not Jack.'

She fell silent when she felt a cold steel blade press against her neck. A knife. She froze, feeling his breath in her hair. His hand was steady at her throat.

'Enough with the questions,' he whispered in her ear as he loosened and pulled off the rope that held her robe together. His cold hands rubbed against her neck and held up her chin. 'Get dressed and be ready to go in half an hour. Pack a bag. You might be there for a few days.'

She stood still as he stepped back from her and headed for the door. She wished for nothing more than to go back in time, to never have loved him, never have kissed him, never have let him into her life. Even more, she wished she'd never left that hospital room with him.

He unlocked the door. 'You know what to do. Don't screw it up. If not for yourself, then for our child.'

His words sent a cold shiver down her spine. Holding her tummy, she crumpled to the floor. She folded herself up in a ball and cried.

She could hear his voice in the distance, telling El what to do and giving orders, just as he had done the past few days, and she hated him so much.

Huddled close to each other on the couch, tucked under a big duvet, Mote and Ara were watching a show on TV and stuffing their faces with food left over from the funeral. Sometimes they laughed, sometimes they cried, but mostly they were quiet.

They were interrupted by a knock on the door. They stared at each other for a few seconds. They weren't expecting anyone.

'Maybe it's Andrew,' Ara whispered.

Mote shrugged and got off the couch. 'Who's there?' she asked.

'Maureen Lewis—I'm a detective from the police department. I have a few questions for you.'

Mote opened the door slowly.

'May I come in?' the detective asked, smiling.

Mote let her in and followed her into the living room. The detective wore a black pantsuit that fit her perfectly. Her blonde, straight hair was parted down the middle and fell just a bit below her shoulder. Her nude lipstick matched her skin, her eyes were dark, and she had a stern look on her face that seemed to fade away once she saw Ara and smiled at her.

Ara sat up straight, but she didn't utter a word. She recognised her—she was the detective from the hospital. She turned her face away from her; she wasn't going to tell her anything. Not after all her father's threats.

She looked at her mum. She knew Mote wanted her to be more responsive, but she couldn't risk saying the wrong thing. She hated to admit it, but he had managed to scare her into silence. She looked at her mum a moment longer, then turned to the screen in front of her.

They both got seated, and the detective began. 'My name is Maureen Lewis, and I'm from the police department. I'd like to ask you both a few questions, if you don't mind.' Her voice was clear and low pitched, with an official tone to every word she spoke.

'That's no problem,' Mote answered. She looked over at Ara, who hadn't turned away from the screen.

'Where were you the night of the murder?' she asked plainly.

Mote froze. Ara turned to see the startled look in her eyes, like a deer caught in headlights, and reached for her mother's hands.

'I need you to answer the question, ma'am,' Maureen said calmly.

Mote let out a deep sigh. 'I was here, at home, on this couch.'

'Alone?' Maureen asked.

'Yes, alone,' Mote replied, agitated.

'What else did you do? Did you call anyone?'

'They left the house right after dinner. Her father was supposed to drop her off at her prom.' The detective gave her a curious look, and she explained, 'Ara's date, Andrew, he couldn't get her, so her father offered to drop her off.'

'And your son?'

'He insisted on going with them.' She let out a slight smile. 'Jack said it'd be no trouble, so they took him along with them.'

She shut her eyes tightly and sobbed. 'He was just a boy.'

Maureen realised Mote might not have as much information as she needed, or at least not as much as her daughter did. Since the day she'd first talked to Ara at the hospital, Maureen had wanted to see her again. Her story seemed to not completely match her father's, and Maureen wanted to find out why.

She was tired, and the last place she wanted to be today was sitting here in front of a grieving mother and her uncooperative daughter.

It was exactly a year since she'd lost Daniel, her partner on the job. The entire day, she hadn't been able to get the images of him lying on the street, bleeding out onto her arm, out of her head, so she'd tried to wash them away with as much alcohol as she could take without losing herself.

She hoped neither of them could smell anything on her breath. She had almost emptied the can of breath spray before pressing their doorbell. She had stood there for about ten minutes, convincing herself that this was the right thing to do. Something was off with the stories she'd heard, and she knew she could uncover the truth if she tried, but that was the problem: she didn't want to try. She knew more than anyone that finding a murderer does not bring back the murdered, nor does justice make loss hurt less.

Perhaps she would be doing them a favour if she just let it be and allowed them to grieve for their son and brother, but she'd finally knocked on the door after minutes of indecisiveness, and now here she was, realising that getting Ara to open up as she had in the hospital was going to be a chore.

She turned to Ara. 'Hi, Ara, I have a few questions for you as well.'

Ara ignored her and continued to stare blankly at the screen. Tears had begun to form in her eyes.

Maureen continued, 'We spoke at the hospital. You told me about a man you saw?'

'You saw someone?' Mote asked, surprised.

Ara sprang up from the couch. 'I didn't see anything. It all happened so fast.' She began to head up the stairs.

'Ara!' Mote called after her, rushing off the couch.

Maureen stopped her by gripping her arm firmly. 'May I speak to her alone?'

A bit confused, Mote nodded slowly and directed her to Ara's room.

Maureen smiled, hoping to ease Mote's edginess, but she knew she was running low on patience. She went up the stairs after Ara and knocked on her door but didn't wait for a response before she entered the room.

She looked around and walked across the room to a shelf where she saw some of Ara's trophies and awards. Then she saw a picture of Ara and Tale placed right beside her bed, and she picked it up to get a closer look.

'He looks like a happy child.' She placed the photo down. 'I know you saw someone. You described him to me—dark, tall, scar on his face.'

'Please stop,' Ara said, her cheeks wet with tears. 'Just stop. I wasn't thinking right in the hospital. I don't know what happened. One minute, we were in the car and the next, my brother was dead in my arms. Anything else and you have to ask my father.'

'Well, I did, Ara, and his story doesn't match yours.'

She was beginning to get agitated. She knew the pain she'd felt when Dan was killed. She would have done anything to bring his killer to justice, said anything to anyone who asked.

'I don't know what you want me to say,' Ara whispered, interrupting her thoughts.

'I want you to tell me the truth,' Maureen demanded. 'Tell me who killed your brother.'

'I don't know. You need to leave now.'

'Why won't you tell me? Don't you want to see them pay? Do you not care about your brother? Does his death mean nothing to you?'

'Leave my room!' Ara cried out loud.

The door swung open, and Mote rushed in. She ran towards Ara and hugged her. 'What is going on here?' she demanded.

'Mum, ask her to leave,' Ara said as she buried her face in Mote's chest.

'I just needed to—' Maureen tried to explain.

'You need to leave,' Mote said sternly.

Maureen sighed. Before she turned to leave the room, she dropped her card beneath the picture of Ara and Tale. 'If you remember anything, please give me a call.'

'We have said all that we have to say,' Mote said.

'I'm only trying to help you.'

'If you want to help, find my son's killer. Leave me and my daughter alone.'

Maureen didn't say anything else. She walked out of the room, but she wasn't done. Not yet.

CHAPTER

15

J ack tossed large files of paper to the ground, shuffling them across the floor, intentionally trying to wake Victoria. She finally opened her eyes, and frowned at him, the sleep lingering heavy on her eyelids. Jack did not let her get a word in.

'What are these?' he asked as she got up slowly from the bed.

'These are the documents we will use to get him arrested.'

'I don't understand. All these are accounts and transactions. Where are the tapes? These say nothing about him killing my son and destroying my life. How is this of any use to me?' he shouted. 'We risked our lives for nothing!'

'No, we didn't. I didn't find the tapes—he must have destroyed them—but I did find something. These are all illegal transactions. If we can show this to someone, we can get him arrested and put in jail.'

His head hung low. 'This doesn't save my family from this man. This can go wrong in so many ways. Where's the proof that he's my brother—birth certificate, recordings, anything? What happens when he claims he is me and I killed Tale? I will lose my family.'

'This will get him out of your house, Jack,' Victoria said, holding the papers to his face. 'Once he's out, you can be with your family. Tell them everything, prove to them that you are you.'

'That's your plan? To tell them that I'm me?' he scoffed. 'You said yourself that if my wife doesn't know that the man she goes to bed with every night isn't me, how then will she believe me when I see her?' He was agitated and continued to raise his voice over hers.

She tried to calm him down. 'I shouldn't have said that. She's your wife, she has lived with you for many years. I've watched you with her, and she loves you. I'm sure she suspects something is off. Jay is good, but his temper gets the best of him. He will slip up, and we will be here to make him pay for all that he has done.'

Jack wasn't convinced. This wasn't the plan he'd hoped she had. He didn't want to be rid of Jay for just some time. He wanted him gone from his life. He wanted him dead.

'Who will we show these to?' he asked.

'Ethan, your friend. He's a lawyer, isn't he?'

'I don't want him to be involved in this.'

'Listen to me, Jack. Jay has already involved everyone in your life in this. It's time to be one step ahead of him, so pick yourself up—we've got work to do.'

She walked towards the bathroom.

'What did you mean about Komi being Jay's mistress? What was she doing at the cabin? What is he going to do with her?' he asked without pausing.

'I'm here with you, Jack; I can't have answers to any of these questions,' she answered, irritated. 'Even more, she isn't who you think she is. I can't tell you any more.'

'No, you must!' he shouted, pulling her towards him by her arm.

She snatched back her arm and leaned against the wall. She glared at him. 'She has been sleeping with him for the past six months. What's worse is that she thought she was having an affair with you.'

'That's not true. That's not even possible. She's Mote's best friend.'

'You don't have to believe me.'

'I don't trust you,' he said plainly. 'You could be working for him or with him. You've done nothing but lie to me all this time.'

'I've told you all that you need to know!' she shouted at him. 'I am tired of your constant bickering and your crippling anxiety and unwarranted mistrust. You need to get it together. If you think you can do this without me, leave. If not, we leave in an hour.'

She entered the bathroom and slammed the door shut behind her.

He sighed and buried his face in his palms. He couldn't believe the turn his life had taken in the past few weeks. He was losing his mind, staying here, doing nothing.

Thoughts rolled in one by one, and eventually, he let one stay and roam in his mind. What would he do when he finally had Jay in his hands? He had to make him pay, but how? Prison suddenly didn't seem good enough for his crimes. He'd taken his son's life, his little boy.

Tears filled his eyes, and he let out a deep sigh. Jay, his brother, had to die.

He got off the bed and picked up the papers that had fallen to the ground. He packed up their clothes in a bag, like he did every day. Every time he left that room, he hoped to never return, but he found himself right back there night after night. However, this didn't stop him from packing up every morning.

Victoria got out of the bathroom just as he was done packing up.

'We'll be back tonight,' she scoffed. 'You don't always have to pack up.'

'This isn't my home. I'll pack up every day, and one day, we won't come back, and I'll leave nothing behind.' He paused. 'Except you.'

She walked over to him, holding her towel to her chest with one hand. 'You know what, Jack, when this is over—and it will be soon—you go back to your home, to your wife and daughter. You've lost your son, but you haven't lost everything. I have nowhere to go when this is done. My helping you has cost me a lot more than you'll ever know.'

'It's hard to feel sorry for you when your husband is the reason we're here. I barely know the guy and I know he's a monster, and you married him. What kind of person does that make you?'

'Exactly! I'm married to him, and you do not have the slightest clue what it means to live in the same house as a monster, to share the same bed with him, to wake up every morning to that face.' She paused. 'To your face.' She pulled even further away from him. 'I have had to wake up next to you day after day, watching you slowly turn into the man you are hunting.'

'I am not Jay!'

'Oh, but you are! What will you do when you find him? When you are two feet away from the man who has taken your son from you and probably destroyed your relationship with your wife and daughter? What will you do?'

'I'll kill him!'

'So you are him. When you go back home, you get to pretend that you don't have the same darkness that he does, but I, I go back to him.'

'You don't have to.'

'Wherever I go, he will find me. I've spent decades with him. It can't get any worse.' She smirked, but tears filled her eyes.

It was the first time he had seen her this way, emotional and vulnerable.

She went on about the things Jay had done to her and the person he had become because of his unending thirst for vengeance, because of his obsession with Jack. He could hear all that she was saying, and for the first time, he could see how much she was hurting. He stared at her as she talked. Sometimes her voice echoed in the room; other times she spoke in whispers as though the walls had ears. She spoke through her tears. He moved in closer to her. She stared out the window, talking to him but not looking at him.

He continued to watch her every move: when she tucked her

hair behind her ear, when she adjusted her loose towel, when she smiled because the irony of something she said amused her. He wished she had shown him more of her. He wished he hadn't spent so much time distrusting her and hating her for being married to the man who had hurt him. He, for the first time, felt her pain and hugged her.

She flinched when he first touched her, and he could feel her holding her breath, but after a few seconds, he felt her shoulder drop and she sobbed into his chest, holding him as tightly as she could.

He let her stay in his arms for as long as she wanted to. He couldn't quite describe what it was that made him hold on to her just as tight, but he did not want to let her go either. Even though he knew they couldn't stay like that forever.

He hated that she saw in him what she saw in his brother. He knew he could probably never convince her that he was different, that he did care about her, no matter how unlikely that was. He hoped that in that moment, she did not feel as alone with him as she did when she was with Jay. He hoped he was better.

She fell asleep in his arms, and he put her to bed and covered her up. Although it felt good to be there for her and care for her, his goal remained the same—getting home to his family.

He continued to go through the papers they had taken from the cabin, hoping to find something before she woke up.

He took glances at her. He wondered what was going on in her head, what dreams she had when she closed her eyes. If she had nightmares, if she was afraid, or if she had become used to them.

His feelings towards her confused him more with every passing moment. He hated her for her part in this. She had confessed to driving Jay to his apartment the night he first met him; her father had made Jay the man he was today; she seemed to be in the middle of everything yet begged to be free. At first he'd thought what he felt was pity, but it was something more. He admired her resilience, her strength, and everything he had complained to her about, he'd begun to see in a different light.

As he watched her, he played back every moment since he had escaped from the cabin with her as he had done a thousand times before. This time, though, he tried to understand her. She could have escaped alone; she could have done all this alone. She had been kind to him, in her own way. She kept him safe. He had battled with himself for days on end; he didn't know if he could trust her, but today, in this moment, he believed that he could and so he did.

She woke up a couple of hours later. He was lying next to her, and she moved closer to him and laid her head on his chest.

'What do you want to do?' she asked quietly.

'You're right. I think it's time to have a talk with Ethan.'

She nodded slowly and lifted herself off him. She began to get off the bed, but he pulled her back towards him.

'About what you said earlier—'

'You don't have to,' she said, moving away from him.

'No,' he replied. 'I won't let him hurt you. You don't have to go back to him. I can protect you. I will protect you.'

She looked into his eyes and smiled. She leaned in and kissed him. He moved back and stopped her.

'Victoria!'

She ignored him, leaned in closer, and kissed him again, and he let her.

They arrived at Ethan's office later in the afternoon. Jack had no trouble getting in. There was no reason for anyone to think he wasn't himself, which he was. The entire thing made his head spin when he thought about it.

He saw a couple of people stare at Victoria as they passed by. He wasn't surprised at all. She was beautiful; she intrigued him. When she kissed him, he had felt something that made him kiss her back. That last thought alarmed him, but he put all that away. He had to concentrate on the conversation he was about to have with his best friend about his long-lost psychotic twin brother.

He walked into Ethan's office. He was filled with so much joy to see his friend; he ran up to him and hugged him, laughing loudly.

Ethan was a bit confused. 'What's going on, Jack? I saw you just a couple of hours ago.'

Jack released Ethan. 'He was here?'

He turned back to look at Victoria, who had come in after him and was closing the blinds around the room.

'Hey, what are you doing?' Ethan asked. 'Who was here? Jack, who is this?'

'This is Victoria,' he answered.

'What's she doing here? Why is she closing my blinds?'

'I have something I need to tell you, Ethan, and I need you to listen. Even more, I need you to believe me.'

'What is this, Jack? You were supposed to go back home to Mote. Why are you back here?'

'Why was he here? What did he say?'

'What did who say?' Ethan snapped. 'You were just here. You know what we talked about.'

'It wasn't me!' Jack shouted.

Victoria ran up to him, holding his arm. 'Calm down, Jack, we don't want to cause a scene. If he knows we came here, it's over.'

He took in a deep breath. 'Ethan, do you remember, I told you about the man that came to the apartment claiming to be my brother? Well, for starters, he was right. He is my brother, and he's on some sort of blind revenge mission to destroy my life.'

'What? Jack, you need to explain this—what are you saying?'

'That man that was here today wasn't me. You must have noticed something, anything, come on! You're my best friend, how can you not know when someone impersonates me?'

'How do I know you're not the crazy one?'

Jack sighed. This was going to take longer than he had hoped, but he was determined. If he could not convince Ethan, then he had no hope of convincing Mote or Ara, so he kept on. He described in detail as much as he remembered from the night of the incident. He went as far back as the first time he met Jay and everything he said to him. He told him Jay's story about his parents, their parents. He said everything Victoria had told him about Jay and his plan for vengeance that had brewed in him for a long time.

When he was done, he could see that Ethan was even more confused than when he'd begun.

'This is me, Ethan. That man that was here today, the man who has been living with my family since the day of the incident —that man is not me,' he said as he walked around the table towards Ethan. 'You have to believe me. You're like my brother. Our children grew up together. I've known you since college. How could you not see past his façade? Why can't anyone see!?'

'Stop raising your voice,' Victoria said. 'If he won't believe you, we have to go. We don't know who Jay has watching this place.'

Tears filled his eyes. He looked at Ethan one last time and walked towards the door.

'Stop,' Ethan called out from across the room. 'I believe you, Jack.'

Jack turned to face him. 'Will you help me get my family back?'

Ethan walked over and hugged him tightly. 'What do you need me to do?'

'Victoria and I have spent the past few days working out how to get him arrested. I don't have proof that he is responsible for everything that has happened, but we have some documents that can prove his illegal dealings. Hopefully, that will get him out of my house for a while.'

Ethan gave her a sharp look, then asked Jack, 'How can you trust her? She's his wife.'

'She's on my side.'

'How can you know that? This man murdered your son. He could have her spying on you. She could be playing you.'

'She saved me,' Jack replied.

'It doesn't matter, she could—'

'It matters to me. I trust her.'

Ethan let out a deep breath. 'You shouldn't.'

'You don't know her.'

Victoria remained quiet.

'I hope you know what you're doing.' Ethan paused. 'Show me the documents you have. Let's get started.'

'First of all, call him.'

'Call who?'

'My brother—I want to know where he is.'

'Why does it matter? You can't do anything now.'

'I know. I want to know if he's with Komi. Have you seen her since the incident?'

'She was at the hospital the night Ara and Tale were brought in. I saw her briefly, but I haven't seen her since then. Anna mentioned that she hadn't come over to the house and she missed the burial.'

'They really buried my son?' Jack's voice broke. 'He is really gone?'

He bent over, suddenly unable to stand upright. He'd known his son was dead, but somehow hearing it from Ethan, hearing that his son lay cold in the dirt, and he hadn't been there, sent a sharp pain through his chest, and he lost his breath. Still leaning over, heaving, he tried to regain the strength to stand.

'I'm sorry, Jack.' Ethan hugged him again. 'This will all be over soon. I will do whatever I can to help. I promise.'

Jack walked over to the window. Furious, he allowed his anger and grief to fuel his hatred for his brother. Jay had to die by his hand.

He looked at Victoria, remembering the words she'd spoken, and he turned away. He knew he was becoming the man she feared he might become, and as much as it pained him, he wasn't going to do anything to stop it, not until his brother had paid with his life.

He wiped his tears and let out a deep sigh. 'One last thing, Ethan—you can't tell anyone. Not even your wife. Not yet.' He turned back towards the window, staring out blankly. 'He will not be able to stop me, not until it's too late. It's time to take back what's mine.'

A ra had called Andrew over to the house as soon as the detective left. The detective had convinced her to speak up to someone about what happened, and Ara hoped Andrew could be that person. She paced nervously back and forth in her room until she heard his voice from the other side of the door.

'Ara, are you there?' Followed by a soft knock.

She hurried towards the door and let him in.

'What's wrong, Ara? You sounded worried over the phone. Is everything OK? Your mum said you've been up here since you spoke to the detective that came to ask questions about the incident. Did she say something to upset you?' he asked.

Ara knew he wanted to know more than she had told him. No doubt he was confused to say the least. And she knew she had been withdrawn from him since the hospital, but how else could she make sure he didn't become a target, caught in the crosshairs of this nightmare?

He continued when she did not reply. 'I feel like you are hiding more from me, Ara. A lot more. You're shutting me out and I don't know what to do with that. I don't know how to help you if I don't know what's really going on. So please tell me. Tell me everything.'

He waited until she was ready to speak. She started her sentences and stopped without completing them. Sometimes she stammered. He continued to wait patiently.

Five minutes later, she still hadn't formed a full sentence. She had paced back and forth, she had stared out the window, cried while looking at the picture of her and Tale that rested on her side table. She had done everything but actually say anything.

He moved in closer to her and hugged her tightly. 'Would you like to go somewhere else? The park, maybe?'

She nodded slowly and buried her head deeper into his arms.

She remained there for a moment and then followed him out of the room.

Downstairs, Andrew convinced Mote that what Ara needed most was to leave the house and clear her head. Everything at home seemed to remind her of Tale, and it wasn't the best for her.

Ara got out of the car first when they arrived at the park. She walked quickly until she reached an open space. She closed her eyes and took in deep breaths. Tears rolled down her face, and she allowed the heat of the sun to dry them up. Andrew stood a few feet away from her for a while, but eventually he walked over to her.

'I'm here for you, Ara, whatever you need.'

She pulled back from him and wiped her tears. 'I want you to help me get my father arrested.'

'What? Why would you want that? What would he be arrested for?'

'Murder,' she said plainly.

She saw the look on his face; he tried to hide his disbelief but failed to. She could always read him. At first, she frowned, angry that he wouldn't believe her, but his disbelief evolved into confusion.

'We were a few minutes out of town, heading towards the city, when they attacked us,' she began.

'I know all this, Ara, your father told us what happened,' said Andrew.

'I'm sure he didn't tell you that he stood above me and Tale and shot his own son in the head.'

His face always said what his heart felt. She paused and watched the confused look on his face change once again to something else: shock and dismay and still a hint of disbelief. She couldn't blame him. Her father was an amazing man; he was the best father she could have hoped for. His patience was remarkable, and he always knew what to say and what to do through difficult times. He truly was the glue that held them together, and she knew Andrew looked up to him as though he was his father, and he loved and respected him. She knew Andrew's doubt wasn't because he thought she was lying but more because he didn't want to believe that Jack could do the things she said.

She continued with her story, pausing when she felt like he needed to let the words he'd heard sink in. When he signalled her to, she continued, on and on through as much detail as she could remember, and she ended with the words: 'Many things happened that night. Some of it I may forget, but I will never forget the look in his eyes when he pulled the trigger. I will never forget the loud bang that nearly deafened me and ended my brother's life.'

She looked at him, and although she was the one who had lost a brother, she felt pity for him.

'I'm scared, Andrew. He made me promise to not tell anyone ever, he threatened to kill my mum, and I know he'll do it. He's not bluffing.'

'I—I don't know what to say,' Andrew stuttered.

'I don't need you to say anything. I need you to help me get him out of our house, out of our lives.'

Andrew frowned.

Ara could see the wheels turning in his mind as she narrated in gruesome detail every single moment of the night. She remembered it all. It was burned into her memory. There was no mistaking it: her father had murdered Tale, and he did not even try to hide or deny it. He had to pay.

Andrew took a few steps back from her and turned in the opposite direction. It was a lot, she knew, so she did not stop him. She turned and brought out her pills and popped one in her mouth.

He turned to face her again, and she answered him as though she'd heard the question he asked in his head.

'Painkillers,' she said softly. 'For the migraines.'

'You took some before we left the house. How often do you take them?' he asked, worried.

'As often as I need to.'

'Are you self-medicating?'

'Self? No, I'm not. I have migraines,' she said with a frown.

'Give me the bottle, please.'

'Why?' she snapped.

'You shouldn't take so many of these. They could hurt you.'

She shrugged and ignored him. He reached out for the pills, and she struggled with him until she finally gave in, letting go of the pills and shoving him in the shoulder.

'I can't believe this! You're supposed to help me. You're my best friend!' she yelled.

'Ara, I *am* trying to help you. How can I believe you when your mind is clouded by these things?' he said, waving the bottle in the air. 'The first time you told me this in the hospital, you were pumped full of meds. I believed you then, but the more I think about it, the harder it is to believe that your dad could do such a thing.'

He looked at her and paused. She turned away from him.

'Is there any way that you're not sure of what you saw that night?' he asked.

'What's that supposed to mean?' she said angrily.

'What you are saying is impossible. This accusation could ruin your father, could ruin your family.'

'Stop it, Andrew!' she barked. 'Do you think I don't know that? Do you think I want this? He's my father.' She paused. 'He was my father until he pulled that trigger. Now he will pay for what he has done.'

She sighed. 'You're either with me or not. I wouldn't make this up, and I wouldn't tell you if I didn't think I could count on you. Please, Andrew.'

He looked at her for a long moment and finally said, 'If he did this, you're not safe with him and neither is your mother.'

She smiled and hugged him. 'Thank you. I have the card of the detective that came over today,' she said while looking for it in her bag. 'Her name is Maureen. She wanted to know what happened, but I couldn't tell her, not when my mum was just a few feet away. I can't go to her either. Please call her, find her, and tell her everything.'

She couldn't find the card. 'I think it's still on the table in my room. We have to go get it.'

She had walked a few steps away before she realised that he wasn't following her. She returned to him. 'What's wrong, Andrew?'

'I'm sorry. I'm sorry about everything. I'm sorry that you're hurting, and I'd do anything for you. Anything other than this. This is ridiculous—I don't think your father would do this. Kill his son? No, that's—'

'That's exactly what he did!' she interrupted him.

She stormed off to the car without saying another word. She was quiet the entire ride home. She was tired of letting her father get away with murder; she was going to do something, anything.

She decided to go get Maureen's card and find the detective on her own, even if it would cost her everything. She was tired of Jack pretending to be the man he once was, deceiving her mother, and ultimately, she was tired of being afraid.

When they got home, she ran out of the car without looking back at Andrew. She crept into the house; she didn't want to make any noise. She knew her father was home—she had seen his car in the driveway—and she didn't want to get caught. Not before she brought the whole world crashing down on him.

Andrew watched her go in. He was scared he might have lost his best friend, the love of his life. He wanted desperately to believe her; perhaps he might have, but how could he be sure she wasn't just imagining all this? Those meds could've really messed up her mind.

He hated being here, sitting in this car, feeling helpless towards everything. He almost wished she hadn't told him. He didn't know how to truly help her or what to do, but he decided to talk to her again. Perhaps encourage her to see someone to help with her grief, maybe a therapist—anything really would do. It broke him to see her like this, out of sorts and seemingly out of control.

He headed for the front door. Ara had left it open when she hurried up the stairs, so he slipped in without making a noise. He was about to climb up the stairs when he heard her father's voice from the kitchen. He stopped and headed back down. He knew he couldn't say any of this to Jack, but he wanted to talk to him still, to see what was different about him that had made her accuse him of murder.

He walked towards the kitchen, stopping briefly to prepare himself for the conversation he was about to have, when he heard him say, 'El, you need to stop this. You are my daughter, and no one could ever replace you.'

Andrew stopped, peeped in to see who Jack was talking to, but he was on the phone. He withdrew and stood by the door where Jack couldn't see him. He continued to listen.

'How dare you question my commitment to this?' Jack

growled to the person on the other end of the call. He sighed. 'I know what the plan was. It's my plan. You know that, don't you? ... I haven't killed her because I need to know. I'll run a test, and by the end of the week, we'll both know. Just drop it!'

After a few seconds of heavy breathing and quietness, he shouted, 'I won't kill my child, El! If you did your job finding my brother, you wouldn't be so bothered about Ara. You will not bring this up again.'

He dropped the phone on the kitchen table and stormed out through the back door to the garden behind the house.

Andrew froze. He could not believe what he had heard; he couldn't even understand it. He hadn't heard what the person on the other side of the call said, nor did he know who El was. But it seemed like she was trying to persuade Jack to kill Ara.

I won't kill my child.' The words rang in Andrew's ears over and over again. He looked up at Ara's room. As much as he wanted to run up and tell her what he had heard and tell her that he believed her, he heard her father coming back in, and he ran for the front door. He got across the street in seconds and drove off as fast as he could.

Ara reached the bottom of the stairs just as her father was walking out of the kitchen. She halted abruptly, almost colliding into him. She regained her footing and took a few steps back. He quickly noticed the card in her hand and snatched it away from her. She tried to recover it but failed.

'What is this?' he asked tensely.

'Nothing,' she stuttered and took a couple more steps backwards.

He rushed towards her and held her neck tightly. 'Do you not take me seriously, Ara? Do you think I will not kill you right here where you stand?'

She screamed and gasped, pulling at his fingers, trying to release his grip.

'Was this woman in this house today?' he asked, still pulling her closer to him.

'Yes,' she said, barely able to speak.

'What did you tell her?'

'Nothing—please let me go,' she begged. 'I didn't tell her anything. You're hurting me. Please, Dad.'

The image of her father before her blurred as she tried to keep from passing out. His hand still held on, and even though he had eased his grip, she still could not breathe. She struggled, trying to pull his fingers off and force air back into her lungs.

From behind her tears, she could see him deliberate on what to do, and for a moment, she really thought that he would never let go. He just stood there, watching her beg and sob.

He released his hand completely when he heard the door to Mote's room crack open. He pulled Ara closer to him and hugged her tightly. 'Hug me,' he whispered into her ear.

She slowly put her shaky arms around him and held on.

'What's going on here?' Mote asked. She hurried down the stairs. 'What's wrong, Ara?'

'She just needed some cheering up,' Jack said quickly before Ara had a chance to answer.

Mote looked back at Ara, who nodded slowly, wiping her tears. 'I want to go to my room now,' she said.

Mote hugged her. 'It's OK, honey. Get some rest. I'll come up soon.'

They both watched her go up the stairs and into her room.

Mote let out a deep sigh. 'I really hope this doesn't break her. I can't lose her too.'

'She's going to be fine. We will make it through this,' he said, kissed her forehead, and walked into the kitchen.

Mote followed him. He brought out a bottle of whisky from a brown paper bag that was lying on the kitchen table. He took a glass from the shelf and poured himself a drink. She rushed over to him.

'Stop!' She pulled the glass from him and spilled some on her hand. 'What do you think you're doing?'

He sighed. 'Mote, not today.' He moved the bottle out of her reach. He took a gulp and let out a satisfied moan.

'Jack, you can't have that in this house.'

'I'm not asking you to drink it. You don't have to be here.'

'What do you mean I don't have to be here? This is my home.'

'Well, it's not my fault you're an alcoholic.'

He regretted the words as soon as they left his mouth. He watched her face, filled with dismay, as she began to tear up. He tried to reach her and hold her, but she backed away from him. She threw the glass at him and ran up to her room.

As soon as Mote left the kitchen, he turned his back and slammed his fist into the fridge door. He remained there for a few minutes, his head resting on its door. He knew he had messed up.

He felt overwhelmed. He could deal with Mote, but Ara was just ... She was going to be the end of him. He knew what he had to do; he was constantly reminded by the hate that consumed him, but every time he looked at her, he felt like he could see himself in her eyes. And the worry that she could be his child had continued to grow with each passing moment, and now it was eating at him.

He needed that drink more than Mote realised, and he knew he had to get her back so she wouldn't begin doubting him, but at that moment, he couldn't spend another minute in this house.

He was so stressed out by everything that had gone off track.

177

His brother was missing, Victoria with him, and he had no idea how much she would have told him. He was losing control of El. She was becoming obsessed with finding her birth mum and wanted him to kill Ara, as she was a distraction. He hated that he wasn't getting what he wanted, and his outburst just now was proof that he was tired of playing husband and father.

He picked up his phone and called El. 'Drop Komi off at the house by noon tomorrow. Mote is becoming a handful, and Komi would be the perfect distraction.' He hung up as soon as he delivered his message. He wasn't going to spend another minute explaining himself to anyone.

He stormed out of the house with the bottle in his hand, not sure where he would go, but he needed to leave for a while. His mission depended on his ability to keep his cool and maintain his cover.

CHAPTER 17

A ndrew finally got home, after taking a long while to think about all he had heard and seen. He stayed in the car outside his house for a while. He tried calling Ara, but she wouldn't pick up. He wanted to text but figured it might be risky if her father had taken her phone from her again. At this point, there was no telling what Jack might do.

After twenty long minutes of spiralling thoughts and plans, he decided to go looking for the detective the next morning. He didn't have her card, but he knew her name was Maureen and she was a city cop.

He finally decided to get into the house and figure out exactly what to do. He couldn't shake the feeling that he should tell his father.

As he approached the door, April stormed out and hugged him. They'd been closer than ever recently, especially during this time, when everything else seemed to have turned sour. She hugged him every time she saw him now. He always hugged her back; he knew she needed it more than he might have.

He smiled and made choking noises as her large mane covered his face. Her hair was a big puff of red. She always experimented with different colours; she had just changed from dark purple a few weeks ago. She was so active and jumpy, and her small physique didn't stop her from being the most adventurous person he knew. There was absolutely no stopping her. 'As alive as spring itself,' her mother often said.

However, this time it felt as though she wanted something from him. He groaned when she hugged tighter and stepped on his toes. He finally peeled her off his body. 'Ha ha ... What's going on, April?'

'Can't I just be happy to see you?' she asked with her eyebrows raised.

'Well, yes, you can, but are you?'

'Nope,' she said plainly.

'Whoa,' he said, smiling.

She laughed. 'That's not what I meant, Andrew. I want you meet my friend Lara.'

He looked towards the door and watched as the girl slowly stepped out of the house. She was breathtaking. He stared at her for a lingering moment and only gathered his words when April shook his arm, bringing him back to reality.

'Uh, hi,' he stuttered.

He truly didn't hear her response. He studied her face, her subtle lipstick and dark eyes, her short shorts and ankle bracelets that made her slender legs look even longer, her low-cut top that revealed more than a shy girl would have—although he had concluded from the minute he saw her that there was nothing timid about this girl, with her mysterious smile and the way she looked at him as though she knew every thought that crossed his mind.

She reached out to shake his hand. Her hands were so soft he thought they might melt into his palm. Her voice was soft as well, and she was absolutely beautiful. Her presence was intoxicating.

He quickly pulled his hand away. She giggled and looked back at April.

'I should get going,' she said calmly.

'Oh, Andrew will drop you off,' April said, her eyes pleading with him.

'Excuse me a moment,' he said as he pulled April away from the porch. 'What are you doing?'

'Please, Andrew. She's my new friend and I don't want her to walk all the way home. You'll be back before you know it.'

'Where did you meet her?' he asked curiously.

'The mall.'

'The mall?' he gasped, and April hit his arm.

He shook his head. It was very like her to invite home a stranger she met at the mall.

'Be nice. I just need you to drop her off. Also, I already offered. It'd be weird if you said no.'

He sighed. 'You can't bring strangers home, April. She could be dangerous.'

'Like a serial killer?' She rolled her eyes.

Before he could reply, she hugged him again and called out to Lara. 'He said yes!' She ran up the stairs and hugged her. 'It was awesome meeting you, Lara. I hope we'll meet again soon.'

Lara smiled. 'We most definitely will. I can't wait to meet the rest of your family.' She walked after Andrew, who had already begun to unlock the car.

They drove off, and April stayed in the driveway, waving until they were out of sight.

A few minutes later, Lara broke the silence. 'She's fond of you.'

'Huh?'

'April?'

'Oh yes. She's a handful too.' He smirked.

Lara laughed out loud. 'She's nice. I like her.'

There was a pause before she said, 'So what's your story, Andrew?'

'My story?'

'Are you dating someone?' she asked abruptly, intentionally avoiding his glance at her. 'I only ask 'cause if you are dating someone, I doubt she'd appreciate her boyfriend drooling over another girl.'

'I wasn't ... I wasn't drooling,' he stuttered again.

Lara laughed. 'Well, I doubt you're a stutterer either.'

He sighed and took a turn, avoiding her questions by focusing on the road ahead of him until he reached a stop sign.

'I'm just teasing,' she said as she laughed and placed her hand on his knees. 'April did say you were uptight.'

He let out a tense giggle. 'Oh really, what else did she say?'

'That you're in love or not in love with your "best friend but not best friend but not girlfriend" person.'

His eyes widened. 'She said that? Oh my goodness.' He sighed and shook his head.

'Well, what's the true story?'

'Uh, she's my best friend but I guess it's just complicated right now. She just lost her brother, so she needs a friend right now, not a boyfriend. So what's your story?' he asked before she could throw another question at him.

'I'm adopted. Never knew my birth parents. My dad adopted me when I was a baby. He's white, so you can imagine he's got a lot of questions. So I could never really hide that I was adopted.'

'Oh, I'm sorry to hear that,' he said.

'Oh, it's OK. You can pull over here,' she said, and he brought the car to a stop.

He thought she was ready to get out—perhaps the conversation was too much for her—she didn't.

She continued, 'He's amazing though, my dad. He's taught me everything I know, and I'm so grateful for him.'

'Do you have a mum? I mean, is your dad married?'

'He is, or he was. I don't know how that's going.'

'How so?'

'Well, she ran away with his brother.'

'What?'

She laughed and he laughed too.

'That's something. Is he OK?' Andrew asked.

'He says he is, but he loved her. I know he did. I hope he never finds her—I don't know what he'll do if he finds either of them.'

She paused. 'That's enough about me. Tell me more about this "best friend, girlfriend" complication.'

He sighed. 'I don't know what to do or how to help her.'

She gave him a moment before asking, 'What do you mean?'

'Well, she's scared of her father. She's terrified.'

'Why would she be?'

'Hmm ...' He took in a deep breath. 'She thinks he killed her brother. She said she saw him do it, and she's losing her mind, she's so scared. I wish I could help her.'

'Whoa! That's intense. What can you do?'

'Well, there's this detective that has been reaching out to her. I think she can help. I'm not sure he actually killed his son, but she can help investigate it and help Ara calm down.'

He watched her smile fade and quickly asked, 'Where's your house? I thought it wasn't too far.' He didn't want to say too much or put too much on her.

'Well, you passed it a few houses ago.' She smiled.

'Oh gosh, I'm sorry. I must have been—'

'Distracted? That's my bad.' She removed her seatbelt. 'I'll walk it from here. It's not too far.'

He offered to drive her but she insisted.

She leaned in closer to him and hugged him. 'Thanks for the ride.' She held on for a moment, before she smiled, got out of the car and walked away.

He watched her in his rearview mirror and shook his head, smiling. She'd been easy to talk to and not as intimidating as he'd first assumed. He figured he shouldn't have said so much, though. He'd just been happy to talk to someone, but it had probably made her uncomfortable.

He sighed and cranked the engine, and drove on home.

E xcited and anxious, Jack barely slept that night. He was thrilled that Ethan believed him, and although they had no concrete plans yet, he was one step closer to having his life back. Coming back here, lying on this bed every night was always a disappointment, but tonight was different—and not just because of Ethan, but because the woman lying next to him was no longer a stranger.

He found himself watching her as she slept. She looked as beautiful as the day he had first seen her from the corner of his eye when he was taken into the cabin. She looked serene and calm, even though she was really nothing like that. He smiled at the thought. She had become a completely different person from who he had thought her to be, and although he'd hated her and then distrusted her, in that moment, he found himself leaning in closer to her until her soft breath brushed against the arm he placed across her chest. He finally closed his eyes and drifted off to the flowery smell that filled her hair.

Morning came faster than he had hoped. He liked being in her embrace and she ... well, she was clear about what she wanted. She led him into the bathroom and he followed her like a lamb to the slaughter—those were the exact words that echoed in his head when he halted at the door of the bathroom. Although she pulled slightly, he remained unmoved, and she closed the door, leaving it ajar, just a crack.

He closed his eyes and breathed heavily. He remembered his wife, he knew what he was fighting for and why he was here, but every time Victoria touched him, everything seemed to fade away. All his problems, all the pain he had caused, all the lies he had told and the truths he had hidden were lost to him when he looked into her eyes. She had her demons too, and perhaps that was why he found comfort in her embrace, but he knew he'd have hell to pay if he gave in.

He peeped in through the crack and caught a glimpse of her in the shower. He quickly closed the door, holding on to the handle for a moment before finally letting go.

She got out of the bathroom shortly after and didn't say anything of what had happened before. He avoided looking at her and went into the bathroom. The air was filled with her scent, and he stood there before the mirror, taking it all in. He looked at his reflection, and for a fleeting moment, he thought he saw his brother.

It was just past six in the morning when they left the motel room, once again all packed, with hopes of not returning. At first she had fought him on this—they had so much to carry every time they left the room—but she soon gave in.

They were on their way to see Komi. He wondered if Victoria had only agreed because of this new phase in their relationship that had blossomed out of thin air.

He could feel his heart beating faster as they approached Komi's apartment. He knew she had spent the most time with Jay since the incident and might have some information that could help—anything, really, would help. At this point, he was grasping at straws, but he needed to know why his brother had taken her hostage.

Victoria pulled him to a stop before he entered the building.

'Breathe,' she said, holding his hand. 'We don't know who else is up there, so be careful.' She pulled out a gun and tucked it beneath his shirt. 'Shoot anyone that's not Komi.'

He gasped in shock. 'You've had a gun all this time? And you didn't tell me?'

'I picked it up from the cabin, and you haven't needed it,' she said quietly. 'Until now.'

He took in a deep breath and nodded.

'I'll wait here. I'll call you if I see anyone coming up.' She kissed his lips and released him.

He walked into the building and ran into the elevator just before it closed. There was a woman in the corner of the elevator, and glancing at her, he moved closer to the other side. His movement was rigid; he had never held a gun before, and he felt as though she could see it right through his shirt. His backpack felt heavier and he felt hot. He began to sweat. He felt as though his legs would give way. He took deep breaths and held on to each breath tightly until the elevator reached Komi's floor, and he sprang out without looking back at the woman.

When he got to Komi's door, he tucked the gun tighter into his trousers and knocked lightly. Though he hoped she had answers for him, he was even more worried that she might. He was about to knock again when Victoria sprang up on him. He was so startled that when he tried to draw the gun, it fell to the ground. She picked up the gun and held his hand. 'Don't knock.'

His hand was trembling, and she wrapped her hand firmly around his. 'It's going to be OK. I'm here,' she said, moving him away from the door and kneeling by the door handle.

She brought out a small purse. In it were different kinds of small tools for picking locks, and she set to work on the door, trying to get it open.

'Where did you learn that?' he whispered.

She laughed softly. 'It was the first thing my father taught me,' she said.

The door clicked open, and they walked in slowly. The place was a mess. He walked faster towards Komi's room and opened the door. She was asleep in her bed. He walked towards her and sat beside her. He whispered her name and tapped her hand, trying to wake her up.

Komi jumped at the sight of him, and immediately he knew who she thought he was. She had the same fear that Victoria did when she opened her eyes to see him most mornings. That moment in between consciousness where the face they saw was that of a monster.

Victoria stayed at the door. She had seen a couple of familiar clothes around, so she knew El had been in the apartment or might still be there. While Jack tried to wake Komi, she checked out the rest of the place with the gun in her hand.

The apartment was beautiful—sparse, but still beautiful. The warm brown colour on the wall gave the room some warmth. The furniture was in different colours, like a well-arranged rainbow splashing all over the chairs and throw pillows. Although there wasn't a lot of furniture, the decor was nice and cosy, she admitted to herself.

She searched behind the flat-screen TV and underneath the chairs and pillows for anything, really; cameras or hidden weapons —she wasn't taking any chances. Jack might have trusted Komi, but she was never going to make that mistake.

She panned across the room, searching every corner, every painting—there were a lot of them, many of which were by the same artist: Mote. She scoffed. As though buying Mote's work made it easier on Komi's conscience when she lay with her best friend's husband. It didn't matter that Komi had actually been sleeping with Jay; she was still scum and deserved whatever wrath Jay poured down on her. He was always very quick to dispose of what he no longer needed, and whether Komi knew it or not, it was unlikely he would let her live, knowing so much about him already.

Victoria cracked a half-smile. In another world, they might have been friends. They could have talked and laughed and maybe cried over hot cocoa as they shared the pain Jay had caused them, but unfortunately for Komi, in this world they couldn't be further apart.

She stopped when she got to the painting hanging on the post closest to the kitchen counter. It was painted all blue with just a few dim spots of yellow.

It reminded her of her father—he'd loved to paint. It reminded her of the good times she'd had with him, the life she could have had if Jay hadn't taken him from her, if he hadn't been so consumed with this mission of his. A bitter anger boiled in her, and she turned away. She hated being here, standing in the apartment of her husband's mistress.

She'd thought she'd seen the worst of Jay. He'd killed her father, and still she'd stayed with him. The pain she'd felt when she held her father's dying body in her arms was indescribable, although someone else would probably have killed him if Jay hadn't done it himself. But all of that hurt and betrayal was nothing compared to what she had felt when she found out about Komi. She'd felt like her heart had exploded, she was enraged, but she couldn't even bring herself to confront him.

She wasn't sure what had stopped her. Whether it was her fear of him or her love for him, he had her bound to him with something she could not explain. She'd wanted to leave but always found herself back in his arms—at least, until now.

She'd believed she felt the anger that burned inside of him, and she let it be what held her sanity together. She let it feed off her, and she let the vengeance brew and consume her. She couldn't wait till the day she would take everything from him, and when he'd ask why, she'd have the exact words to say to him, words she'd searched for the courage to say for a long time.

She moved on past the kitchen to the door on the other side of the apartment. She opened it slowly and saw El asleep on the bed. Some of Stig's clothes were lying around; she could recognise his odd sense of style anywhere. She woke El up with the gun pressed to her face.

'Shhh,' she said, placing a finger on her lips.

El sprang up. She tried to reach for the knife beside her pillow, but Victoria beat her to it. She took the knife from the bed and put it in her back pocket. El managed to knock her down, but soon, Victoria had her pinned to the ground. She tied her wrists to the bed frame, her ankles together, and gagged her with a piece of cloth.

Komi sprang up from the bed, and Jack followed her up.

'It's me, Komi. It's Jack,' he said quietly.

'I know who you are. Stay away from me!' she yelled.

'No, no, no ... Komi. That wasn't me. The man who took you to that cabin, the man that kidnapped you, Komi, that wasn't me,' he tried to explain.

She threw the pillows at him and ran out into the living room. She bumped into Victoria, who threw her off. She stumbled into one of the chairs and finally fell face first on the carpet.

She scrambled off the floor and was running for the door when Victoria pulled out her gun.

'Don't take another step,' she commanded from across the room.

Jack ran out of the bedroom after Komi and tried again to get her to calm down.

In the midst of all this, El stepped out from the other room, ripping a rag from her mouth. There was a gun in her hand, and before Jack could move, she'd grabbed Victoria. She held the gun to Victoria's head and forced Victoria's gun out of her hand.

'Sit down now!' she demanded. 'All of you.'

Komi rushed towards the nearest chair, and Jack followed after her. El picked up her phone and made a call.

'Stig! Where are you?' She paused for a response, but she was clearly dissatisfied with whatever he said. 'I don't care. Get here now. I've got her.' She hung up.

She looked at Jack and he could see the same conflict in her gaze that he'd seen the first time she aimed a gun at him. It seemed liked she couldn't quite decide what she wanted to do with him.

Then he saw it. The recognition. The look he had seen in Victoria and Komi's eyes. The look he saw in his eyes when he looked in the mirror. She saw the face of the monster too.

She turned to Victoria. 'He will kill you,' she said mockingly. 'How far did you think you could go?' She glanced at Jack again. 'Obviously not very far.'

Victoria didn't respond. She remained quiet, but Jack saw her hand creeping towards a knife in her pocket.

Komi was a mess. She whimpered and sobbed and ranted about how she didn't deserve to be caught up in all of this. She wouldn't even look at Jack.

Jack placed his hand on his forehead. He knew El wouldn't listen to him; he had tried before at the cabin, and he knew exactly what she thought of him. He looked around the apartment, and his gaze settled on Victoria. They might not leave this place alive.

Victoria finally broke the silence. 'I have what you want,' she said.

'There's no talking your way out of this one,' El scoffed. 'You don't have anything I want.'

Victoria moved slowly. El quickly pointed the gun back at her. She raised her hands. 'It's in my bag. I'm going to take it out now.' And slowly, she reached for it.

El nodded but moved closer to her, the scowl on her face now permanent.

Victoria brought out a small white envelope.

'What's that?' El asked.

'The answers you've been looking for. It's a copy of your birth certificate and adoption papers signed by your mother.'

El stared at her in disbelief and walked closer to her to take the envelope, then Victoria jumped her. She forced the gun from her and slammed it into her head, knocking her out.

Jack turned to find Komi pointing the gun at him. She must have run for it while they were distracted. He tried to speak but no words came out. He just froze, hands raised above his head.

Victoria shouted, 'Drop the gun, Komi, or believe me, I will hurt you!'

'No, please—' Jack begged, finally finding the words stuck in his throat.

Komi shook her head. She held her stomach. 'You have ruined everything!'

'We can fix this, I promise, just put the gun down,' Jack said.

Komi kept shaking her head as if tossing out every word he spoke.

There was a loud noise in the corner of the room, and when Komi turned to see what it was, Victoria jumped her and forced the gun out of her hand. She had tossed her shoe to create the distraction, and with a hard shove, she sent Komi to the ground.

She turned to Jack. 'You need to leave now. Stig will be back any minute. He cannot meet you here.'

'What about you?' he asked.

'I'll be right behind you,' she assured him.

'Don't hurt her,' he pleaded again.

She simply nodded.

'Promise me, Victoria,' he insisted.

She sighed. 'I promise.'

He took one last glance at Komi and hurried out the apartment.

As soon as he left the apartment, Komi's eyes widened. 'You're Victoria. You're his wife.'

Victoria ignored her and walked back into Komi's room, where Jack had left his bag. Komi came in after her. She had dropped the gun in the parlour.

Victoria went straight for the bag. She picked it up, and underneath it was a pregnancy test pack torn open. She looked at Komi with disbelief. She could barely get the words out of her mouth.

'Are you pregnant?' she asked with anger in her voice.

She felt the rage build in her as Komi slowly nodded and moved away from her. Victoria's hands began to quake. She had spent so many years trying to get pregnant, hoping a child would return them to their good times. She had hoped to have a family with him; she had tried and tried, and she had failed. She stood still, watching as this woman who was nothing but a mere pawn folded her arms across her stomach, unconsciously protecting her child, his child.

She lost all control and lunged at her. Screaming, she knocked her to the ground.

One moment, she had Komi pinned beneath her, struggling to hold her hands, and the next she was holding El's knife in Komi's stomach.

Victoria froze. She stared at the crimson that stained her hands, and realisation knocked the air of out her. She looked at Komi still screaming beneath her. Her ears rang as blood rushed to her head, and the scream felt like it was coming from miles away. She panicked and tried to pull out the knife, but the shrieking sound that came out of Komi made her jump off her.

She tried to speak but did not know what to say. She would have stayed, but the thought of what Jay would do to her if he found her there with his child's blood on her hands made her more afraid than she had ever been in her life.

She picked up Jack's bag, washed her hands in the bathroom as quickly as she could, and ran for her life, leaving Komi bleeding out on the bedroom floor.

As she approached the door that led out of the building, she saw Stig rushing in. She stopped right in front of him. In that moment, she didn't know what to expect from him. They'd been very close when he'd lived with them many years ago. Her father had bought him from some human traffickers when he was very young. He could barely speak when he first arrived, and although her father didn't raise him a slave in the actual sense of it, Stig became his fiercest fighter and cruellest assassin. He'd had a soft spot for Victoria; he'd always said that whenever he had done the worst things, he found solace in her company. Of course, all that changed when Jay took over.

He looked at her sternly, then at the elevator doors, waiting to see if anyone came after her. He took a step back and allowed her to go free.

She let out the breath she didn't know she was holding as he moved out of her way.

'Thank you,' she breathed.

She moved to pass, and he said, 'You saved my life once. Now we are even. If I see you again, I will follow my orders.'

His words were cold. He may have let her go because of his lingering affection for her, but she knew his threat was real. It broke her heart to know that yet another man had been led astray by her husband's ill-placed search for vengeance—redemption as he called it.

CHAPTER

19

J ay had called El nearly twelve times that morning, and each time, she just let it go to voicemail. She had begged Stig to not say anything until they were sure that Komi was OK. She had woken up to find Jack and Victoria were long gone and Komi passed out in a pool of blood.

She'd rushed Komi to the hospital, claiming that Komi was her mother and she'd found her lying on the floor when she got home. She'd panicked, and quite frankly she was terrified of what her father would do when he found out. She had also seen the pregnancy test and knew that the thought of Komi carrying Jay's child would have been enough to drive Victoria over the edge. She didn't need to have witnessed it to know that Victoria's rage had driven the knife into Komi's stomach. She knew from experience exactly what Victoria was capable of. She could be about to lose a sibling that two hours ago she didn't even know existed.

She waited for the doctor to return with a report on Komi. It took hours and it felt like forever, waiting to hear the fate of a woman who she previously could not care less for. Now, she found herself praying that they would both be OK, Komi and the baby.

She finally picked up Jay's call, and as expected, he began to shout before she could even get a word in. He hurled questions at her. He had overheard April talking to Ara about her new friend Lara, and he knew it had been El. She'd known she couldn't keep that secret for much longer, but today was the worst day for that to happen. She just let him go on about all he had overheard as he over-exaggerated and overanalysed the situation. He couldn't be reasoned with when he got all worked up—she had learnt that the hard way. It seemed as though she would always try to please him but somehow ended up doing the exact opposite.

'I know you mean well, but you're just not strong enough.' Those were the words he'd said to her shortly after Victoria first escaped from the cabin. She remembered them every time she spoke to him, and they cut even deeper every time. Knowing that he saw her that way, she felt as though she could never truly be a part of his world, and it broke her.

She let out a deep sigh. 'I'm in the hospital, Dad. Komi was hurt badly, and she's in surgery now.'

She paused to hear what he would say next. Shouts, insults, threats—whatever it was, she was ready for it, but he simply asked in a low tone, 'Is the baby OK?'

'I ... I don't know, Dad,' she stuttered. 'I'm still waiting to hear from the doctors.'

'Give the phone to Stig,' he ordered.

She walked over to Stig on the other side of the room, and handed him the phone. He held the phone to his ear and waited to hear his orders.

'Who did this?' Jay asked. His voice was filled with anger.

'El said Victoria came over with your brother to see Komi. Victoria attacked her and knocked her out, and when she came to, she found Komi on the floor bleeding.'

'Where were you?' he shouted so loudly that El heard him through the phone.

'I was taking care of the other thing, boss. You said first thing in the morning,' he said carefully.

He hung up and gave the phone back to El. 'He'll call back with instructions. He wants you to stay here.'

'Where are you going? You need to stay here with me!' she shouted.

He towered over her. 'I don't take orders from you. Stay here and fix this.'

As she watched him walk away from her, it was all she could do to not punch his smug face. He'd never respected her, and he believed he was more important to Jay than she was. And honestly, sometimes she felt that way too. She was Jay's daughter, but he continuously lied to her and kept secrets from her and she was tired of it all.

She rolled her eyes and murmured under her breath, 'Fix it.' As though she'd be the one to patch up Komi.

She called Jay back, hoping the information she'd got from Andrew was enough to earn some part of his trust back. The phone rang a couple of times before he picked up. She didn't let him say anything before she began. 'Dad, Andrew told me something when I was at their place. He mentioned that Ara was planning on revealing the truth she knew to a detective that came over to her house. Maureen—I think that was her name. I think you should look into it.'

'You should have never gone to see that boy,' he said coldly and hung up.

She stood still in shock, the phone still held to her ear, listening to the disconnecting tone beep over and over again until it finally stopped.

She reached into her bag and pulled out the white envelope Victoria had given her. She had always disliked Victoria, but she admired her for one thing: she always stayed true to her word. The envelope could have vanished with her, but she'd left it for El.

She held it in her hands for a very long time, wondering whether she should open it, if she could even bring herself to.

All she had ever wanted was to know her birth mother, to find her, to know why she had given El up. She had so many questions, and they had only grown over the years. Her father had always found a reason to hide the truth from her, but now she had the answers she'd sought in her hands.

She couldn't bring herself to open it. Tears trailed down her cheeks, and she buried her face in her palms and sobbed.

She remained there until one of the doctors got her attention.

She sprang up and cleaned her tears, grateful for them because she was sure the man thought she was crying for her injured 'mother'.

He placed his hand on her shoulder in an attempt to calm her down. 'She is going to be OK.' He paused and frowned. 'However, we found that she was pregnant. We did everything could, but the wound was too deep. She lost the baby.'

Her world collapsed around her as she took in his words. She held her chest, trying to stop her heart from beating fast. She cried into his arms. She cried for many reasons: she cried because she had hoped for a brief moment that the child would live, and she would get to meet it and have a brother or a sister, even. She cried because she didn't have the courage to open the envelope and find out the answers to the questions that had haunted her for years. Most importantly, she cried because she knew her father would be enraged and grief-stricken and someone would pay for this. She dearly hoped that it wouldn't be her.

Jay was back home with Mote and Ara. He'd got in late in the night before and snuck into the house. He slept on the couch, as he knew that was what his brother would do after a fight or an argument with Mote. He'd got up early and cleaned up the house, made breakfast—pulled out all the stops to make sure he got back on track with her.

Although Ara had started off as merely part of the mission, he found himself caring for her, which only destabilised him more while waiting for the DNA results to come back from the lab. He had taken her hairbrush and replaced it. She didn't seem to notice, which didn't bother him at all; he was quite content with the distance she kept from him. But he knew she was hiding something from him, and the call from El confirmed it. Ara had been talking with that detective from the hospital. It was a good thing he'd had someone look into the detective as soon as he saw her in the hospital with Ara.

He picked up his phone, agitated.

'Pick up, pick up ... Do you have information on that detective I told you to look into? ... Good, send everything to me. I'll wire the rest of the money to you once the information is confirmed.' He hung up and dropped the phone on the kitchen counter.

He paced around the kitchen for a while before he stopped at the sink and just stared out the window. He watched the flowers in Mote's garden. The wind blew against them. Some remained in its wake, and some fell off so easily it was as though they were never there. Tears built in his eyes. How could Victoria do this to him? How could she hurt him this way, take away the one thing that she could not give him? He hated her more than he'd ever thought he could.

He remembered how much he'd loved her when they first got married. He'd been sure, once, that she knew every part of him, all of his heart's desires, and yet she resorted to this, to attacking the woman that carried his child? She knew how much he wanted a child of his own, which among other things had driven him to adopt El—but what a disappointment she was turning out to be. He desperately wanted to have a child of his own blood. Maybe he already did, if the one night he spent with Mote all those years ago had conceived Ara. Soon—soon he'd know.

He sighed in despair. So many things had gone wrong. He had hoped that he would seamlessly ease into his brother's life, kill him and the two children, and start a new life with Mote.

All that seemed far away now. He'd just lost his child, and he felt pain he'd never thought he could. He tried to breathe, but he felt like the room was closing in on him. He began to pant heavily, holding back the tears in his eyes.

'Dad?' he heard Ara call out to him. She was standing just a few feet away. 'Are you OK?' she asked, staring at him but not moving any closer.

He nodded quickly and tried coughing to clear out his lungs. They felt clogged up. She tried to help him when it seemed like he wasn't getting better.

'Don't! Don't come any closer,' he barked at her.

She froze up, then frowned. 'I have to leave the house for a bit. I'm going to April's,' she stated, watching him struggle to breathe.

He nodded and waved her off. She watched him for a bit longer, and once he had the coughing under control, she filled a cup with water and pushed it to him before storming out of the house.

He knew she was probably lying to him, but there was nothing he could do at the moment. He fell to the floor slowly with his back up against the counter and took deep breaths. He continued to do so until he regained his strength. This had never happened to him before—a panic attack. It felt like his heart was being squeezed out of his chest.

Once it was over, he sighed in relief and got up slowly. He wondered why Mote hadn't got up yet. Normally, she would be downstairs already. Surely she must have heard him yell at Ara?

He walked as fast as he could up the stairs, still holding his chest and regulating his breathing. In the bedroom, he found Mote passed out on the bed. A nearly finished bottle seemed to have fallen out of her hand and spilled onto the floor.

He rushed towards her and tried to wake her up. He held her, calling her name, tapping her lightly on the cheeks. She didn't respond to anything he did. He carried her off the bed into the bathroom and poured water on her face while continuing to call her name. She finally responded slowly. She peered at him with her eyes half open and looked around.

'I'm sorry, Jack,' she whispered.

'Shhh ... it's OK,' he replied, pushing her hair back. 'Just breathe.'

She struggled to hold herself over the toilet bowl and threw up while he held her hair behind her. He eased her to her feet when she felt better, helped her rinse out her mouth, and carried her to the bed.

She was weak and pale; she could barely get any words out.

'I'll get you some coffee,' he said and hurried out of the room.

When he got to the top of the stairs, he sat on the first step and buried his face in his palms. He blamed himself for this, and it hurt him to see her this way. She had broken her long streak of sobriety, and it was his fault. He felt the guilt tug at him, and he knew that he was now undeniably in love with her.

He shouldn't have brought that drink to the house. He shouldn't have stormed out. He should have never left her alone. He had done many terrible things in his life and had been responsible for more ill than he could recount, but nothing had ever made him feel the way he did right now.

He got off the stairs, went to get her the coffee he had offered, and remained with her until she felt better a few hours later.

CHAPTER
20

Maureen woke up to the sound of her phone's ringtone. It was a soft melody, but this morning, it sounded like a hundred church bells being rung in unison. She opened her eyes slowly to the blinding light and squinted for a few seconds before she could see the screen. She didn't recognise the number, but she picked it up anyway.

Her voice was low and husky, still trying to find its way back to life. 'Who is this?'

'Hello, this is Ara. You gave my mother your card.' Ara's voice sounded even louder than the ring that had nearly deafened her.

Maureen sprang up. 'Yes, yes, I remember ... What? Are you sure? ... But you said ... OK, OK, I'll meet you there. I'm on my way now.'

Ara had asked to meet up somewhere near Maureen's house, and she was grateful for that. She wasn't sure she could have made it down to the suburbs that morning. Ara said that she was finally ready to speak with her and tell everything that really happened. She explained that her dad had taken her card from her, but she was able to find the one Maureen had dropped with her mum.

Maureen wasn't sure exactly what had changed her mind, whether it was what she had told her in her room or something else. Either way, she was relieved to hear that Ara was ready to talk, because she'd truly been about to give up on the entire case.

She had fallen off the wagon, again. She had not yet managed to stay on for more than forty-eight hours. She always found herself stuck in search for something she never found at the bottom of the bottle.

She sighed and sat up slowly, tossing the empty bottle off her bed. Hopefully, the case would be resolved soon; she could feel herself fading away more and more with every morning that passed with it hanging over her.

She had a splitting headache and she could barely get her feet off the bed. She dragged herself to the bathroom and had a cold shower, hoping it would wake her up and give her the strength she needed to get through the day without looking like what she felt on the inside. In a loose silk robe, she settled with a cup of black coffee on the floor in the living room with a lot of papers in front of her. All the files she had on the incident that killed a seven-year-old boy one hot summer night in July, the father who had a spotless record yet hid secrets that could lead to finding his son's murderer, the girl who claimed to have watched her brother get shot but was too frightened to speak.

She shuffled all the papers, reading them over and over again, all the statements and reports from that night up until this moment. She was caught up in this when her phone rang again. She thought it was Ara again but she couldn't recognise the number.

'Hello?' she said in a soft voice when she picked up the phone.

'Maureen Lewis?' said a man's voice.

'Who is this?'

'I want you to stop investigating my family. We have gone through enough! There's no need to drag this on and open wounds that are trying to heal.'

'I'm sorry, who am I speaking to?' she asked, although she had a guess who it might be.

'You were at my house, asking questions that have already been answered. Your relentless intrusion has thrown my wife into despair. She's drinking again, and that's because of you!'

'Sir, if you have any complaints, please report them to the station,' she said, ignoring his loud voice.

He paused before continuing: 'It would be a shame if the circumstances surrounding your partner's death surfaced again.'

'I don't know who you think you are, but you cannot threaten an officer of the law. I have nothing to hide,' she said, agitated.

'Oh, but you do, detective,' he mocked. 'I'm sure the police would find it interesting to know that you lied about your alibi the night your partner was killed.'

'Listen to me: your threats mean nothing,' she replied. 'If you have nothing to do with your son's murder, you wouldn't be calling me to make such ridiculous claims.'

'Tell me, Maureen, where were you when your partner was gunned down in the street and stowed away in an alley to rot for days?' he asked.

She hung up and sprang to her feet. She picked up the papers and flung them across the room with a loud cry. She squatted down and buried her face in her lap. This couldn't be happening. She'd always blamed herself for Daniel's death, but that had never felt as true as it did now.

She was terrified, even though she wouldn't admit it to herself.

She grabbed a large plastic bag from her kitchen cabinet and began to throw her bottles of alcohol in it. They were hidden all over the house, in drawers, in cabinets, in the sofa, in her room, in her medicine cabinet, in her dressing table. When she was done, the bag was about half full of bottles of various sizes. She slumped on the chair, staring at the bag and what she had become.

Her first instinct was to destroy all the evidence, anything that might show negligence on her part or that could be used against her. Tears filled her eyes as she looked at the bag full of bottles. Her head hurt more than it had when she woke up. She needed to clear her head and think properly if she was to get ahead of this and solve this case without damaging her career, which she had fought hard to keep even after she lost everything else.

She lay down on the floor beside her sofa and closed her eyes. The smell of alcohol filled the small room. Her mind drifted into the past, thinking about the first time she'd had a drink. At first, she'd sometimes drink with friends after work at the bar, but soon enough, she'd go alone to the bar, then she brought the bar home with her. She couldn't say exactly when, but at some point down the line, she'd realised that she needed a bottle of vodka or two a few times a week. And now here she was, lying on the floor, weak and tired. She had lost her friends; she had lost her partner. She was in debt and was now at the brink of losing her career.

She sighed as tears rolled down her face. She'd thought she would stop after Daniel died, but she had felt like she might die; it hurt too much to remember him and how he was killed. It broke her heart when they'd found his body with a ring in his pocket. She knew it belonged to her, but no one else did. She had insisted that they keep their relationship a secret. It hurt so much more because unknown to the whole world, she had lost her partner and lover. Shortly after his death, she had returned to the bottle to find solace in it, but it did nothing but turn her into someone even he wouldn't recognise.

Ara's next call sprang her out of her spiralling thoughts. She told Maureen that she was already at their meeting spot. As soon as she hung up, she hurried into her room, got dressed, and left her apartment in the mess she had made.

Ara waited about twenty minutes before she finally saw Maureen in the distance. As Maureen got closer, Ara noticed she looked different from the last time she'd seen her. She wasn't in her perfectly tailored suit, and her hair wasn't in a sleek bob. She wore black jeans, a loose top, and a black jacket. She had her hair up in a ponytail, and her eyes looked pale and weak.

'Are you OK?' Ara asked as Maureen approached her.

'Yes, yes, I'm fine. Let's find somewhere to sit and talk,' Maureen said, leading her to the nearest bench.

As soon as they sat down, Ara began to talk. As she described the events that had occurred that night, she began to feel like she had told this story too many times and yet not enough, because her father still remained in their house. She watched Maureen's face as the story unravelled and ended with her father murdering her brother and forcing her to keep his secret and threatening her mum. Maureen's reaction, however, wasn't anything like Andrew's.

She was much calmer, her expression neutral. It bothered Ara that she listened as though she was listening to a tale for a bedtime story.

'Maureen,' she said, shaking her knee. 'Are you listening to me?'

A bit startled, Maureen replied, 'I am, Ara. It's a lot to process. Are you sure about this? Are you sure you saw your father do this?'

Ara stood up, agitated. 'Why does everyone keep asking me this? Why would I lie about this?' she shouted. 'I thought I could trust you. You begged me to tell you the truth, and now you don't believe me.'

Maureen got up and stood before her, holding both her shoulders. 'Ara, calm down. I believe you. If we do this ... No, *when* we get your father and pin this on him, you will have to testify against him. So many people will doubt you. And if you let it get to you, you will begin to doubt the truth, and he could go free.'

She calmed down as she listened to Maureen's words. She knew it sounded unbelievable every time she thought about it or had to say it out loud, but she knew she could not continue to live with him, and he had to pay for what he had done.

Until this morning, she'd believed in her heart that he deserved to die, and she wanted him to. Not only that, she wanted to be the one who shot the gun that killed him, just as he had her brother. No mercy, no pleading, just a life for a life. However, when she saw him struggling to breathe this morning over the kitchen counter, she'd panicked, and she was reminded of the man she loved, the man she had lived with all these years, the man who loved her. He had refused her help and she couldn't understand why, but she was just happy she could leave the house that morning to meet with Maureen. His pride had obviously got the better of him.

She still hated him, but that moment when'd she seen him choking, she'd been scared that he might die. Somehow, she no longer wanted him dead; she no longer wanted his life for her brother's. She couldn't explain how she found herself wanting him to live—he deserved no mercy.

'What has he been up to? In the house, does he go out often? Whom does he talk to?' Maureen asked.

'He's been trying to keep me in the house—both of us actually, my mum and I. He insists that we shouldn't go out, for our own safety. He goes out late sometimes. He visits Andrew's dad too, but that's not surprising. He's his best friend and lawyer. I hear him shouting on the phone sometimes, but I don't know who he talks to.'

'Your friend's dad—what's his name?'

'Ethan Johnson,' Ara replied. 'Andrew should be here too. I asked him to come. I told him about my dad, but he didn't believe me. I was hoping he'd know I was telling the truth when he knows that I've spoken to you.'

'You need to be careful whom you talk to,' Maureen warned. 'If his dad is together with your dad on this, you could have just put his life in danger.'

'Uncle Ethan would never do such a thing,' Ara replied. 'He's a good man. He was Tale's godfather.'

'Your father was a good man. He doesn't have a single record, not even a parking ticket. Without hard evidence of this, it's all hearsay, so this isn't going to be easy. So until we know exactly what's going on, you shouldn't tell anyone else. You could be putting them or yourself in danger.'

'All right, but Andrew has nothing to do with this. He's my best friend,' Ara said confidently.

'I'm not saying that he does, but you need to be careful. When he gets here, I don't want you to tell him that I asked about his father. I don't want him to panic and call him or anything like that.'

Ara nodded reluctantly.

'Do you know if they meet up at his office or his house?' Maureen asked.

'His office, I think.'

'All right, give me his address. I'll start from there.'

Andrew arrived shortly after Maureen scribbled down the address and tucked it in her pocket. He introduced himself to her and answered her questions. She asked just a few, nothing out of the ordinary so he wouldn't get curious.

Then she left, and headed for Ethan's office.

CHAPTER

21

A ra looked at Andrew and smiled. He seemed to grow more handsome with every passing minute. Even in times when she couldn't stand his guts and he made her furious, looking at him, staring into his eyes, and being held in his embrace always seemed to make everything better. She hated being mad at him; she needed him now more than ever. She allowed herself to move past his folly and tried to understand him.

The truth was, she knew why he doubted her. She knew hers wasn't an easy truth, and honestly she was happy that he believed in her father even more than she had thought he did. However, she needed him to rid his thoughts of all kinds of sentiment; it was time to be a man and stand by her and believe her absolutely.

How she wished that he had come for her that night. She'd been ready to tell him all that she knew he wanted to hear. She was in love with him. She'd wanted to tell him since the moment he'd told her, but she'd been scared and now it was too late. It had been weeks since he told her that he loved her, weeks since she ran away from him. She closed her eyes and wished she could go back in time to that moment, imagined how she would hug him and not let go till she found the courage to say those words back to him. She felt the tears begin to build up in her eyes; she smiled and looked away.

'Are you OK?' he asked worriedly.

His voice made the slumbering butterflies in her stomach awaken. His touch sent chills down her spine. She could feel her face burning up; she loved him so much her heart ached because she knew she'd hurt him and he was probably only here because he felt he had to be.

She nodded. 'I just ... I just don't know what to do.'

'It's going to be OK, Ara. I believe you. We will get through this together. I am here for you, whatever you need.'

'Why did you leave?' she asked, remembering when she'd told

him about this a few days ago. She had hoped that he would at least stay and figure it out with her, not leave her all alone, knowing how scared she was.

'I freaked out. I'm sorry. I was eavesdropping on your dad. He was on a call in the kitchen. I didn't mean to, I just did, and what he said scared me.'

'What did he say?' she asked, curious and frightened.

'I can't remember every word, but he was arguing with someone over the phone. He said he wasn't going to do anything until he got the results back. He said he won't kill his child.'

'What does that mean? I'm his child. We both are.'

'I don't know. I freaked out and left—that's why I left. I thought he saw me, and I panicked. I'm sorry.'

She stared at him in disbelief. 'He thinks I'm not his child? Is that why he killed Tale? Did he think he wasn't his child? Oh my God,' she sobbed. 'This is ridiculous, I can't believe this is happening.

'We should tell Maureen,' she continued. 'Why didn't you tell me he could have hurt me? If this test he's talking about said I wasn't his child, he could have killed me.'

She got off the bench and walked away from him.

He ran after her. 'I'm sorry, Ara, I needed to be sure of what I heard. All of this is a lot for me to process. I didn't mean to hide it from you or anything, I'm sorry.'

She sighed and nodded reluctantly. She wished he had told her, but she couldn't dwell on that now. She picked up her phone and was about to call Maureen, when her mum's call came in.

'Ara!' Mote called out to her frantically over the phone. 'I'm on my way to the hospital. I got a call that Aunt Komi was attacked in her home. I'm listed as her emergency contact. There's someone there claiming to be her daughter.'

'Oh, Mum, is she OK?' Ara asked, concerned.

'I don't know, I'll call you when I get there.'

'No, I'll come meet you. I'm with Andrew now,' Ara replied.

'All right. Please be careful, Ara, I love you.'

'I love you too, Mum.'

Ara hung up. She closed her eyes and swung her head back, looking up to the sky.

'What's wrong?' Andrew asked. 'Is your mum OK?'

'Yes, she is. Aunt Komi is in the hospital. She was attacked. I need to go and see her. Will you take me there?'

'Of course, Ara—of course I will. Come on, let's go,' he said, holding her hand and leading her to his car.

Mote arrived at the hospital before Ara and Andrew. She rushed towards the reception, asking to see Komi. After Mote described Komi, a nurse led her to Komi's room.

'She might be asleep for a bit longer. Try not to make any noise,' the nurse said to her.

She nodded while peeping into the room, trying to catch a glimpse of Komi's face. 'Is she going to be OK?' she asked.

'She lost the baby, but she is fine. She just needs to rest,' the nurse replied.

'She was pregnant?!'

'Please keep your voice down, ma'am,' said the nurse. 'I'll ask the doctor to come by and answer any questions you might have.' She turned away.

'Wait, please,' Mote begged. 'On the phone, someone told me her daughter was here with her. She doesn't have a daughter.'

'A young girl brought her in, but she left about an hour ago. I'll get the doctor,' the nurse said and left hurriedly.

Mote walked in slowly, trying to be quiet as the nurse had

advised. She sat on the chair beside Komi's bed and held Komi's hand. She squeezed it lightly, bowed her head, and cried. She felt terrible that she'd been upset with her all this time; she hadn't bothered to try and find her while her phone was disconnected. She knew Komi would never have left her during the hardest moments of her life. How could she have ever thought Komi would intentionally hurt her?

She smiled through the tears as she remembered the years they had spent together, all the times Komi had come through for her. Komi truly was the best friend she could ever hope for.

She remembered when she had just given up her child, how Komi pulled her out of her darkest nightmares and led her to the light. Komi had become a sister to her, her confidante.

Komi was Ara's godmother; she couldn't have picked a better person. Komi was strong, she was exceptionally beautiful, she was intelligent, and she was brilliant at her job. She loved that Ara looked up to her; she was the perfect role model.

It saddened her even more to find out that Komi had lost a child. Komi had always had a tough time holding down a good relationship. She seemed to always find herself in sticky situations with men that weren't worth her time.

Mote placed her hand over Komi's stomach and sobbed. She knew how happy Komi would have been to have that child. Who could have done this terrible thing to her?

Suddenly, she felt Komi squeeze her hand. She sprang up from the chair, wiped her tears and hugged her close. Overcome with joy, she held Komi's face.

'I'm so sorry,' she whispered.

Komi's eyes shone with tears. 'I'm sorry,' she said, barely audible. 'I'm sorry about Tale, I'm sorry about everything.'

'Oh, Komi, it's all right. You don't have anything to be sorry for. I love you, just get better.'

Komi looked down and held her stomach. 'My baby?' she asked, her voice cracking.

Mote cried, 'I'm so sorry. The nurse said—'

She couldn't say the words. They would break Komi's heart. She just shook her head and squeezed Komi's hand tighter. 'I'm sorry, Komi.'

Komi sobbed loudly, holding her tummy, and groaned in pain. She turned her head towards the window and stared out until her tears dried on her face, leaving faint marks that ran from her eyes to the tip of her nose and onto the soaked pillow.

'I need to tell you something, Mote.' She paused. 'I need to tell you the truth.'

Mote was confused. 'What are you talking about?'

Komi paused for a long while, and more tears drenched her pillow. Mote leaned in closer, unsure of what was troubling her. So she just rubbed Komi's hand and listened.

'You shouldn't trust Jack. I think he knows more about what happened to Tale than he's letting on.'

Mote removed her hand slowly from Komi's. 'What are you talking about?

'He has another daughter, another family, a wife. He has been lying to you all these years,' she said, struggling to say every word.

'I don't understand, Komi, why are you saying these things?' Mote asked, even more confused than before. 'This cannot be true, how do you know this?' She sighed. 'You need to rest.'

'No, you need to believe me!' Komi shouted, trying to lift herself off the bed but failing. 'You need to believe me,' she repeated, panting.

'He is my husband!'

'He is the father of my child!'

'What?' Mote stepped away from the bed. 'What do you mean he's the father of your ... oh God, Komi, what did you do?'

Komi went quiet, sobbing, staring at her as though she was scared that the next words would make her finish what her attacker had started.

'Talk to me, Komi! Now!' Mote shouted.

'We've been together for the past few months. Everything changed a couple of weeks ago when he abducted me and threatened to kill me. I don't know what's going on, but he's not the man you think he is.'

'What do you mean "together"? He's my husband!'

'I didn't mean to hurt you. I didn't want any of this to happen!' Komi cried. 'I lost my child.'

'Am I supposed to feel sorry for you? You were pregnant with my husband's child. How could you do this?' Mote didn't wait for a response; she could no longer stay and listen to anything Komi had to say. 'Whoever did this to you should have completed the job. At least you'd be with your bastard child.'

Her words cut deep and she intended them to. She stormed out of the room, ignoring Komi's calls and pleading. She walked and then began to run until she saw Ara and Andrew rushing towards her. Her face was filled with tears and she could barely get a word out. She hugged Ara and asked Andrew to drop her off at home after they had seen Komi; she lied and said she had an errand to run. Only one thing was clear to her in that moment, and it was that she should get as far away from Komi as possible.

Ara rushed towards Komi's room and found her struggling to get off her bed.

'No, Aunt Komi, don't get up. Andrew, get a doctor,' she said, calling out to him as he approached the door.

She helped Komi lie back down on her bed. Her stomach had

begun to bleed out through the bandage to stain the loose gown she wore. Ara tried to apply a little pressure to stop the bleeding, and Komi groaned in pain.

The doctor rushed in with a nurse who took over from Ara. Asking her to step back, she dabbed off the blood that had spilled and gave Komi an injection that put her to sleep.

'She should still be asleep. You shouldn't have woken her up,' the doctor said sternly.

'We didn't,' Ara responded. 'When we got here, she was trying to get up.'

'You should leave, she needs to rest. She might be out for a while,' he said, leading them out of the room.

'Is she going to be OK?' Ara asked.

'Yes, she just needs to rest. You can come back tomorrow. She should have regained some strength,' he said before closing the door and leaving.

Andrew held her hand. He didn't say anything, just stood there with her as they looked at Komi through the window.

'She looks so tired,' Ara said after a while.

He turned towards her, assuring her, 'She's one of the strongest women I know; she will be fine. You know that, there's no need to worry.'

He led her away from the window, and they left the hospital. Andrew stopped in his tracks when he saw someone approaching them. He let go of Ara's hand and hurried towards the girl. Ara stopped too, looking down at where his hand had held hers, now swinging empty beside her. She followed slowly after him, hurt that he'd left her and curious as to who this mystery girl was. The girl's eyes were swollen from crying.

'Are you OK?' he asked, holding her arm.

She tried to speak but couldn't. She began to cry again and fell into his arms. He hugged her and patted her head, whispering to her, when Ara caught up with them.

She stopped in front of them without saying anything. The girl pulled away from Andrew and wiped her tears.

'I'm sorry,' she whispered, only taking a glance at Ara while trying to avoid eye contact. 'My friend was hurt this morning. I was staying with her while my dad was out of town. I don't know what happened—I just found her on the floor bleeding. I think someone attacked her,' she sobbed, looking straight into Andrew's eyes.

She held on to his hand even though he'd pulled away when Ara joined them.

'I don't know what to do. I can't go back there. I'm scared,' she said, whimpering.

Andrew looked at Ara and back at the girl. 'You can come with us. I'm sure April would love to have you around, at least until your friend gets better.'

Ara cleared her throat, bringing Andrew's attention back to her. He quickly apologised and introduced them. 'Ara, this is Lara, she's April's friend. She came by the house a few days ago.' He turned to the girl. 'Lara, this is—'

'Ara,' Lara finished. 'It's nice to meet you. I've heard a lot about you.' She smiled.

'Oh really,' Ara replied. 'I've heard nothing about you,' she said plainly.

Lara paused. 'I'm sorry to hear about your brother, and your father.'

'My father?' Ara asked, confused.

'Uh ... being involved in your brother's murder and all that. That must be a lot to deal with.'

Ara froze, dumbfounded. She turned to Andrew, who clearly knew in that moment that he had messed up. He closed his eyes slowly, and before he could say a word, she stormed off.

Ara waited by the car, and they all got in. She didn't say a word the entire ride back. Lara was also quiet in the back seat. When she wasn't staring at Andrew through the mirror, she was looking out the window to avoid looking at Ara.

They finally arrived at Andrew's house and got out of the car. Ara came out last. She watched through the glass how Lara moved close to him, whispering into his ear. She hugged him and strolled into the house slowly so Ara could overhear what they said.

'Ara, please come out of the car,' Andrew begged, leaning into the car through the window.

She stormed out angrily and slammed the door.

Before she began to shout, he blurted out, 'I'm sorry.'

'You're sorry you told her, or you're sorry she told me?' she shouted.

He paused for a bit. 'Both?'

She was furious. 'How could you do something so stupid? She's a stranger. You literally met her a few days ago, and you're already telling her things about me.'

'No, Ara, that's not it. We were talking about me, and it just came up.'

'My father murdered my brother. I have no way to prove it. You wouldn't even believe me when I told you, but you would make small talk with Little Miss Pouty Face over there?'

'You don't need to do that. She hasn't done anything wrong.'

'You're defending her? Why in the hell are you defending her? Are you seeing her?'

'What do you mean? No, I'm not seeing her. What has that got to do with anything? I told you I loved you, and you literally ran away from me.'

That stopped her cold. 'I was ... I was going to tell you. I was going to tell you that I loved you.' She fuelled up again. 'But I'm happy I didn't because my brother is dead because of you.'

'Ara, don't say that. I wasn't even there.'

'Exactly, you weren't there. If you had come to get me instead of making me go with that man, maybe, just maybe my brother would be alive.' Tears filled her eyes.

He was crying as well; his voice was shaky. 'You cannot blame me for this, Ara.'

She knew she had crossed the line. She was just so angry. 'If you loved me ...' she said, sobbing.

'I do love you, Ara. I love you!' he said, shaking her.

She peeled her arm from his hand and stepped back. She didn't say anything else, just turned and left him standing in the middle of the street. She felt her heart break, and she knew she had hurt him. She was so hurt and confused by everything that had happened she broke down crying and ran to her house, as fast as her legs could go.

CHAPTER

22

M ote left the hospital and went straight to her gallery. It had been closed since the night Tale was killed. She hadn't come by since, but she couldn't think of a better place to be alone with her thoughts.

She cried the whole drive there. She cursed and shouted to herself in her car, honking loudly at anyone who crossed her path. When she finally got there, she stayed in the car for a while, staring at the entrance to the gallery. Her thoughts took her back to the day she had had her first exhibition in there. How happy she'd been to have accomplished so much by doing exactly what she loved: painting. She remembered thinking how lucky she was to have married this man who was with her every step of the way, encouraging, guiding her, pushing her until that moment they put up the sign 'The AM Gallery'. She scoffed at the thought of the man he had now become: the father of her best friend's dead child.

She got out of the car and slammed the door loudly. She walked inside the gallery with the bottle of whisky she had bought on the way over. The smell of paint and canvas hung in the air; she opened up the windows to air out the room and turned on the lights and air conditioners. She brought out every piece she had in storage, arranging them in order as though she was expecting a crowd.

She always had spare clothes in her wardrobe at the gallery, suitable for a show at any time, so she wasn't ever caught unprepared looking any less classy than her high-end clients expected. She pulled off her blue jeans and her loose T-shirt in full view of the entire gallery. Should anyone have been there, they would have witnessed more than their money's worth. Without a care, she pulled on a backless royal-blue dress, carefully easing it over her knees, slipping both arms through, and zipping it up. The gown fell all the way to the floor. It had a deep-cut neckline, almost as low as the back, and showed off the curves of her slender figure.

She took off her shoes and walked around barefoot. She picked up the awards that sat on a shelf one by one and tossed them to the ground. As she walked the halls of her sanctuary, she closed her eyes and took one slow step at a time. She could remember that night so clearly, the night she first welcomed the world into her space. She could almost see everything in front of her as it was then. Most of the paintings were different—but not this one. This one had been here since the very first day.

She stood before it, barefoot and half drunk, loosely holding the bottle in her hand. It was her favourite piece; she had painted it the morning she married Jack, and although she never did finish it, she loved it so much that it had hung in this very spot for many years.

As she stared at it, she felt a rush of emotions. Her love for him was overwhelming, her hate for his betrayal fuelled her anger, and she felt weak struggling with both sides. Did she hate him or did she love him? Overwhelmed and confused, she rushed towards the painting with the bottle in her hand and smashed it into the canvas, carving it open with sharp edge of the broken glass.

She stared at it for a while. It looked much better this way, she thought to herself. It was always supposed to be a representation of their love, and this was exactly what that love felt like: broken and torn.

Ara arrived at home when the sun was beginning to set. She ran in and found nobody home. The quiet walls echoed with Tale's voice, his laugh, and his joyful squeals. She'd always loved being alone in the house with him; he was the most precious child in the world. He knew how to make her laugh, how to make her scream and chase him down the flight of stairs. He had brought life into her life and into their home.

She decided to get an early night. She wanted to switch off her phone, but she couldn't. Some part of her hoped Andrew would call to talk to her, but he hadn't yet and she feared that he wouldn't. She was about to go into her room, when she realised ... her father wasn't here. This was her chance.

She hurried towards her parents' bedroom, hoping it was unlocked, and it was. She crept in, scanning the room and searching the drawers for the test results he had spoken about. Some part of her hoped she wouldn't find them, but she did. They were hidden under a pile of papers in one of her mum's old shoeboxes.

As soon as she put down the box and started to open the letter, she heard someone walking up the stairs. A few seconds later, the person stumbled into the door, making a loud thud, and struggled with the handle. She quickly returned the envelope into the box and ran towards the door. She opened it and found her mum sitting on the floor in front of the door. Her eyes were red and her breath was filled with the smell of whisky. Ara struggled to lift her and dragged her on to her bed. She noticed her hands were slightly bruised.

'Mum, are you OK?' she asked worriedly.

Mote nodded, slowly smiling. Ara wasn't convinced but she knew she couldn't hold a conversation with her in this state. She got off the bed and walked towards the door.

'Ara,' Mote called out to her. 'Stay with me,' she whispered and smiled.

Ara smiled and returned to the bed. She knew that once upon a time, her mum had struggled with alcohol, but she had never seen her this way before, and it broke her heart. She lay next to her, hugging her and trying her best to hold back her tears until they both fell asleep.

Maureen had just got to Ethan's office and was about to get out of the car when she saw him leave the building in a hurry. She hoped to follow him in the car and catch up with him before he got home. She had a lot of questions for him, everything she would have asked Jack but couldn't at the moment. For Ara's sake, some part of her hoped he had nothing to do with the boy's death. She didn't know exactly how much Ethan knew, but she was ready to find out.

She followed him closely but still far enough back to not be noticed. He seemed to be going in a completely different direction from his home. She continued to follow him until he stopped at a motel just outside of town. She wondered what he was doing there and why, but most importantly, who he was meeting with.

She kept her distance and watched him walk into room 1511. She waited patiently, hoping that he would come out with whoever he was meeting. After about half an hour, he hadn't left the room, so she decided to go in for herself. She was grateful that she hadn't left her badge and gun at home—she might need to make arrests tonight.

Her head still hurt and she felt sick, but she knew this was something she had to do. She considered calling in for backup, but she realised she didn't have a solid case against either of them: a well-respected defence attorney and a record-free family man.

She got out of the car and walked towards the room. She stood outside for about a minute, trying to eavesdrop, but she couldn't get any clear words, only the vague sound of voices.

She knocked on the door, and the voices on the other side went quiet. She waited for a few seconds and knocked again.

Someone on the other side asked, 'Who's that?'

It was a woman's voice she didn't recognise.

'I'm looking for Mr Johnson,' she called out.

She wasn't sure what the plan was, but she needed answers as soon as possible, so she was going to wing it until someone told her something she could use to put that man away.

She almost turned back when no one answered. She still heard whispering—maybe he was having an affair, and that wasn't what she was here for. However, she stayed and knocked again.

'My name is Maureen Lewis, I'm from the police department,' she said.

She heard someone walk slowly to the door and unlock it. Ethan tried to look calm but was clearly agitated.

'May I come in, sir? I have a few questions for you,' she asked politely.

'Uh ... Now isn't a good time,' he said, shaking his head.

She flashed him her badge. 'I'll have to insist, sir. A young girl's life may be in danger.'

He continued giving excuses and asked her to meet with him at his office at another time. She grew tired of his charade.

'Do you know a young girl—Ara?' she asked plainly. She continued without waiting for a response, 'She has reason to believe that her life and that of her mother are in danger, given her brother's murder. She seems to believe that her father was responsible and now threatens to hurt her.'

His eyes widened with surprise. At what, she wasn't sure, whether it was the fact that Ara had accused her father of murder or that she knew about it. He hung on to the door tightly.

'Is anyone in there with you?' she asked curiously.

'Let her in, Ethan,' she heard a man say from inside the room.

239

'No!' shouted the woman she heard earlier.

'She said he threatened my daughter, Victoria. Ethan, let her in!' the man shouted.

Ethan sighed. He pulled the door open slowly, allowing her into the room. She stepped in, and as soon as she saw Jack, she drew her gun and pointed it at him.

'Put your hands up,' she shouted. 'All of you!'

She waved the gun across the room from Ethan to Jack to the woman—Victoria?—and back again.

'You need to come with me,' she said to Jack.

She had hoped she wouldn't have to meet him until she had proof against him, but this was where she found herself and she had to handle it the best she could. She figured if she could get him to the station, she could have him in holding for at least twenty-four hours, which would give her time to run this investigation properly.

'What are you arresting me for?' he asked rather confidently.

'We'll start with threatening a police officer,' she snapped.

'I haven't threatened you,' he replied.

'I believe that was your intention when you called me this morning, talking about my partner, Daniel?'

'Maureen,' Ethan said. 'I remember you. I was at his memorial last year. I knew you looked familiar.'

'You knew Daniel?'

'Yes, we went to high school together. I'm sorry for your loss.'

She looked at him curiously; she wasn't sure if he was telling the truth or just trying to distract her. However, she knew she could not keep them standing here forever. She pulled out her phone and began to dial the station's number, when Jack quickly moved closer to her, interrupting her.

'Stay back!' she shouted, dropping the phone and holding the gun with both hands.

'You cannot arrest me—that's what he wants. Please, just let me explain,' he begged.

'You can say all you need to say down at the station.' She reached for her phone on the ground.

'I'm not him!' he shouted. 'I'm not the man you are looking for.'

'I think you are exactly who I'm looking for. Your daughter is terrified of you. How can you threaten and hurt your own family?'

She turned to Ethan. 'Ara was so sure you had nothing to do with this, but here you are,' she scoffed, and turned to Victoria. 'Who are you?'

Victoria looked away without saying anything.

'Please put the gun down and let me explain,' Jack begged again. She didn't respond to his plea. 'If you don't believe, call Ara and ask where I am.'

'Don't play games with me,' she said, agitated.

'No, no, no, he's not lying,' Ethan said. 'Call her, ask where her father is. You'll understand that he's not who you think he is. It's his brother.'

She looked at them, trying to understand what they were talking about. There was no record of Jack ever having a brother, and neither Mote nor Ara had mentioned anything like that.

'You don't have a brother. This is ridiculous. Do you think I would fall for this?' She picked up the phone again and began to dial.

'Wait.' Victoria finally spoke. 'He's telling the truth; they both are. Just make the call. If you still don't believe us, then we'll go with you.'

She hesitated. 'How do you know I won't just call for backup?'

'I'm trusting you,' Jack said softly. 'Make the call.'

She dialled Ara's number and held the phone to her ear. She could feel the tension in all of them. She wasn't sure what they hoped to accomplish, but she was willing to indulge them.

'Hi.' Ara's voice was soft and calm, like she had just woken up.

'Hi, Ara. I'm with your dad right now.'

'Please hold on. I can't hear you properly,' Ara said, still whispering.

Maureen heard a door close, and Ara continued. 'What did you say?'

'I said I'm with your dad. I want to—'

'Maureen, my dad just walked into the house. What are you talking about?'

'Are you sure? You're looking at your father right now?'

'Yes, he just walked in. Maureen, what's going on?'

Maureen froze; she stared at Jack. 'Nothing, Ara. I must have been mistaken.'

She was about to hang up when she heard Jack's voice on Ara's end, shouting, 'Who are you talking to?'

She heard Ara deny talking to her. She heard a scream, and the phone went dead.

'Ara, Ara! Are you OK? Ara?' she called out to her, but there was no response.

Jack was agitated. 'Is she OK? Did he hurt my daughter?'

Maureen was still trying to understand how this man could be in two places at the same time. 'I don't know,' she said under her breath.

'You need to get her out of that house. You need to go now!' Jack said.

Maureen tucked her gun into her belt. 'I can't just pull her out of the house. It may put her in more danger.'

'Yes, you can!'

'No, she can't,' Victoria said. 'She isn't in any danger. He won't hurt her.'

'What? How do you know that? I will not gamble with my daughter's life.'

Victoria paused, then said, 'Jack, he won't hurt her. He won't hurt her because he believes that she is his daughter.'

'What?' he asked, confused.

'He believes that Ara is his daughter,' she repeated.

'I heard you the first time! How is that possible? Why would he think that?' he asked, even more furious.

'That doesn't matter right now,' Maureen interrupted.

'What do you mean it doesn't matter?' Jack shouted at her.

'What's important is that he continues to believe that, so she's safe. Isn't that what's important, your family's safety?'

Jack went quiet.

She turned to Victoria. 'Are you sure about this? He truly believes this?'

Victoria nodded.

'Does he have reason to believe this?' Maureen asked.

Victoria nodded slowly. Maureen noticed how the woman's eyes avoided Jack's. And when she looked at him, his trembling lips told her why Victoria could not look at him as she confirmed the truth.

'How are you sure of this?' Maureen asked.

'I'm his wife. I am sure he believes this,' Victoria replied, still avoiding Jack's gaze. Maureen could see tears in his eyes.

'You are his brother's wife? The brother that killed his son?' she asked in disbelief. She let out a deep breath.

'Well, everybody, sit down,' Maureen demanded. She turned to Jack. 'Tell me everything. From the first moment you met your brother.'

CHAPTER

23

J ack sat on the edge of the bed in the drab motel room, looking at the only people in the world that could help him get his life back. His hands grazed the itchy sheets he sat on, and he looked at the yellowing curtains by the window where Victoria was leaning her head, gazing into the distance. He noticed the chipped bathroom door that Ethan was standing next to, and of course, the police officer seated opposite him—detective Maureen with her notepad in her hand, waiting patiently for what he had to say. He took a moment to organise his thoughts, because this was it. He was on the verge of destruction, and these people before him here were his lifeline.

He began with the day he had first met Jay, through to the night he believed Jay had broken into his house, which was when he'd had his family start taking self-defence classes, and all that had led up to this moment here in the motel room on the outside of town, hiding from his brother yet trying desperately to save his family.

He could see from the way the detective looked at him that she did not believe everything he said, or at least she struggled to. He couldn't blame her. His narrative of the events that had occurred the night his seven-year-old son was murdered was probably one she hadn't heard before. If he hadn't been there, he too might not have believed his own words.

Jack told her how he'd been separated from his family. He described the man with the scar who'd stopped them, the smell of the van they put him in and the cries of his children, which were the last thing he heard before someone struck him on the head and he passed out.

Jack paused, the words too heavy for him to say. He looked at Ethan's glassy eyes, and his mind instantly took him back to the night of his wedding, when Ethan had begged him to tell Mote all that was happening. Damn it, he should have. He would live the rest of his life regretting keeping that secret to himself.

Ethan's voice cut through his thoughts. 'Why are you still with her?' he asked, pointing to Victoria. 'What exactly do you need her for?'

Jack looked at her, then and turned back to Ethan and Maureen. 'Nothing,' he said calmly. 'I don't need her anymore. She has done nothing but lie to me.'

'Why did you save him? Why are you here right now?' Maureen asked Victoria. 'If your husband found you with him, I doubt he'll be so forgiving.'

'I don't have to answer any of your questions,' she said angrily.

'Yes, you do,' Maureen insisted, 'if you're a suspect in this investigation. Your name sure does seem to come up a few times in this story.'

'Is that right, Jack?' Victoria asked. 'Am I a suspect?'

'I don't know,' he said under his breath without raising his head to look at her. He knew she would have been shocked to hear that. It hurt him to feel like he couldn't trust her again and they were back to being strangers. He might have been furious with her.

He knew it only hurt him this much because of how much he cared for her.

She stormed out of the room and slammed the door shut.

Maureen tried to run after her, but Jack stopped her and went after her himself. He found her in the car park near the street, sat on the floor beside the car they were currently using. They had got through a few since they began this journey together.

He sat beside her, and for a while, neither of them said anything.

'I didn't lie to you,' she said in a low voice.

'You didn't tell me the truth either.'

'Honestly, I don't want to be the one to tell you anything about Jay or what he has done.'

'That's why you're here, Victoria. That's why I stayed: you promised to tell me all that I had to know, all that I needed to know to help me get my family back.'

'I tell you the truth, and every time you get so mad. You want to know the truth, the whole truth, but you can't handle it. I risk everything telling you what I know, and what do you do? You lash out and scream and shout and go on about how you can't trust me. I know I may have played some part in making all of this happen, but I never meant for things to be this way. Killing your son—that wasn't part of the plan. I don't know what changed, and I am trying to make up for it.'

'I am trying to trust you, I really am.'

'Then trust me,' she said, now facing him and holding his face. 'I would never do anything to hurt you,' she whispered.

He turned away, but she turned his face back to her and kissed him. 'I don't want to lose you,' she said, letting the tears that had filled her eyes roll down her face.

'I'm not yours to keep,' he said calmly, peeling her hands off his face and getting off the floor.

He could hear her quiet sobbing as he walked away, and as much as he wanted so desperately to run back to her and hold her in his arms and wipe her tears away and kiss her again, he was so close to getting his family back. He couldn't risk anything for that, not even for her.

He walked back into the room without saying anything.

After a long silence, Ethan's phone rang. He brought it out of his pocket and checked the caller ID. 'It's Anna,' he said before answering.

The call didn't last very long. He told her he would be home soon and they would talk more then. After he hung up, he turned to Jack. 'Mote is having a dinner of some sort in honour of Tale tomorrow. She just called Anna and asked her to come over in the morning to help her prepare for it.'

'What? Why does she want that? Did you know about this?' Jack asked.

'No, I didn't,' Ethan replied. 'Anna said she called her about half an hour ago. She's not been doing very well. I think she just needs the company.'

The words fell heavily on Jack. He felt responsible for all that had happened, and his guilt roiled in him.

'This might be a good thing,' Maureen said. 'If you wear a wire tomorrow and get Jay talking privately, he might slip up and say something that might help us.'

Victoria walked in while she was talking. 'He can't do that,' she interjected.

'She's right,' Ethan said, frightened. 'I can't wear a wire. I haven't seen the man since the day Jack came to my office. I don't even know how to be around him. He'll figure it out—he could kill me.'

Victoria scoffed. 'He definitely will.'

'Do you have a better idea?' Maureen challenged.

Victoria remained quiet.

Maureen turned back to Ethan. 'You don't have to do anything risky, just wear the wire. If you can get him talking about anything, really, it would go a long way. You don't have to pry, but anything you can get us would be helpful.'

'The entire plan sounds risky,' Ethan said, not convinced.

'Please, Ethan,' Jack begged. 'He's already done enough damage, and I need to get back to my family.'

Ethan let out a deep breath. 'OK, I'll do it. What do I have to do?'

'I'll meet up with you tomorrow and I'll walk you through everything,' Maureen replied.

He nodded slowly, looking like a heavy burden had just been put on him. He got up to leave and Jack followed him out.

'I'm sorry to put you in a difficult spot,' Jack said to him.

'It's all right, Jack. I'll do whatever I can to help you get your family back.' He smiled faintly.

Jack hugged him, and for a moment, they remained in each other's embrace.

Jack walked him to his car and returned to the room. Maureen got up to leave.

'One last thing before I go,' she asked. 'Your wife's friend Komi—when last did you see her?'

'Why? Is she OK?' He figured he shouldn't disclose yet that he had seen her earlier that morning.

'She was rushed to the ER this morning. She had a stab wound to her stomach. She appears to have been pregnant.'

His eyes opened wide. His mouth felt dry; he could not speak or move. He closed his eyes and shook his head. 'I don't know anything about that. Is she OK?'

'Yes, she's fine, but she lost the child,' she replied. 'I'll see you both tomorrow. Get some rest. If this goes well, you'll be with your family soon.'

She walked out and closed the door.

Jack walked slowly towards the door and turned the key.

'Did you do it?' he asked quietly.

'What?' Victoria asked.

'Don't play dumb, Victoria! Did you hurt Komi?' He walked towards her, eyes red with anger. He pushed her and pinned her to the wall. 'Did you hurt her?' he whispered.

Her eyes shone with panic, but she kept her mouth set in a

hard line. She tried to fight him off but failed. She continued to struggle until he finally let her go.

'I didn't mean to hurt her,' she said. 'It just happened. I was just so angry.'

'What do you mean, it just happened?'

'She was pregnant with his child, Jack. She was having his baby. He's my husband.'

'I thought he meant nothing to you anymore.'

'He doesn't,' she whimpered.

'You killed a child! Clearly he still does.'

'I gave that man everything. I stayed with him through every high and every low. He killed my father and I stayed with him, and he just had a child with another woman?'

'That's not her fault and you know it. She was a victim in all this.'

'No—no, she wasn't. One way or the other, she brought this upon herself. She was sleeping with either you or Jay, and that baby could just as well have been yours. Tell me, what would Mote have done if she thought Komi was having your child?'

He paused and looked at her. She was wrong—Mote was not a murderer. She would never kill a child out of spite or vengeance.

'My wife is nothing like you,' he said coldly. 'Unlike you, she has a heart.'

He knew his words hurt her, and he watched her try desperately to not crumble before him. She always wanted to be strong, and show no weakness. That's what had turned her into this person, someone capable of murder.

He hated his brother because he killed his son, but though Victoria had just killed someone's child, he couldn't bring himself to hate her as he did him.

He ignored her completely the rest of the night. It was as

though she wasn't even there. He did not look at her once, although he felt her presence and her occasional glances at him.

He spread a blanket on the floor beside the foot of the bed.

'What can I do?' she asked quietly.

'Make me hate you again,' he said before he closed his eyes and allowed himself to drift off.

CHAPTER
24

M ote woke up very early that morning. The day before remained a haze she tried to piece together; she could barely remember most of it. She had slept through nearly half the previous day. She turned and tossed on the bed and finally lay still on her side, staring at her husband as he slept peacefully beside her.

She watched his face for a very long time. All kinds of thoughts raced through her mind. For a brief moment, she felt as though this face wasn't the one she had woken up to the past sixteen years.

She closed her eyes and rubbed them. She staggered out of the bed, still feeling woozy.

She remembered going to the hospital; she remembered every word that Komi had said to her. She doubted she would ever forget hearing her best friend say that she was pregnant with her husband's child.

Why did all of this have to happen? She was barely getting through living with the fact that her little boy was gone, and now she had lost her husband and her best friend. She wouldn't forgive them, either of them. If that meant they were lost to her, she didn't care.

Even in her rage, she could not stop the tears from flowing down her face.

She put on her robe and tiptoed out of the room. She opened Ara's door quietly and saw her sleeping in her bed. She shut the door and went down the stairs.

She walked around aimlessly, looking at the photos on the wall, the paintings. She stopped at the couch in the living room and lay down on it. She remembered calling Anna last night and asking for help with the dinner she planned to have. She couldn't remember why she'd made the call then—she had planned to do the dinner a few weeks later.

She drifted off on the couch and woke up about an hour later. She felt his hand touch hers, and she opened her eyes. Jack smiled at her and lifted her up, resting her back against the couch.

'Did you sleep well?' he asked, handing her a cup of coffee.

She nodded and put the cup to her mouth so she didn't have to speak to him.

He placed an empty bottle of whisky on the centre table with a loud bang that made her head hurt. She groaned in discomfort.

'Did you drink all that?' he asked calmly.

She continued to sip the coffee without answering him.

He sighed. 'You can't do this again, Mote. You can't fall back into old habits.'

'I'm an alcoholic, remember?' she said spitefully.

'I shouldn't have said that. I shouldn't have brought that bottle home. I'm sorry, I had a really bad day.'

'We all have really bad days, Jack.'

'I know, I know, and I am sorry,' he said. 'You need to stop this. Ara needs you, and you can't be the mother you ought to be if you're drunk half the time.'

She heard the words he said, but they were like thorns in her side. He sat here pretending to care about her and her daughter when he had been sleeping with her best friend. She rolled her eyes and ignored him.

'Tell me what to do, Mote, and I will do it,' he continued. 'I will make it up to you. I'll do whatever you ask of me, please. We need to be stronger together, now more than ever,' he pleaded.

She could feel herself begin to give in. He always knew what to say, what comforted her, and what brought her back from the deep end if she ever wandered off. She hated that he knew her so well; she wanted to throw her coffee in his face. That was what she wanted, not these meaningless words.

'I think we should go away for a while, take a vacation maybe,' he said. 'Just me and you.'

She could not believe her ears. She wanted to reach out and slap him across his face.

'What good is that going to be? What about Ara?' she asked, irritated.

'She can stay at Ethan's. We need some time alone, Mote. You've been distant. I feel you withdrawing further and further away from me.' He held her hand in his palm. 'Please think about it.'

She removed her hand from his and got off the sofa. 'I have invited Anna and her family over this evening. I want us to have a memorial dinner, for Tale.'

'Tonight?' he asked.

'Yes, tonight. Anna should be here anytime now to help me prepare.'

'Why didn't you tell me? Tonight isn't good.'

'I'm telling you now. What do you mean, tonight isn't good? It's for your son. Or would you rather be somewhere else than be with your family?'

He sighed. 'Why are you being so difficult?'

'I'm being difficult? How dare you say that!'

'I can't make it tonight,' he said, putting on his jacket and walking towards the door.

'Where are you going?' she yelled at him. He didn't answer her. 'If you're not here tonight, Jack, don't bother coming back at all.'

She heard the door close with a loud bang. She stood up and threw her cup at it. The cup broke on impact, spilling its contents. Hot tears filled her eyes, and she crumbled to the floor.

An hour passed, and still she lay on the floor, staring at the ceiling, consumed by grief and self-pity. Finally, the smell of spilled coffee pulled her from limbo, and she decided to distract herself with sorting and cleaning the house. That always helped her on bad days, and this was a very bad day.

She began to arrange and dust obsessively, still speaking to herself and hating her husband. As she worked her way through the living room to the dining room, she continued to wonder how she hadn't seen the signs earlier, how he could do this to her. She was infuriated at the thought that he was going to see Komi.

She was rearranging the space under the stairs when she stumbled upon it. A gun. She picked it up and looked around to see if Ara had woken up. She called out to her, and when there was no response, she rushed back underneath the stairs.

She had never held a gun before—not a real one, anyway. What would it be like to pull the trigger? To shoot, to hurt, to kill? She let herself picture it, Jack's horror as she took aim. She was so consumed by her thoughts that she didn't think to wonder why he had the gun in the first place.

She heard the doorbell ring and tucked the gun underneath her robe.

Taking short, deep breaths, she wiped her tears. She didn't want anyone to see her like this. She walked to the door and let Anna in.

Anna had come with bags of groceries, ready to help with the preparations. Mote smiled faintly. She admired Anna; she knew that this was difficult for her as well, but she had been with her all through these difficult times. They went into the kitchen and dropped everything on the counter.

'I saw Jack leaving. Will he be back in time?' Anna asked.

Mote tried to speak, but the words would not come. She began to cry loudly, and Anna ran towards her, hugging her and patting her back.

'It's OK, Mote,' she whispered.

She held her until she stopped crying.

———

Ara woke up later and went down to the kitchen to help with the preparations, but as she got there, Andrew, April and Lara arrived.

April rushed towards Mote and hugged her and then Ara. Andrew hugged Mote as well but withdrew from Ara. He completely avoided her gaze as he introduced Lara.

'This is Lara, she's April's friend,' he said warmly as Lara stretched out her hand to shake Mote's.

'And your friend too, I hope.' Lara smiled at Andrew and he smiled back.

'Her father is out of town, so she's staying with us for a few days,' Anna jumped in.

'It's nice to have you here,' Mote said. 'Well, you guys get settled. I should go change out of this robe.'

Anna followed her, and they both went upstairs to her room.

'Andrew, can I talk with you alone for a minute?' Ara asked, pointing towards the garden at the back of the house.

He looked at Lara. 'I'll just be a minute.'

He walked in front of Ara and into the garden behind the kitchen. She followed, closing the door behind them.

'I'm sorry,' she blurted out. 'I am so sorry. I shouldn't have said any of those things. I was sad and angry and a bit jealous, and I am sorry I hurt you.' She let out a deep breath and waited for his response.

He looked at her. 'Ara, I was trying to be your friend and you blamed me for your brother's death. You know I blamed myself for not picking you up that night, and you still blamed me for it.'

'I was angry, I wasn't thinking.'

'No, you weren't,' he said plainly.

261

She looked at him. She tried not to cry, but she couldn't help herself.

'You had nothing to be jealous about, and you made it clear how you felt about me, so I don't know why it bothered you so much.'

'Andrew, I shouldn't have left when you told me that you loved me. I panicked and I'm sorry and I was going to tell you that night ...' She paused and wiped away her tears.

'Ara,' he said, looking into her eyes. 'I love you,' he said with a pained smile.

'I love you too,' she whispered beneath her soft sobs.

'The only thing is, I think you're only saying this because you're jealous, or you feel threatened by Lara.'

'No,' she said. 'This has nothing to do with her.' She leaned in to kiss him.

He pulled back from her. 'I want you to love me because you do, not because you're scared of losing me,' he said and walked towards the house.

It hurt him to leave her there, to walk away from the girl he loved. He had dreamed of this moment many times, the moment when she would reach out to him and kiss him, and although he loved her, it hurt him terribly to think that she might not care for him as much as he did her.

He walked back into the kitchen, where April and Lara were cutting up some vegetables for the salad. He smiled weakly and sat on one of the empty stools near the centre counter. He noticed Lara's gaze when he sat down. He kept his eyes down. He could feel her coming closer to him; her scent was strong and arousing. He couldn't deny that she was a distraction from how he felt about Ara, and he knew that she might be one of the reasons he'd left his best friend crying outside in the garden. He wanted to be sure that he loved Ara not just because he had known her his whole life but because he chose her.

He was drawn to Lara and he knew it. It was strange for him; he had met many other girls since he started college, but he knew his heart belonged to a young suburban black girl with beautiful eyes and the most enchanting smile. Yet, for the very first time, he found himself confused about his feelings. It was almost as though he could see bits of Ara in Lara; he couldn't quite put his finger on it. She was easy to talk to, she was free as a bird, and she was beautiful. He wanted to stare at her every time she looked at him.

He sighed and hung his head.

She finally stopped behind him. 'Are you OK?' she whispered, rubbing his shoulders.

He flinched when she touched him. She giggled and so did April.

'He's all so sensitive,' April mocked, before picking up her phone.

Ara walked in while they were laughing. She saw Lara leaning over Andrew's back and rubbing his shoulders. She took a deep breath and walked past them out of the kitchen. She walked out the front door and shut it with a loud bang.

Upstairs, Mote showered and put on a pair of blue jeans and a white loose tank top. She packed her hair up in a ponytail and fell back into the bed.

'Get up, Mote, we have a lot of work to do,' Anna said while going through her closet. 'Have you picked out what to wear tonight?'

'Yup, the black one in the corner, hanging above the red shoes,' Mote replied.

263

She knew Anna wouldn't talk about her breakdown earlier in the kitchen if she didn't bring it up herself. Anna didn't like to pry, but she was a great listener.

'This? Are you sure?' Anna asked. 'It's so ... umm .... open.'

'Yup. Maybe it'll bring my husband back to me.'

Anna sighed. She dropped the dress and went to sit beside Mote. 'Do you want to talk about it?' she asked.

Mote nodded. 'He's been sleeping with Komi, and until yesterday, she was having his baby.'

'What? Jack?' Anna asked, her eyes open.

'Yes, Jack.' Mote nodded. 'Jack, my husband, having an affair with Komi, my best friend.' She laughed. 'That's my life now.'

'Oh God, Mote, how do you know this? I mean, you have to be sure.'

'I'm sure. Komi told me herself. I saw her at the hospital yesterday. Someone attacked her in her house, we don't know who yet, but she lost the child.'

Anna placed her hand over her mouth and gasped. 'I'm so sorry,' she said in a whisper.

'Don't be. That child should never have existed.'

Her words clearly shocked Anna, perhaps even more than the truth she had just revealed.

'Don't say that, Mote. I know you're hurt and angry with Jack and Komi, but that child was innocent and didn't deserve to die. I can't imagine what Komi is going through.'

'What I can't imagine is how she could do this to me,' Mote said angrily. She got off the bed and stood in front of Anna. 'She deserves this; they both do.'

'Mote!' Anna scolded her. 'Please don't say things like that.' She paused. 'Have you asked Jack about any of this?'

Mote walked to her side of the bed and brought out the gun she found.

'My goodness! Mote! What are you doing?' Anna screamed.

'Calm down, I'm not going to use it.'

'Is it yours?' Anna asked, still in a panic.

'No.' Mote shook her head. 'It's his. I can't believe he brought a gun into our home. I knew he was paranoid after the break-in, but I can't believe he would keep it here. Anyone could have found it.'

'Where did you find it?' Anna asked.

'Beneath the stairs.'

'Are you going to use it?'

'I don't know. I really don't know,' Mote replied. 'I haven't figured that out yet.'

'Here.' Anna stretched out her shaking hands. 'Please give it to me.'

Mote shook her head. 'No, I will keep it safe. I won't use it— I'm not stupid.'

'Mote, our children are downstairs. Anything could happen, someone could get hurt. Please give it to me, Mote, just for tonight.'

Mote refused again. Anna got furious. 'Can you promise me that when you see him tonight, you won't want to use this? Are you really in the right frame of mind to hold a gun, Mote? Think about all the kids downstairs. My husband will be here soon. I cannot let you keep this. Not now.'

Mote knew Anna was right. She had thought of shooting Jack dead the minute he walked in the door, or hurting him if he lied about Komi when she finally confronted him. And though part of her wanted it, longed for it, she didn't want to lose any more parts of herself.

She dropped the gun into Anna's hands.

Ara went back into the house after a few minutes. She could hear the three of them still talking and laughing in the kitchen. She was about to go in, when she saw Lara's bag on the dining table. She couldn't resist opening it. She wanted to know more about this mystery girl that seemed to have them all swayed into her corner.

She went through the bag and brought out a white envelope. She was about to open it when she heard Andrew's voice behind her. She froze.

'What are you doing?' he asked her, then walked around her and took the envelope from her. 'That's Lara's bag. Did you take this from her bag?'

He didn't let her say a word. 'Damn it, Ara, you are impossible. You can't just go snooping in people's belongings. And I thought this wasn't about her.' He looked at the envelope. 'Clearly it is.'

He was about to return it to the bag when Lara walked out of the kitchen.

'Hey, Andrew,' she said then stopped when she saw Ara. 'Is everything OK?' she asked.

Andrew quickly tried to slide the envelope into his back pocket. It slipped to the floor. Ara dropped the bag and turned to face Lara. She stared her down and then walked past her, brushing her shoulder.

'Everything is fine, Lara,' Andrew said. 'She's just—'

'Jealous?'

'Upset,' Andrew corrected her.

'Well, she shouldn't be.' Lara smirked and walked back into the kitchen.

CHAPTER
25

Mote and Anna came down to continue prepping for the dinner.

Everyone got to work. Andrew helped retrieve the good china from the cabinets high on the walls. April prepared the chicken and baked a small batch of muffins. She loved to bake and used every opportunity in the kitchen to try out a new recipe, so no one bothered her when she brought out the flour and bowls. Lara prepared the fruit punch and salad. She'd confessed earlier that she wasn't very good at cooking, so Mote guided her through it.

'Andrew?' Mote called out, handing him a short piece of paper. 'Could you please run down to the store? I had this list out for Jack, but he left so early this morning I forgot to remind him,' she said, smiling.

'It's no problem, ma'am,' Andrew replied.

She smiled even wider; she always had liked him. Unlike some of Ara's other friends, he was always well behaved. He was Mote's favourite, not only because he was Anna's son, but also because she could tell from the way Ara's eyes sparkled and widened every time she heard his name that he might be her favourite too.

'Check on Ara, see if she'll go with you,' Mote said.

'I'll come with you,' Lara said from the other side of the kitchen as she washed her hands and dried them with the towel hanging from her apron. She removed the apron slowly and hung it on the door that led to the store.

'OK, that's fine. I doubt Ara is up for it anyway. We'll be right back,' Andrew said to Mote.

'I'm going to watch some TV, Mum, please call me when the oven bell rings,' April said, walking out of the kitchen.

'You had better listen for it,' Anna shouted after her, laughing.

They laughed and talked some more, never staying on one topic for too long. Mote had appreciated the company, but she was glad to be alone with Anna for a while. She could speak without censoring herself, mostly.

Anna asked if Mote was going to see Komi again, and if she could go and see her. She didn't talk much about Jack, instead steering the conversation into safer territory. They talked about Ara and Andrew, and Anna told her a little more about Lara. Soon the conversation drifted, and they somehow ended up talking about flowers.

It was an unusual conversation. It had short pauses and long ones; it had quiet laughs and giggles, sometimes a few tears that filled the eyes but refused to fall. Mote could admit that it was refreshing to get her mind off the terrible thoughts that clouded it anytime she had a moment alone to think, so she indulged Anna. In every topic that came up, meaningful or not, she laughed, and every time, she felt as though she had left her body and stood in the corner of the kitchen, watching herself laugh, trying and failing to forget her pain.

'I think we should get some flowers from the garden,' Anna said, delightfully looking out the window. 'It'd be good for the table tonight.'

Mote shrugged. 'All right. I haven't had flowers on the table in a while.'

Anna moved towards the pantry and put on the garden gloves that were in the basket that hung on the inner wall. She walked out of the kitchen, still smiling. Mote wondered how that came so easily to her, smiling. She did it as though she had no demons tugging at her heart and no sorrow that caused her great pain. Mote envied her, but only for a moment. This pain she felt had grown on her; she almost couldn't imagine herself without it.

She turned back to continue what she'd been doing before she got distracted talking with Anna, when she found a white envelope on the floor, near the spot where Andrew had got the plates out from. She bent over and picked it up. The envelope wasn't addressed to anyone and was already unsealed, so she opened it up. Inside were two papers and a small photograph of a little baby not more than a few days old.

She opened the papers and began to read, and then she froze. She felt her heart stutter. She frowned and squinted and rubbed her eyes and read over and over again, but the words did not change.

Baby Lara born this day, Sept. 18, to Motopeda Adewale.

She almost passed out. She held on to the counter and screamed, 'Anna!'

Anna rushed inside. 'What is it, Mote, what happened?' she asked in a panic.

Mote tried to speak but she began to tremble and cry.

April and Ara ran into the kitchen. Ara ran towards her mother, holding her.

'What's wrong, Mum?' she asked, frightened.

'Oh, I'm sorry, both of you. It's nothing,' Mote said, wiping her tears. 'I just ... I just hit my leg against the stool and it hurt badly. You can go now,' she said, hiding the envelope and the papers beneath the table.

Ara tried to stay and figure out what had really happened, but Mote insisted that they both leave and they did, although reluctantly.

When they had finally gone, Mote looked to Anna and handed her the papers.

'What are these?' Anna asked, still confused about everything.

'She's my daughter,' Mote said frantically. 'I remember signing this paper. I remember. Oh God, I remember giving my baby girl away.'

Anna dropped the papers and held on to Mote. 'I don't understand what you're saying. Please tell me what's going on.'

Mote didn't hesitate to tell her everything. Anna was her confidante now, since Komi had proven unworthy. She told her about the child that she'd been pregnant with when she first settled in the US all those years ago. Her father had wanted her to get an abortion. He would always remind her of the shame she'd brought to their family even till this day, although more subtly now. She told her about her aunt who'd lived here and taken care of her until she had her baby, and that she'd had to give the child up for adoption. It was the only way her father would not disown her, and she confessed to Anna that although she was strong-willed and had tried to not let her father know, she'd been terrified. She'd been terrified of being a mother—a single mother and a struggling artist. She told Anna that even if she hadn't been forced to give up the child, she still might have.

She spoke in hushed tones and sobbed. She couldn't let any of the girls know what she had just discovered, especially Ara. She knew she had no answers that could justify giving away her child, Ara's sister.

'Where did you find this?' Anna asked as she folded the envelope.

Anna stared at her as though she was seeing her for the first time. Mote couldn't hear her clearly, the ringing in her ears too loud to pick out Anna's words. Her heart ached with hope and fear at the same time. Could this be really be true?

'Does Jack know?' Anna asked quietly.

Mote nodded. 'I told him a few weeks after the wedding. I remember that night so clearly, it was the moment I was convinced that I could not and would not live without him. I told him everything,' she said, holding her stomach tightly. 'I couldn't bear to keep lying to him. I was so scared that he might leave me, but he didn't. He just said never to speak of it again, and we haven't since then.'

Anna just kept the questions coming; Mote's head began to spin. 'Do you think she knows? Is the envelope hers? Perhaps that's why she's here?'

Mote shrugged. 'I don't know. She could know. If she doesn't, should I tell her?' She sighed. 'What would I even say? Where do I start from?' She began to cry again.

'Mote, calm down, please,' Anna said, hugging her. 'Don't say anything yet. Not tonight, just get through today first.'

Mote could not take her eyes off the letter. How was this possible? Her daughter, her baby, had found her when she most needed something to pull her out of her despair. It was a miracle.

Ara had gone upstairs right after her mum sent her away from the kitchen. She knew her mum wasn't OK but also knew she would tell her the truth later.

She was about to go into her room when she discovered that there was no one else upstairs. She quietly entered her parents' room and went straight for the envelope in the shoebox. It hadn't been open last time she saw it, but now it was. Without waiting for a moment, she read through the results.

She fell to the floor, buried her head between her knees and cried. The results said there was no DNA match. Her father wasn't her father, and she couldn't bring herself to get off the floor.

She lay down and curled up in a ball. She cried until her eyes hurt, and then she suddenly remembered Andrew's words, saying that her father had told someone over the phone that he would not kill his child. And she was not his child. He could kill her; he could do whatever he wanted. She wiped her tears. If the envelope was open, then he had read it.

She returned the envelope in a panic and ran out the room.

Andrew and Lara had just got back, and she ran down the stairs to meet him. 'I need to talk to you,' she whispered in his ear.

He walked around her with the bag of groceries in his hand. 'I think you've said enough, Ara,' he said and followed Lara into the kitchen.

Ara followed behind them, not too close, so it didn't seem like she was intentionally stalking their every move. When she entered the kitchen, she saw them huddled together, and his eyes met hers. He was still angry, she could tell. She sighed and walked out of the kitchen. This girl was ruining everything.

Jay walked in just as Ara got to the bottom of the stairs. Her eyes were red, so he hugged her tightly and kissed her forehead as soon as he saw her.

'Are you OK?' he asked her, holding her close.

She held her breath until he let go. He was still trying to find out why she had been crying when El walked out of the kitchen.

He stood straight and froze.

He could not believe his eyes. If Ara had not been in his path, he might have launched at El and knocked her to the ground. However, he held his composure. He knew he wouldn't have to keep up this façade for much longer, so he cracked a smile.

'Oh hey,' he said, walking towards El. 'Who is this?' he turned to ask Ara.

Andrew stepped in. 'This is my friend Lara. She's staying with us for a few days. Her father is out of town.'

'Is that so?' he asked, smiling. He stretched out his hand. 'It's nice to have you here with us,' he said, shaking El's hand so firmly he could feel her bones rub against each other.

El smiled through the pain, just as she had been trained to do, and avoided eye contact with him.

'What are you doing here?' he said under his breath.

She ignored him and pulled her hand out of his grip. 'It's nice to meet you too, sir,' she said as she turned and walked away.

He tried to keep his calm as he followed her into the kitchen, hoping no one else was there so he could show her exactly how he felt about this little prank she'd decided to play.

Anna called out to him as soon as she saw him walk through the door. 'Oh, welcome back, Jack, just in time,' she said, smiling. 'Is Ethan with you?'

'Uh ... no,' he said, still trying to get El's attention, but she continued to ignore him. He decided to let her be for now.

He walked up to Mote and hugged her tightly. 'I'm sorry,' he whispered in her ear, kissing her cheeks.

She ignored him and continued to mix the sauce she was making.

'Everything looks really good, Mote,' he continued, but she still ignored him, just cracking a little smile, which he saw right through.

He fell to his knees dramatically. 'I'm sorry, please forgive me,' he declared.

They all stopped what they were doing and stared at him.

Mote stopped and smiled. He had her, he knew he did. She couldn't hate him; he would not allow her.

He noticed all the eyes on him, so he got off the floor and pulled her in for a kiss. He spun her around and she laughed, easing the tension that had built between them. Her brows furrowed when she finally bumped into his chest, but as he reached down to kiss her again, she let him and in that moment he knew: he had her.

'I love you, Mote,' he said, staring into her eyes. 'I'm in love with you.'

Jay felt his heart beat faster as the words came out of his mouth. This was his biggest and most unexpected surprise: he was in love with her, and in this moment, for the first time in a long time, he felt a glimpse of happiness.

He loved the way she smiled at him. When she looked at him, he felt like she could see who he truly was, which was in itself an irony.

'I think we should give these two lovebirds a moment,' Anna said and cleared the kitchen, closing the door behind her.

Mote smiled at her and looked back at Jay. 'I love you, Jack, and I'm sorry too.'

'What are you sorry for, my love?' he asked. Baiting her.

'For everything, for everything I've done.' Her voice sank lower. 'And for the things I might do.'

Jay smiled, and from her reaction, that was not what she'd expected, but to him, the only thing better than being in love with a perfect woman was knowing she had a little bit of darkness in her. Then they would truly be soulmates.

'You have nothing to apologize for. I'm lucky to have you in my life.' He could not stop grinning as he said the words.

She nodded, and he wiped the tears that had streamed down her face.

He'd moved to turn off the stove when he heard her question. 'Have you met Lara?'

He froze, unsure of how to answer what he knew was coming.

'Andrew's friend? Yes, she's a nice young girl,' he replied as he turned back to face her.

'Does she remind you of anyone?' She smiled.

'Uh ... no. I don't think so. Although I did just meet her.'

'She's my daughter,' Mote said with the widest smile on her face.

His eyes widened. He'd already known, of course. He'd hunted down the child she'd confessed to having years ago. It was all part of his plan. The real question really was: how did she find out? That was the real surprise.

'What do you mean, she's your daughter?'

She walked towards him. 'Did you know? Did you go looking for her, Jack?'

'I don't know what you're talking about! I've never seen that girl in my life.'

'Remember that night, weeks after the wedding?' she asked.

He nodded slowly. He almost smiled—he could never forget that night. It was the first time he had met her, the first time he made love to her, the first time he had hope of having the life he'd always wanted, with her as his anchor.

'I told you I gave up my daughter when I moved here,' she continued. 'That's her, Jack. That girl is my daughter.' She spoke with both guilt and excitement, her hands moving rapidly in the air as she explained how she'd found the envelope on the counter and read its contents.

He thought about a thousand ways to deal with this. He shook his head. Yet another unforeseen event—he could almost scream. He could have sworn that he had this plan all figured out, but somehow he seemed to be the one holding the short end of the stick. For a brief moment, he almost began to regret coming here, being in their lives. He wished he had killed his brother all those years ago and stayed with her, raised her children, and loved them all as he knew he could if he tried. That would have been much better, because right now, they were doing a fantastic job of ruining everything.

He hugged her tightly when she began to cry. Tears of joy, he presumed. He held her for as long as she would let him.

'After the dinner, maybe sometime during the week, we could have her over and talk to her. Find out where she's been, who adopted her, if anyone did at all.'

Mote nodded. 'She mentioned that her father was out of town. I don't know if she had a mother.' Her face fell. He could see that she was about to start crying again.

'Hey, hey, don't cry. She does have a mother—you are her mother. That cannot change,' he said, holding her hands and wiping her tears.

She cleaned her face. 'We're almost done here. You should go and get ready. I'm sure Ethan will be here soon and we can start.'

'All right,' he said, smiling at her.

Before he left, he asked if she knew why Ara was crying. She shook her head, but she guessed it might have something to do with Andrew. She said she thought they were having a fight, but it'd probably blow over.

He agreed with her and went out of the kitchen.

Anna and April went in to check on Mote, while he went through to the living room, where El was on the couch. He sat beside her.

'I spent the entire morning looking for you, El. What is this? What are you doing here?' he asked in a low, stern voice, turning up the volume of the TV.

She ignored him and turned her face away. He pulled her arm, held her face in his palm and squeezed it. She gasped and frowned.

'You need to leave, now,' he said.

'What were you two talking about?' she asked, pointing towards the kitchen.

'That's none of your business, El. You need to get out of here before—'

'She's my mother, isn't she?' El asked, furious.

He paused. He looked at her and wondered what he should do. He could lie and deny it, but he knew from the look on her face that she had read the contents of that envelope. Although she'd asked a question, she'd meant it as a statement to him.

'I will explain everything to you, El. I will, I promise I will, but not now. Not today.'

'You're in love with her, aren't you?' she asked, tears falling down her cheeks.

He paused again and sighed. She was the first person to ever ask him this question, and for some reason, he couldn't bring himself to deny it. He stared at her like a deer caught in the headlights.

'Is that why you came here? Not for revenge but for love?' she asked bitterly. 'Why didn't you just tell me about her? You've known all this time. Every time I asked, you just ignored me. You let me think I didn't have a mother.'

'You did have a mother. Victoria was there for you,' he said, holding her hand.

She pulled her hand out of his grip. 'She was your wife, and she was never my mother,' she said, and pointed in the direction of the kitchen. 'She doesn't love you, you know, right? She loves her husband, Jack, not you. When she finds out who you are, she will hate you.'

He slapped her across her face as soon as the words came out of her mouth. She gasped in shock and got up from the couch. He had never hit her before. He also had never been as scared in his life. The thought that she might, for any reason, be inclined to tell Mote the truth scared him so much that he'd reacted before he could think it through.

He got up and tried to hug her, apologising furiously, but she wouldn't listen to him. He tried to speak but he knew nothing he could say would make up for what he'd done or make her feel any better. He knew she felt betrayed and she had reason to, but he still needed her to just behave herself.

He wanted nothing more than for this dinner to pass quickly so he could go somewhere far away with Mote, and they could be alone, and maybe she would love him. Not Jack, not as Jack, but truly love him. James Mulder.

CHAPTER
26

A ra and Andrew had been outside the whole time. She tried to get him to listen to her, but he was so upset, he just ranted about how she had invaded Lara's privacy and she was being jealous and rude. He went on saying all kinds of things.

'He's not my father,' she blurted out. 'I saw the test results and he is not my father.'

Andrew went quiet.

'What?' he asked. 'When did you find out? Does he know that you know?' He kept the questions coming. 'Have you called Detective Lewis? I think we should—this is the kind of evidence that she could use to get him out of the house, at least for a while. It could be motive to harm you and your brother.' He paused. 'Do you think you can get the test results? Maybe we can get it to her before he finds out. You can go for it when everyone's downstairs during the dinner.'

He knew he didn't have the liberty of not believing her. He paused and waited for her to respond.

She nodded. 'I will try and get it during dinner. I'll text her to come over, and I'll give it to her before he knows it's gone.'

He sighed. 'Please be careful, Ara,' he said and tried to hug her.

She shoved him off. 'I don't need you to be nice to me because of this,' she said. 'You've made it clear that you no longer care about me, and that's fine. Just don't pretend to. I just needed to tell someone. I'm scared, and I don't know what to do,' she admitted. 'You said you heard him say he won't kill his child, but I'm not his child, so what's he going to do?'

'I won't let anything happen to you, Ara, I promise,' he said, holding her face, and he meant it. He knew he did; he knew he loved her. He hated that they were falling apart, he hated that he wasn't there for her when she needed him, and he didn't know how to fix it.

He knew she was scared, and although she might not have seen it, he was scared too. He knew he ought to apologise for the way he'd reacted when she took that envelope from Lara, and for the things he had said to her.

He knew his words might not mean much at this time, but he said them anyway. Not until this moment had he realised how hurt he would be if he ever lost her. He had pushed her away over the past couple of days, and he knew that if she did pull away from him, he would be lost without her.

She was his best friend, and more than that, he was in love with her. Somehow, he still found himself feeling unworthy of her. He had been distracted by Lara, and although he still couldn't tell exactly what it was he felt for her, it paled in comparison to what he felt for Ara.

He didn't know how best to say what he wanted to, but he figured it was better to try than not.

'I'm sorry. I don't want you to feel like you have to do any of this alone. When I say I'm here for you, I want you to trust me. And I know ...' His words trailed off as he tried to arrange his thoughts in the best possible way. 'I know I have been distracted lately, and I'm sorry.'

When he finally stopped to breathe, Ara had a blank stare on her face, and he worried he had said too much or not enough— definitely not enough, he concluded.

'You really hurt me,' was all she said.

He shut his eyes; the words stung. But he wasn't giving up. He opened his eyes, about to speak, but she was already gone.

Ethan parked outside the house and noticed his son standing near the doorway. His hands were shaking; this wasn't going to work.

He would slip up, he just knew he would. He was never good at pretending.

He took in deep breaths. 'It's going to be OK,' he said, repeating the words Jack had said to him earlier that day. He did not believe it, but he needed it to be true regardless.

As he got out of the car, Andrew rushed to hug him. 'Where have you been?' he asked.

It felt like it had been ages since he'd seen his son and he had missed him, but now was not the time.

'Dad, I need to talk to you about something. Ara—'

'Andrew, let's talk later,' Ethan said, interrupting him. 'I know you and Ara have had a rough time—your mum told me about that—but let's not keep everyone waiting.'

'It's not that, Dad. I think—'

'Andrew, please, not now,' Ethan said. 'Go inside—I'll be right after you.'

He saw the disappointment in his son's face, but he could not listen to what Andrew had to say. He could not focus on anything other than the wire he wore underneath his shirt. He hoped that it hadn't got disconnected when Andrew hugged him.

After he watched Andrew walk in, he turned away and unbuttoned his shirt to check the wire. Maureen was listening to him a few blocks down, and he was ready to shout for help the minute he felt that his cover was blown.

He took short breaths. He was nervous—surely Jay would see right through him. He wondered what he should say first. He hadn't seen Jay since he found out he was an impostor.

Jack and Victoria weren't too far away either. Jack insisted on using this opportunity to search their room in the house. He believed that Jay would keep any implicating evidence closest to him. Jack and Victoria weren't listening to Ethan's wire, and he just realised he didn't have Jack's burner number.

He sighed. He felt more uneasy with every passing moment. The plan felt hurried and unstable and, honestly, unreliable—and it was. Just yesterday, he was still trying to wrap his head around all that Jack had told him, and now Jack was breaking into his own home in an attempt to find any incriminating evidence that would get his murderous brother arrested.

Ethan walked towards the door slowly. Sweat was building on his arms, and his palms began to shake. He hid them in his trousers and opened the door.

The house looked different from the last time he'd been there, which was the day of the funeral. It looked brighter and happier. Everyone seemed to be smiling or laughing and talking about something.

April was the first to meet him. She hugged him and walked him over to the living room. He saw Anna and Mote in the corner, placing down some glasses and napkins, and he smiled and waved at them. April introduced him to Lara; he had heard about her but hadn't seen her yet.

Ara called a greeting as she came down the stairs, and he responded to her from the living room. April seemed keen on keeping him next to her.

Everyone looked beautiful and happy, and he felt more at ease. He wished Jack was here to see this, to see his family healing and trying to move past the difficult times, together.

He listened to April as she tugged at his hand for his attention. She told him more about her new friend Lara. He smiled at her and indulged her.

Shortly after, everyone gathered around the table and settled into their seats. Everyone but Jay.

Ethan sat at the end of the table. Beside him to his right was April, and beside her was Anna, and beside her was Mote. He knew that Mote probably wanted Anna by her side tonight, and he was sure that April wouldn't ever be too far from him. She was her daddy's girl, and he was happy to have her close, especially tonight.

Jack's seat on the other end of the table was empty. Next to the empty chair sat Ara, Andrew, and El, in that order. Ethan had noticed the tension between Andrew and Ara, and he wished he had been able to talk to Andrew earlier, but he was too tense.

'Where's Ja— hmm, Jack,' Ethan asked.

'He's on a call outside at the back,' Mote replied.

He hoped no one noticed the fact that he almost just said Jay. He knew he couldn't keep this up; he knew he wasn't the best person for this job.

He got up from the chair and walked through the kitchen to the back door. Jay was in the corner of the garden near the fence. This was it; this was Ethan's moment of truth. He could not mess up. If for any reason Jay suspected him, he could be putting the lives of everyone here at risk. The more he thought about it, the more it seemed like a risky plan, and he wanted to rip out the wire and toss it in the plants. And he almost did, when he heard Jay's voice call out to him.

'Ethan,' he said, smiling. 'You're late.' He walked over to him and hugged him. 'Where have you been?'

Ethan paused before he spoke. 'I was at the office,' he said slowly, almost picking at his words.

'Are you OK?' Jay said jokingly and tapped his shoulder.

Ethan nodded and smiled. He somehow couldn't get out as many words as he had hoped.

They were about to enter the house when he got a text from Maureen. It read, 'GET HIM TO TALK!' in capital letters.

'Uh ... hey,' he said nervously. 'Anna told me about Komi. Is she OK? She said she lost a baby. I didn't even know she was pregnant. Did you know?'

Jay froze. He turned and looked at him. 'Anna told you?' he said as he moved closer to him.

'Yes—I think she said the hospital called Mote, and she went to see her. I hope she gets better,' he said. 'Do you have any idea who attacked her?'

Jay stared through the kitchen door and back at Ethan. 'Why would I know who attacked her?'

'Uh ... I don't ... I just ... I hope they find them,' Ethan stuttered. He could feel his heart beating so fast he thought he might pass out.

Jay walked away without another word. Ethan ran after him. He was disappointed in himself; he had succeeded in pissing Jay off instead of getting any information from him.

He tried to calm Jay in the kitchen, even though he wasn't sure what had upset him; he couldn't risk him throwing any kind of tantrum. Jay was a murderer, and Ethan's wife and kids were in the other room.

Jay just kept walking until they reached the dining room. Ethan was startled by Ara's loud scream. It came from the bedroom upstairs. 'Dad!' she shouted.

Mote looked at Jay in shock, and he ran up the stairs.

Ara ran out of the room, bumping into Jay halfway down the stairs. He was leading her back down, when Jack ran out of the room after her and Victoria after him.

The room fell silent.

'What is this?' Mote asked, breaking the silence.

Ara ran towards Andrew and stood by him, holding his arm.

Ethan pulled Anna closer to his end of the table, where April was. Whatever hell was about to be unleashed, he was determined to walk out of that house with his entire family alive.

288

Mote stood alone as she walked towards Jay. 'Jack?' she said quietly.

'Yes?' they both answered.

The room fell silent again.

Mote's head spun as she looked at her husband and his doppelgänger on the stairs. She barely noticed the woman at the top of the stairs. She wanted to say something, anything; she wanted to scream, but she had nothing. What was going on? She remained where she stood, staring at both men over and over again until she was sure she'd pass out. She felt out of breath; she began to breathe heavily, holding her chest and trying to force out words that simply would not come.

The man on the stairs rushed towards her.

'Mote!' he called out to her.

She rushed into her husband's arms. He pulled her towards the table and stood protectively in front of her, shielding them from the crazy person on the stairs.

'Get away from my wife!' The man launched himself at Jack.

'Jack, stop!' the woman called out from behind him and ran down the stairs.

Before the doppelgänger could reach Mote, her husband—the man she had run to for refuge—pulled a knife from the table and held it to her neck. She screamed. 'Jack, what are you doing? Let me go!' She tried to struggle out of his grip, but he held her tightly.

Fear gripped Mote's throat tighter than her husband did her neck. She did not understand anything that was happening. She had stopped struggling, and watched the scene play out in front of her like a movie. It was like she had left her body and she was observing this insane moment in her life from someone else's perspective.

The doppelgänger's eyes reflected the fear she felt, and even though he was a mirror image of her husband, as she looked into his eyes, he felt more familiar with every passing moment.

She watched as the red-haired woman clung to his arm—no, that could not be her husband. But neither could this person threatening to spill her blood with a steak knife.

'Dad, stop!' Lara cried out from the other side of the table, rushing towards them.

'Sit down, El!' he said, pressing the knife harder against Mote's neck.

Mote choked. She tried to pry his hand off her body, but even with all her strength, he did not budge.

Why did he call Lara El? That was not her name. Why she did call him Dad, when they had never met? The questions would have continued to rage through her mind if the pain did not distract her from the rabbit hole.

Ethan pulled his wife and daughter further into the corner behind him. He stepped forward. 'Jay, it's over. Just put the knife down,' he said, calmly trying to reach out to him.

It was no use, Mote thought as she begged him to stop. His fingers dug deeper and her vision blurred.

Wait, who is Jay?

That was the question on her mind when he flung her to the floor, releasing her from his grip. She forced air into her lungs, trying to take as many deep breaths as possible.

The doppelgänger ran towards her and she kicked him off, scurrying away from him.

Jay stood above El like a giant. 'You told him?' he said coldly, yanking her hair back, exposing her neck, and pressing the knife against it.

'No, Dad, I didn't. Dad, I promise I didn't!' she cried out.

'Stop, you're hurting her!' Andrew shouted, leaving Ara standing a few steps behind him.

'Don't hurt her, please,' Mote begged. 'Don't hurt my daughter.'

Mote did not realise what she'd said until she noticed the stares. She ignored them and turned to the man holding her daughter's neck.

The man—because she realised now that she had no idea who her husband was. He was not the monster who threatened to kill her, but he also couldn't be the one who'd left her with a monster.

'Please, I just got her back, please don't hurt her.'

The man laughed. 'I guess it's a family reunion, then,' he said, pressing the knife deeper into El's neck, drawing blood.

'Help me, Mum, please!' El cried.

The red-haired woman walked towards Jay slowly. 'Let her go, James. It's over,' she said calmly.

She pulled El from his grip, and he let her.

She moved in closer to him, once Lara was free from his grip, and hugged him. She kissed him and said, 'Let's go home.'

Yeah, that was not her husband. Mote was sure of it.

Jay closed his eyes. If Victoria had come to him a few days earlier, if she had said these words earlier, he knew he would have crumbled in her hands as he had many times before. She had a hold on him, and for as long as she lived, she would. She would be his greatest love and his biggest weakness. She had betrayed him in ways he could not fathom, and even in this moment she was probably only trying to save herself, but he could not deny that he wanted her to do all that she did.

She closed the gap between them and kissed him again.

'Please, Jack,' she whispered.

Jay's eyes widened. And just as she realised the slip, he plunged the knife into her stomach. She groaned and ached, gasping for breath, and slowly fell to the ground.

'That's for my child,' Jay said.

Jack ran towards her, holding her head and pressing on the wound to keep it from bleeding. He called out to her to make sure she stayed awake. He patted her and whispered quiet words to her.

Mote finally spoke again. 'What the hell is going on?' She directed her question to Jay. 'Jack, who is this man?'

'That's not your husband. He is,' Ethan said, pointing at Jack on the floor, who was still trying to keep Victoria conscious.

Jay turned on him. 'You need to be quiet.'

'I think you need to come in now, Maureen,' Ethan whispered in fear.

'Who are you talking to?' Jay asked. He tore open Ethan's shirt and saw the wire. He hit him hard over the head, knocking him unconscious.

Anna screamed and pulled Ethan closer to her. Andrew tried to intervene, but El held him back.

Mote approached Jack cautiously. She stared at him as he held Victoria close to his chest.

'Jack?' she whispered. Her hands began to tremble.

He looked up at her, and tears filled his eyes. He turned back to El, asking her to take over holding Victoria. 'We need towels, Ara!' he called. 'Please get towels.'

Ara froze when she heard him call her name.

'Dad?' she said, sobbing.

Jay watched as Jack and his daughter were lost in each other's gaze. And the moment Ara turned to look at him, he saw the realisation in her eyes. She knew he was not her father, and he felt a pang of jealousy followed by rage.

'Dad,' she said again.

'The towels, Ara,' Jack said again, urging her to go.

She ran into the kitchen, and Jay shouted, calling her to come back.

Jack sprang up and pulled Mote behind him to his left side while Victoria and El were to his right.

'Don't threaten my daughter,' he growled. 'You are done here, leave now, and I won't kill you.'

'Kill me?' Jay laughed. 'Is that what she said, that you could kill me? She has led you to your slaughter,' he mocked.

Jack looked back at Victoria. 'If she dies, I will kill you.'

Jay noticed something in his eyes. He recognised that look; he had seen it many times. It was the look of a man who had fallen in love with Victoria Sherman. He laughed even louder.

'You're in love with her. Oh, you are even more stupid than I thought.' Jay looked at Mote. 'I would never do this to you. I would never fall in love with another woman. He left you. He knew who I was, and he didn't tell you. He didn't come back for you. Come with me, and we'll go away from here, far away from here, like we planned, just the two of us.'

'I will not go anywhere with you!' she barked at him.

Ara came out of the kitchen, bent down, and handed the towels over to El, who placed them over Victoria's stomach. Victoria groaned in pain and panted weakly.

Jay scoffed as he watched them fussing over Victoria. None of them knew what that woman was capable of. She'd got what she deserved.

Jay turned back to Mote, still trying to convince her to run away with him. 'I found your daughter. I protected her for you,' he said, pointing at El. 'What else can I do to prove that I love you? I love you, Mote.'

'What's he talking about?' Jack turned and asked Mote.

She frowned. 'I told you, Jack, when we just got married. I told you I had a daughter that I had given up for adoption.'

'What are you talking about?' He raised his voice.

'Ahem.' Jay cleared his throat. 'That would be me you told that little secret.' He smiled.

'What?' Mote asked, confused.

'You should be happy you told me and not him. See the look on his face. See how he looks at you. I accepted your truth. I found your daughter and raised her as though she was mine. Now we can be a family—you, me, and Lara, just as it should have been all these years.'

Mote did see the look on Jack's face. He looked broken and betrayed, even more than he did earlier. Her heart broke. She had gone all these years thinking her husband knew the truth about her past, and he didn't.

'Who are you?' she asked Jay.

He smiled, as though he had been waiting for this moment to introduce himself. 'A long time ago,' he began his story, 'two boys were born to a young woman, and when she had to choose, she took one and left the other behind to be burned up by the flames that destroyed their home.' He paused.

'I am James Mulder, the one left behind, and I am here to take everything that should have been mine. You see, our mother chose my brother, your husband, and clearly she made the wrong choice. Don't be like her, Mote. Don't choose the wrong man.'

'I had nothing to do with that!' Jack roared. 'We were children. I didn't leave you behind—she did. I don't even remember that day.'

'No! You don't! You weren't left behind!' he screamed back at Jack. 'I've always been here, lurking in the darkness, a reflection of your worst fears!' He paused to collect himself. 'One way or the other, brother, I will get the life I deserve. *You have lived our life. It's my turn.*'

They were interrupted by a loud knock on the door.

'This is the police!' Maureen shouted, banging on the door. 'Open up!'

Jay ran to the door and bolted it. 'If you come in, I will kill everyone in this room.'

'I know you won't do that, not with your wife and daughter in there,' Maureen shouted through the door.

Jay turned back and looked at Victoria. She was growing weaker by the minute.

'It's a bit late to play that card, detective,' he said. He scanned the room.

'Andrew, lock up that door.' The boy did not move, so he shouted at the top of his voice. 'Lock up that door! Lock up all the doors leading out of this room! Don't try anything funny,' he said, pointing the knife at Ethan, who was waking up slowly. 'Three seconds. Go now!'

Andrew ran to lock the door and was back as quickly as he could. He also locked the door leading from the kitchen to the dining room.

'Dad, please stop this,' El begged and sobbed, still holding Victoria's bleeding body in her arms. 'Please, let's just go. I will come with you, I will, I promise. Let's go, please.'

'No one is leaving with him,' Jack said angrily.

'Let her go with him,' Ara spat.

'How can you say that? This man is a monster!' he asked in disbelief.

'She's his daughter, so what does that make her?' she shouted back at him. 'She lied to us—she deserves whatever she gets!'

'Oh damn ... that's cold, Ara. I didn't know you had that in you,' Jay teased. 'Perhaps you really are my daughter, after all.'

Jack stared at Ara, and his eyes widened with dawning horror.

CHAPTER

27

The look in her father's eyes made Ara shrink back. The imposter was lying.

Her mother's voice cut through her thoughts.

'Ara is not your daughter!' Mote shouted at him, stepping out from behind Jack.

'I know, I know. I checked. I was pretty disappointed though,' he said, shaking his head. 'She would have made for a much better daughter than the one I got,' he said, looking at El. 'Oh well, better luck next—'

'What do you mean, you checked? Why would she be your daughter?' Jack asked furiously. He turned back to Mote. 'You slept with him?'

Ara shrank back even further, trying her best to physically remove herself from the horror that played out before her. Watching as her mother tried desperately to prove whose child she'd borne.

'I thought he was you, Jack. I thought he was my husband!' Mote cried.

'That was just weeks ago. Ara is seventeen!'

'Oh, stop shouting, brother,' Jay said. 'Let's just say we did a little more than talk the night she told me her darkest secrets.' He paused and smiled at Jack, allowing his words to sink in. From the look of despair on her father's face, it worked. 'We had a connection—we *have* a connection. I mean, she didn't even know you were missing. None of them did. What does that say about you? You are replaceable, insignificant—you are nothing!'

'Why would you do this? I have done nothing to you! I didn't even know I had a brother, and you just came into my life and destroyed everything.'

'Well, you did do something to me. You slept with my wife,' Jay replied.

'No, no, I didn't ... I didn't ...'

'Don't lie to me. You think I don't know that look? That's the look of man who has fallen for the same tricks that I fell for. You know what the best part is?' he added, looking at Mote. 'You will spend the rest of your life wondering when you were with me instead of him. You will take every moment you hold dear and dread it, because every time you see him, you will see me. I may not be able to be with you again, but you can be sure, Mote, that I have had my fair share of being your husband for days, maybe even years, and you'll never know when or where.'

Mote gasped, backing away. Jack tried to pull her closer, but she moved even further away from him. She looked at him with tear-filled eyes. 'He's a monster, and you knew that when you left, and you didn't come back.'

'I didn't leave, Mote, he kidnapped me,' Jack replied. 'All I have done is try to get back to you.'

Mote looked at Victoria bleeding out on the floor. 'Is she why you didn't come back for us?' she sobbed. 'Oh God, you knew he was here pretending to be you, to be my husband and father to your children, and you stayed with her?' she said, pointing at Victoria.

Jack tried to explain, but she wouldn't listen to anything he said.

Ara watched her mother break down, recoiling from her father, sobbing and shaking uncontrollably. She saw Anna and April try to keep her uncle Ethan awake, wiping the blood from his temple where he'd been struck.

On the other side of the room, El knelt behind Victoria, applying pressure to the wound. Ara tried to pity her; she saw the tears that filled her eyes, but she felt nothing. El had lied to them and put her family in danger. She couldn't help but blame her for all of this, whether she was her mother's daughter or not. It all meant nothing to her; she hated her just as much as she hated her father.

Victoria soon began to bleed from her mouth and gasp for breath. She called out to Jack, who ran to her side to comfort her. He begged Jay to let her out to the police, but Jay wouldn't budge. He laughed and mocked and revelled in the pain he caused.

Ara looked at her mother, the one person who was as broken as she was in this moment. She had finally got her husband back only to lose him again. She was also the one with the least information. She had no idea what had been going on; she'd had no idea about the threats and how scared Ara had been all these weeks, how alone she was in her grief.

Her thoughts were interrupted by Jay's loud voice. He laughed loudly as he watched Jack crouch at Victoria's side.

'I see you cannot choose which woman to save,' he mocked.

Ara was tired of it all. She was tired of him; she wanted it all to stop. She let out a deep sigh and took Andrew's hand. She squeezed slightly and looked up at him.

'I love you.' She mouthed the words so no one else heard her.

He smiled and squeezed her hand back.

She let go of his hand and walked towards Jay.

'Stop!' Jay shouted. 'Don't take another step.'

'Ara, what are you doing? Please stop,' Jack pleaded.

'Listen to your father, little girl. Don't get yourself hurt.'

'You have no idea what he has done, Dad. I have spent the last few weeks in this house, with this man, this impostor!' she cried out loud. 'He is a murderer. He killed my brother, and I will kill him.' And she pulled the gun out from beneath her shirt.

Mote screamed, 'Ara! Please put the gun down. Ara!'

Jack managed to hold Mote back. He took slow steps towards Ara. 'Look at me, Ara—look at me!' he shouted. 'Please.'

She ignored all their cries and pleas. She could hear El crying and shouting behind her. 'Ara, don't kill him! Don't kill my father, please!'

Ara heard Maureen's voice from the other side of the door, trying to appeal to Jay. She told him the police were right outside and they would let him go if he released the hostages. He ignored her, as though the loud bangs on the door were nothing but whispers.

She could hear them all loud and clear; their voices screamed in her head, but there was only one voice that echoed through them all, silently calling her name. Tale's. When she closed her eyes, she could hear him scream and beg when Jay pulled the trigger. She tried to shake it off, but that moment played over in her head again and again. She was crying as she pointed the gun at Jay.

She hoped he would be scared; she wanted him to be scared. She wanted him to beg as she did; she wanted to hear him cry out loud like Tale did, and when he didn't, when he smirked instead, she pulled the trigger.

'For Tale,' she whispered under her breath.

The sound of the gun was deafening. She let the gun fall out of her hands and she dropped to her knees. Immediately, two police officers broke the door open and Maureen rushed right in.

Louder than the gun was El's scream from behind Ara. She didn't look back, but she felt El rush past her to Jay, right as he hit the ground.

Jack ran towards Ara and hugged her. She cried loudly in his arms. 'I'm sorry. I'm sorry,' she repeated over and over.

Mote hugged her as well. 'It's OK, Ara. Shh ... It's OK, everything is going to be OK. It's over now.'

The paramedics rushed in a few minutes after and carried Victoria out on a stretcher. She had passed out from blood loss. Her skin was paler than usual, and her pulse was weak.

The shot that Ara had fired went right through Jay's forehead, killing him instantly. It was almost exactly where he had shot Tale.

Maureen checked his pulse.

'Get away from him!' El barked at her as she held him closer, crying over his body.

Ethan, Anna, and April were the first to leave the house. Maureen asked an officer to drive them home, while Andrew insisted on staying over.

El stayed glued to Jay's side. She called out to him, 'Dad, Dad, please wake up. Dad, wake up, let's go home,' she cried. 'Please don't leave me.'

Andrew lifted her off the body so they could carry Jay out as well. She screamed and struggled, but he finally peeled her off the body. She held on to Andrew and cried in his arms.

He tried to get her to calm down, but she got even angrier. She shoved him away and ran towards the door. She ran as fast as her legs would take her. In seconds, she was out of the house.

Andrew started to chase after El, but stopped when he saw Ara and their eyes met.

Ara kept her eyes fixed on him, begging him with silent cries for him, for his embrace, to be there for her as he had always promised her he would. Somehow, he heard her and reached out for her. In a single move, she was in his arms, holding on tightly to his shoulders.

As he carried her up to the stairs, Ara could hear the detective ask a multitude of questions, and she shut her eyes, to shut it all out. She knew that this was far from over.

Ara curled into a ball as Andrew dropped her on her bed. He turned to leave, but she called out to him.

'Please stay.'

He returned to the bed and lay down beside her. She rested her head on his chest and cried. Her tears soaked into his shirt. He held her close and stroked her hair. She could hear his heart thump faster and faster beneath his chest. He was afraid.

He remained quiet for as long as she did.

'I didn't mean to kill him. I never wanted anyone to get hurt,' she whispered beneath her sobs.

'I know,' he reassured her.

'I know they are talking about me downstairs. They are going to ask why I killed him.' She paused. 'I don't know why I did it, Andrew. He just ... He took so much from me.' She cried even more.

'It's OK, Ara, it's OK. Just close your eyes and try to get some rest. You were protecting your family, you have done nothing wrong.'

She remained quiet the rest of the night.

She could not sleep. Her mind refused to rest. Like a broken tape, the moment she pulled the trigger played on a loop in her mind. She had nothing more to say, and neither did he. They just lay there in the dark, staring at the thin lines that the dim lights outside shone in until he fell asleep with her in his arms.

CHAPTER
28

It had been three weeks since the night of the incident, the second one. Not the one when she lost her son, but the one when her daughter murdered his killer. That was all Mote could think about as she sat in that chair, next to a judge, explaining to the court how her seventeen-year-old daughter acted in self-defence, killing the man who had intruded into their lives, into their home, and killed her brother.

The prosecution had assumed that although it was a tense situation, Ara was moved to kill Jay because of what he did to her brother.

Mote spoke softly and confidently. She was the last of all of the witnesses to speak on behalf of Ara, and although she feared that there might be an ounce of truth in their accusations, she knew Jay had deserved to die. She was only sad she hadn't pulled that trigger herself.

She wished she could shield her little girl from all the backlash and gossip that had risen from this case. Everyone had an opinion on all that had happened, and unfortunately, whether it was solicited or not, they felt compelled to share. There were those who believed Ara had been consumed with rage and others who believed she'd planned it all along.

As Mote sat in that chair looking at her family—her husband, Ara, Andrew, Ethan, Anna, April, and even Komi—she knew what she was fighting for and so she knew exactly what to say to make sure her daughter never had to worry about spending another day proving her innocence to anyone.

She kept her gaze on Komi and cracked a faint smile. They weren't yet back to where they used to be, and honestly, she felt like they never would return there, but Komi had paid enough for her foolishness. It had helped to find out that Komi wasn't actually sleeping with her husband, but the mere fact that she'd thought she was ... that burnt bridge was yet to be rebuilt.

She moved on from Komi to Jack, who sat right next to her. He had told Mote everything, and although she was grateful that she was no longer in the dark, no longer the only one who didn't know that the man she'd lain with was not her husband, she could not help but feel like it was all a little too late.

She smiled at him, slightly wider than she had earlier. She loved this man, but his brother was right: he might not have fired the shot that killed her son, but he had the face of the man who did. As the weeks went by, it mattered less and less that he was once again the man of her dreams.

She sighed. It hurt to know her dreams had changed, and she wasn't sure what they were now, but she knew she might not get to forever with him. She wondered how long it would be till she could no longer wake up next to the face that had destroyed her life.

She turned her gaze back to the man in the grey suit who stood before her, asking her questions about that night. She answered every question as well as she could. She cried when she felt it was necessary. The irony wasn't lost to her: faking tears before a judge, when just a few weeks ago, she couldn't keep herself from crying from the minute she woke to the minute the sun went down.

She was all out of tears. She had grown these past few weeks, and she was different now. She wasn't sure how, but she knew she felt a lot less weak and out of control.

She walked out the box and walked back to her family.

After a few minutes of deliberation, just as she had expected, the judge ruled in their favour. All the charges against Ara were dropped.

The court was in an uproar. She watched as her family rejoiced and shouted, hugging each other. It was an odd thing to bind them together, murder, but it seemed to be just as strong as—if not stronger than—the love they'd started out with.

She saw El through the crowd, trying to leave the courtroom, and she ran after her.

'Lara!' she called out. Nearly out of breath, she caught up with her. 'Please wait,' she said. 'Where have you been? I've looked everywhere for you. I am so sorry about Jay.'

'No, you aren't,' El said coldly.

Mote was shocked, but she wasn't going to lie to her. 'You're right. I'm not sorry he's gone, Lara. He was a horrible person; he ruined my family. He should never have adopted you.'

'He took me when you abandoned me; he raised me when you were too scared to. He was my father, and you, you all took him from me.' Anger filled her words.

Mote stopped. Jay was a monster, but there was no point in telling his grieving daughter that. Instead, she said, 'I am sorry I gave you up. I was young and I was scared. I didn't know what I wanted and I was so unsure of the future, I couldn't risk not being able to take care of you.' Tears stung her eyes. 'I promise you, Lara, I will never leave you again. You are my daughter, my first child; I could never live without you now that you are back in my life. Please forgive me, let me make it up to you. Let me get to know my little girl,' she said, holding El's face.

El cried and nodded. She threw her arms around her mother. She had waited for this moment her entire life, and she was not going to let it go. She couldn't stop the tears from falling, even though she tried. She, for the first time in forever, felt like she had a home that was not enclosed in the walls of a house but in someone's heart.

She wasn't sure what the next step would be, but she knew she did not want to spend another minute alone in the streets, looking for a home she would never find.

She had spent the last few weeks looking for Stig and Victoria, but they both seemed to have disappeared without a trace. She'd searched every hideout, every house they'd ever moved to, and she'd found nothing, which was why she was here today. She had run out of places to go, and a part of her had hoped she would end up right where she was, in her mother's arms.

Victoria had run away from the hospital shortly after she recovered. Although they didn't have any charges to arrest her on, the police were hunting her because she was Jay's wife and they assumed she was with Stig, who had also been missing. El hadn't seen him since that day he'd left her at the hospital.

There was something her father was hiding from her. There had to be. Something he had had Stig take care of for him, one final plan, one last move. She just couldn't figure out what it was.

Eventually, they all left the courthouse and headed home. The moment she walked into the house, Ara knew that this was the start of another phase in her life. Every bit of the house reminded her of the terrible things that had happened there, and she knew her parents felt the same way, which was probably why they'd put the house up for sale. She was going to miss this place, her memories with Tale, his treehouse out front, his handprints on the wall; she would miss it all.

She was happy to leave still. Every time she stood on the spot where Jay fell, she felt like if she squinted hard enough, she could still see the image of him lying dead in their dining room. It was all she saw when she closed her eyes.

She was happy to have everyone support her the way they had at the court hearing, but she was most grateful for Andrew. He truly had proven himself to be her knight in shining armour. He'd stayed by her side every step of the way, listening to her rants and wiping her tears, helping her get through each day as it came. She knew she had fallen in love with him all over again, and this time, she was not going to let anything get between them.

And especially not her, she thought to herself as she watched El talking with him in the corner of the room. Her first instinct was to pull her by her hair and throw her out of her house, but after weeks of compulsory therapy, she walked over and tried to join the conversation.

She had always wanted to know what it was like having a sister, and perhaps this was her chance. It was a long shot but she was willing to take it.

She had come to pity El, more than anything else. She often wondered what would have happened if her mum had given her up instead of El, if she'd been the one Jay raised to be like him. She could never forget the words he'd said about her: that she would have made for a better daughter. What did he mean? Would she have been like El? Or worse?

She smiled as she approached El and Andrew. She stretched out her hand to El, who in turn hugged her. They both giggled, and Andrew laughed; she could see the relief in his face. She wondered why it was so important to him that they got along, but she didn't put too much thought into it. She hugged El back and waited for her to let go.

Andrew excused himself and went to talk to his sister while Ara tried to start a conversation with El.

'Don't do that,' El said coldly.

'What?' Ara asked, surprised.

'I'm not interested in whatever you have to say.'

'But .... you just hugged me,' Ara said, still smiling, still trying to fix whatever she had done to cause this reaction.

El smirked and moved in closer to her. 'You killed my father.

He was my family and you took him from me. I begged you to not kill him.'

'He killed my brother. I was protecting myself,' Ara said in shock. She could not hide the fear and confusion she felt.

'You don't have to tell me that lie, Ara. The court may believe you, and your family may lie for you, but I was here, Ara. I know the truth, and you will pay for what you have done. Now I will take everything from you, and you will know what it truly means to be alone.'

She brought out her phone and played a five second clip to Ara. It was a silent video showing Ara shooting Jay in the head in the middle of their dining room.

'Remember that break-in a couple of months ago?' El whispered. 'You shouldn't only have checked if anything was taken, but if anything was left behind.'

Ara gasped, and before she could utter a word, El snatched the phone back from her hand.

She could not believe what she'd seen. She hadn't been able to forget the image of Jay lying dead on their floor, but for the first time, she'd watched herself shoot him. She couldn't recognise herself, and in this moment, she was more afraid of who she had become than El's threat. She looked around the house as though to search for any cameras.

'Don't bother. There's no need for cameras anymore, I have all that I need,' El said.

'Get out,' Ara hissed.

'I'm not going anywhere, sister. I am here to stay. Your mother is my mother, your friends are my friends, and him ...' El said, smiling at Andrew. 'I think I'm in love with him. When I am done, Ara, you will have nothing and no one to call home.'

'You cannot do this. I will tell him,' Ara said. 'I will tell everyone.'

'Good luck with that. You've spent every moment since you met me angry or jealous about one thing or the other. Now you're still picking on me even after I lost my father? Even after you took him from me? I'd like to see you convince even one person in this house. You see, to everyone here, I am the lost sheep welcomed back home with open arms. You don't want to be that spiteful little girl now, do you?'

Ara froze as she watched her walk away. She wanted to scream, but once again, her voice did not come. She had turned a full circle back to where she started from, once again being threatened, once again in fear for her life, once again keeping secrets for and with the person that would destroy her family.

The doorbell rang, and Mote went to the door.

It was Maureen. Mote let her in and offered her some food.

'Oh no, I won't be long. Is Jack in?' she asked.

'Yes, he's upstairs in the room, should be down any minute. Can you wait?'

'No,' Maureen replied. 'I just wanted to tell him, some of the guys down at the station believe that he is in contact with Victoria, and that might not be the best thing for him—for any of you. Please tell him that if she does contact him, he should call me immediately.'

Mote nodded and smiled, closing the door after her.

She had tried to remove any thoughts from her mind that her husband might have truly fallen in love with that woman. Her heart hurt every time she thought about it. She no longer cared that he'd lied to her or let her believe that his brother was him for all those weeks, but she could not comprehend why or how he could fall in love with Victoria. She was the enemy; she was his brother's wife.

She tried to pretend that she did not see the way he'd cared for her and looked at her the night she was hurt; she chalked it up to his big heart. But it would seem his heart was getting way too big.

She quietly walked upstairs and into their room.

Jack stood on the balcony and stared down at the garden. She thought he was just staring and thinking, but then she heard him say the words that confirmed her greatest fear.

'Please call me, Victoria. I need to know that you are OK.' He paused. 'I love you.' He paused, sighed again. 'I love you.'

He let out a deep breath and tucked the phone back into his pocket when he saw Mote standing behind him.

'Detective Lewis was here. She wanted to know if you've been in contact with Victoria. She thinks it might be too risky,' she said plainly.

She didn't realise she was crying.

He walked towards her. 'Mote,' he said quietly.

She shook her head and smiled. She tried to speak, but the words she truly wanted to say could not find their way out of her mouth.

He tried to say something, but she knew that there was nothing he could say, not in this moment anyway.

She hugged him and kissed him passionately, and then let go. 'Your family is waiting for you downstairs,' she whispered.

She turned around and walked out of the room. She didn't know what he would do; she knew what she hoped he would, but she could not say that she was sure of anything. She wasn't sure of her love for him, and she most definitely wasn't sure of his love for her. She felt like she had lost him so many times now that he might not be hers to keep anymore.

She stayed behind the door for as long as she could wait for him. If only he would open the door and see her and choose her. She waited, and waited, but finally went downstairs. She checked a couple of times to see if he was out yet, but he remained in the room. Soon she stopped checking, and later she forgot that he was up there at all.

~~The End~~

DISCUSSION QUESTIONS

JAY

1. Do you consider his anger justifiable? Was his quest for vengeance warranted?
2. The story tells us that he murdered Victoria's father. Do you believe that he ever loved her?
3. He adopted El based on the story Mote revealed to him. Should he have told her who her birth mother was earlier?
4. What was his biggest regret? What could he have done differently to change the outcome of his story?
5. Jay's drive for vengeance leads him to his death. Who else acted out of anger and wanted revenge? What did you learn from this?
6. How did he feel when he lost his child? Did you feel pity for him, knowing that he had killed a child a few weeks earlier?
7. Among Victoria, Mote, and Komi, who do you think Jay loved most? Who do you think loved him most?
8. What do you think Jay told Stig to do at the end of the story?

JACK

1. How did the secrets he kept destroy his family?
2. Victoria helped Jack escape from the cabin. Should he have continued to live with her?
3. Do you think he loved his family? If yes, did his actions reveal this?
4. Was there any other way to save his family from his brother? What alternative decisions could he have made with regards to this?
5. Do you think he loved Mote more than he loved Victoria?
6. Should he have trusted Victoria? Do you think she played him?
7. At what point did you realise that Jack did not murder his son?

MOTE

1. How did the secret she kept destroy her family?
2. Did she do the most she could to find out what happened to her son the night he was killed? What else would you have done?
3. She lived with Jay for weeks before his identity was revealed. Do you think she ever suspected that he was not her husband?
4. Did she allow herself to properly grieve the loss of her son?
5. Compare her relationship with Anna and her relationship with Komi.

6. At the end of the story, do you think Mote still loved Jack?
7. Do you believe in redemption? Do you think Mote's family can be what it was before Jay came into their lives?

ARA

1. She witnessed her brother's murder. Did she do the right thing by keeping the identity of his murderer a secret? Would you have the courage to tell?
2. Do you think that she loved Andrew, or was she simply jealous of El?
3. Would you consider Ara to be brave?
4. Did she make the right decision shutting Andrew out when he did not believe the story she told him about her father? Would you have believed her?
5. Should she have killed Jay? Did he deserve to die? Should Ara be convicted of murder?
6. What should she do about El's final threats?

KOMI

1. Do you consider her a victim in the story? Did she get what she deserved, or was she mistreated?
2. Do you think she was in love with the father of her child? Should she have left the hospital with him that night? What would you have done?
3. Should she have told Mote about the child she had by Mote's 'husband'?

4. What could she have done differently to change the outcome of her story?
5. Can her relationship with Mote ever be restored?

VICTORIA

1. Did she have any ulterior motives for helping Jack escape? What were they?
2. Do you think she fell in love with Jack?
3. Describe the relationship she had with Jay.
4. Were her actions against Komi justified? Should she have attacked her?
5. Do you think she would ever come back to Jack?

EL

1. Do you think El is anything like the man that raised her?
2. Do you think El intends to hurt Ara or just scare her?
3. Do you think El is in love with Andrew or she only seeks to spite Ara?
4. Describe El's relationship with her father.
5. Do you think she wants to be a part of their family or she has ulterior motives?

ANDREW

1. Do you think Andrew was a good friend to Ara? What would you have done differently? Do you think their relationship will survive all they have been through?
2. Should Andrew have disclosed things that Ara told him to El? Soon his feelings for El began to grow. Do you think he truly loved Ara?
3. Do you think he will continue to explore the feelings he has for El?
4. What is his biggest flaw?
5. Describe his relationship with his father.

NOTE FROM THE AUTHOR

Photographed by Tosan Andrew in the Michael Family Library
(2017)

Hi there! Thank you so much for reading! I hope this was a real page-turner for you and kept you holding your breath until the very last page!

If you enjoyed reading this book, I would really appreciate you taking a moment to leave a review on Amazon and Goodreads. It would mean even more people get to read and enjoy this book as you now have.

To stay in the know about new releases, freebies and signed copies, **sign up to my newsletter at www.justmarve.org**.

All my best,
Marve

ABOUT THE AUTHOR

Marvellous Michael Anson, the best-selling author of *Birthmarked,* is devoted to giving her readers fast-paced, high-stakes stories that explore the multi-faceted human condition. She has been writing poems and short stories for over a decade, as well as directing short plays and being a writer's favourite soundboard.

Marve is not limited to the art of stringing words together; she wrote and produced her award-winning short film in 2016. She is a recipient of the 2017 AFRIFF Film School Scholarship Program.

Marve works as a technology consultant during the day and a storyteller at night. She is a member of the Society of Authors, Alliance of Independent Authors and Abuja Literary Society. She hosts an online writing group called Writers Connect on Facebook (all are welcome!).

Marve was born and raised in Nigeria and lives with her husband in London.

Her website is www.justmarve.org

facebook.com/JustMarve

twitter.com/justmarvewrites

instagram.com/justmarvewrites

tiktok.com/@justmarvewrites

ACKNOWLEDGMENTS

I would like to thank God for everything this book is and all that it will be, for giving me the words to write and strength to finish. In the process of putting this book together, I realised how true this gift of writing is for me. I could never have done this without the faith I have in you, my Saviour and Redeemer.

I want to thank everyone who made this book what it is today, my editors and early readers. This story only keeps getting better because of you.

To my grandma, Omobamitale Ayodele Adewale. Words are not enough to express my gratitude for the love and support you have shown me. Most importantly, your wisdom and guidance have made me who I am today. You held my hand and taught me to write, and you guided my thoughts and taught me to create.

To my husband, David Anson. Thank you for being my sounding board, for listening to my ideas and refining them until they're perfect. Thank you for the original illustrations for the book's cover. I am so thankful that I have you in my corner, encouraging me even when I am ready to give up.

To my mother, Temitope Adenike Michael. You have been by my side every step of the way, and I find myself speechless. You have relentlessly motivated and encouraged me to finish this book. Thank you for waking me up in the middle of the night to write and for allowing me to take over your study room. I am blessed to have you, and I am eternally grateful for you.

To my father, Olusegun Adejare Michael. Most assuredly, this book would have remained a manuscript under a pile of books on my shelf without you. I thank you for giving me the opportunity to share this with the world. You are amazing. I could not have wished for a better father.

To my brothers, Emmanuel Mololuwa Michael and Eriayooluwa Mogboluwaga Michael. You are both blessings to me. Thank you for helping me to unwind when I felt stuck on a page. Every moment with you both is a story in itself.

To Ewaoluwa Eni-Odunjo. Thank you for staying up every night and listening to me read out every chapter of this book. Thank you for being so committed to this project and for falling in love with my characters.

To Temilore Orekoya. Thank you for your edits and critiques and, most importantly, for believing in me.

To my support group, because you are more than just friends. I love you all so much. If you read carefully, you will all find pieces of yourselves in here.

God bless you all.

Printed in Great Britain
by Amazon

19620563R00196